Chance tip

Jenna would be lying if she said the need wasn't there. The need ... ... since she'd been kissed, held close. Being with a man was one thing, but being with a man like Chance?

She stared at him, trapped by his gaze, watching as he lowered his head toward hers but stopped just short of kissing her.

Say no. Say no.

Instead she parted her lips to take in more air and Chance closed the distance. His tongue nudged into her mouth to touch hers and then—the way it had earlier—everything slid away. All thought, all worry, all fear.

Her insides coiled tight, heat flooded every cell and she gripped the material of his shirt, holding on, instead of shoving him away.

No, no, no.

The litany sounded in her head, screamed out warnings, but her body refused to cooperate. She didn't want this. Didn't want to want him.

But she did.

Dear Reader,

Thanks for picking up *Christmas in Montana,* the third book in my North Star, Montana, series. Each book stands alone, so if you haven't read the previous titles, no worries. More information about those titles and work can be found at my website, kaystockham.com.

So what is this book about? When I started writing it, I thought it was a book about fear and how, if we let it, fear controls us. But then I discovered the story was about so much more. It's about self-worth and how we find it. It's also about rock climbing, moving on after the death of a spouse and how the worst person for you to fall in love with can also be the best person for you. As one character says, sometimes you have to let the crazy out and remember to have fun.

This book wasn't what I had planned when I began writing it, but as Jenna discovers, life doesn't always go as planned.

I love to hear from my readers! Let me know what you think of Jenna and Chance's story by writing to me at P.O. Box 232, Minford, OH, 45653. Or email me at kay@kaystockham.com. And follow me on Twitter—@kaystockham—and Facebook at Kay Stockham Fan Page.

God bless,

Kay Stockham

Christmas in
Montana
Kay Stockham

TORONTO NEW YORK LONDON
AMSTERDAM PARIS SYDNEY HAMBURG
STOCKHOLM ATHENS TOKYO MILAN MADRID
PRAGUE WARSAW BUDAPEST AUCKLAND

Recycling programs
for this product may
not exist in your area.

ISBN-13: 978-0-373-71740-8

CHRISTMAS IN MONTANA

Printed in U.S.A.

ABOUT THE AUTHOR

Kay Stockham has always wanted to be a writer, ever since she copied the pictures out of a Charlie Brown book and rewrote the story because she didn't like the plot. Formerly a secretary/office manager for a large commercial real-estate development company, she's now a full-time writer and stay-at-home mom who firmly believes being a mom/wife/homemaker is the hardest job of all. Happily married for more than fifteen years and the somewhat frazzled mother of two, she has sold ten books to the Harlequin Superromance line. Her first release, *Montana Secrets,* hit the Waldenbooks bestseller list and was chosen as a Holt Medallion finalist for Best First Book. Kay has garnered praise from reviewers for her emotional, heart-wrenching stories and looks forward to a long career writing a genre she loves.

Books by Kay Stockham

HARLEQUIN SUPERROMANCE

1307—MONTANA SECRETS
1347—MAN WITH A PAST
1395—MONTANA SKIES
1424—HIS PERFECT WOMAN
1453—A CHRISTMAS TO REMEMBER
1477—ANOTHER MAN'S BABY*
1502—HIS SON'S TEACHER*
1552—HER BEST FRIEND'S BROTHER*
1587—SIMON SAYS MOMMY*
1621—SHE'S THE ONE*
1728—THE SHERIFF'S DAUGHTER**
1734—IN THE RANCHER'S FOOTSTEPS**

*The Tulanes of Tennessee
**North Star, Montana

As always this book is dedicated to my family.
I'm glad God gave me you.

It's also dedicated to the
Sisterhood of the Traveling Plot.
Ladies, you make me smile.
Here's to Marine balls, supermodel legs, funky
songs, late night plot sessions and PF Changs.

Your friendship means the world to me.
Thanks for making this so much fun.

CHAPTER ONE

THE COWBOY SANTA CLAUS inside McKenna Feed
ogled her like a kid eyeing the year's most popular
and impossible-to-find toy.

Jenna Darlington stood at the checkout counter inside
the family-owned store and tried to ignore the blatant
stare coming from the man in red. Hard to do when he
wasn't making any attempt to hide his perusal.

And what was with Santa being here already? It
wasn't even Thanksgiving. Didn't most stores wait until
after Turkey Day? Couldn't they finish one holiday before starting another?

Sitting in a high-backed chair covered in rich bur-
gundy velveteen, Santa had propped his cheek on his
fist, the position skewing his bushy white beard toward
the left.

"I'll be right with you," the employee behind the
counter told her, making an apologetic face because of
whoever was on the other end of the phone.

Jenna could hear the woman's loud voice from where
she stood, so she checked her watch and tried to control
her fidgeting. She had a small window of opportunity
to complete her transaction before school let out and,
given her humiliating task, she'd prefer to finish with
no one in line behind her and close enough to overhear.
Especially her children.

Jenna leaned her hips against the counter to stare

outside the long stretch of windows at the front of the store. The picturesque scene of North Star, Montana, looked like a photograph. Big, fat snowflakes drifted down lazily, and store windows were filled with color.

But she was like one of the leaf-bare trees lining the street, colored lights tossed haphazardly through the limbs. Yeah, she could pin a smile on her face and pretend all was well, but it wouldn't change the fact she felt naked and vulnerable. While everyone else called out greetings and gathered into stores bursting with music, she struggled to hold herself upright.

What was she going to do? Winter hadn't taken a firm hold of Montana, yet, but it was shaping up to be a long one. And despite a day spent checking on possible leads, it appeared every job in North Star from waitress to shampoo girl had been filled with people like her needing extra cash for the holidays.

"Ma'am, let me check on this and call you back. Give me your number and—"

The person on the other end of that call cut off the clerk midsentence and he gave Jenna another apologetic glance.

Jenna counted to ten and checked her watch again. This was ridiculous. If she didn't need the refund so badly, she'd walk out and deal with it another day.

Santa shifted his position and Jenna noticed the move in her peripheral vision despite her best intentions to ignore him. Worst yet, he was still watching her. She could feel his gaze on her like a physical touch and it made her hyperaware.

Oh, for pity's sake, she didn't have the time—or the patience—to stand here and pretend she was merry or tolerant. Not today. Screw the commercialism Christmas had become. How dare they turn the holiday into a money-hungry mess that made every parent who was unable to provide shiny new things for their children feel like the lowest of the low?

The weight on her shoulders grew to mountainous proportions and the rough-hewn edges of her purse dug into her shoulder through the thickness of her coat. Her twins were going to be so disappointed. Last Christmas had been somber because it had been the first without their father. So Jenna had hoped this Christmas they could celebrate like normal—a new normal anyway.

But waiting while the clerk ignored her? "Excuse me? I'm trying to be patient but I'm in a hurry."

The store clerk covered the phone's mouthpiece and said, "I'm sorry, ma'am. I'll be with you as soon as I can." The guy pointed to the handset glued to his ear before he turned his back to the counter.

'Tis the season.

Santa shifted yet again, this time leaning forward in his chair and lifting a hand to the white wig as though to scratch an itch.

Santa could stare all he liked but she absolutely, positively would not make eye contact. She wasn't in the mood for idle chitchat while she was forced to wait.

"Anything I can do to help you?" Santa asked.

Yeah, ignore that, her mind taunted.

Santa had a nice voice, one that was deep and rich and...flavorful, like pit-smoked beef and au jus that melted in your mouth.

And it's familiar. But where had she heard it before?

Unable to place Santa's voice, she shook her head, her gaze firmly focused on the clerk.

"You sure?"

His *you sure* hit her with the force of a fist and the air left her lungs in a gush.

The first time Chance McKenna had said those two words to her, she'd stood outside Jeff's hospital door, reeling from the news of his death. Chance had asked if there was anything he could do then, too. She'd said no, because her husband was dead. At that point what else could Chance or any of Jeff's climbing friends *do?* The damage had been done.

And now? Talk about a cruel joke. The last person she needed or wanted to witness her embarrassing plea for a refund was a member of the Rock Gods, the group of extreme rock climbers her husband had belonged to until he'd fallen to what would be his death. "No, thank you," she managed to say.

"I'd be happy to point you in the right direction. Ignore the cast. It's all for show."

That last playful, boastful comment confirmed her suspicions and nixed any remaining doubts that Santa was indeed Chance McKenna. She gave the store owner more than a passing glance, the knot in her stomach swelling to whale-size proportions.

He had one foot propped on a cloth-covered stool. The cloth didn't reach the floor and revealed three fifty-pound sacks of grain stacked atop each other to the requisite height. The sight of the black wrapped cast made her feel ill.

She'd been lucky the day she'd placed the items in layaway during the Labor Day sale. Chance had been nowhere to be seen at the time—he had been off on a climbing expedition that resulted in the broken foot. Now here it was, barely a week before Thanksgiving, and he was still laid up. When would he or the others learn that their little hobby was dangerous? Hadn't Jeff's death been warning enough? "I'll wait."

She wanted no help from him. It would send her over

the edge of sanity to have to explain to a member of the *Rock Gods* why she couldn't afford Christmas. Neither Chance nor the others understood. And as much as she'd loved her husband, Jeff hadn't understood, either. If he had, he wouldn't have risked his life in the name of *fun*.

"Suit yourself."

"I will," she said.

It wasn't like her to be so rude. Really. She was a nice person. But she had to get out of here. If the clerk didn't get off the phone right this very second, she'd—

"Sorry about your wait, ma'am. What can I help you with today?"

"Santa! Mommy, it's *Santa!*"

The excited cry of a child and the squeaky sound of boot-clad feet running across the polished concrete floor pierced Jenna's brain and left an ache any mother would despise. Her attention shifted to Chance's rapid attempts to right his skewed beard.

She watched as Santa pulled a little boy onto his good leg, the building's interior ringing with several boisterous *ho, ho, ho's* that almost sounded like the real thing.

The boy was around six, maybe seven. Towheaded, with freckles across his nose. Both mother and child were nicely dressed, making Jenna more than aware of her ancient coat with its frayed cuffs and one broken button she'd never gotten around to replacing.

"Ho, ho, ho! Have you been a good boy?"

"Yes."

"Good, good. And what do you want for Christmas, little man?"

"I want a Big Green Fishin' Machine."

Unbidden, Jenna's gaze turned to the large display of the expensive fishing rods stacked against the wall behind the counter. It was the one—the *only*—thing her son had asked for for Christmas. True to its name, it was large and green and had an orange lightning strike on the reel and handle. It came equipped with a matching tackle box with all the so-called necessities.

"Ma'am?" the clerk asked.

"I need to cancel my layaway," she said, before she could call herself too many names for falling short as a parent. She should have tried to better prepare for the situation she found herself in, because she'd known, deep down, something would happen. The same way she'd known, deep down, that she couldn't trust Jeff to prepare for the worst.

But she hadn't, and now her kids were paying for it.

"Name?"

"Darlington. Jenna Darlington."

"What was in it?"

Glaring at the offending products, she swallowed. "A Big Green Fishing Machine."

CHANCE MCKENNA HAD a hard time concentrating on what the kid in his lap was saying. While the boy went yammering on about all the stuff he wanted, Chance tried to tune into the low-voiced conversation taking place at the counter.

"Got that, Santa?"

He looked down at the boy and tried not to notice the snot leaking out of the upturned nose. "Yeah, yeah, I heard you. But remember now, Santa has a lot of children to give toys to, so if you don't get everything, it doesn't mean I don't like you or anything."

The kid's mouth dropped open, his lower lip beginning to quiver. "But I want it *all*. Mommy, I want *all* the toys I asked for!"

Dropping like a rescue helicopter hovering overhead,

the kid's mother grabbed the boy and patted and fussed, looking only slightly embarrassed by the boy's behavior and more than a little ticked off that *Santa* had tried to save mama's bank account.

"I know, sweetheart, I know."

"But, *Mommy*."

An earsplitting wail erupted from the kid and deafened Chance momentarily. Biting back the response he wanted to give, he held up the basket with candy canes. "You want one for the road?"

The kid wiped his knuckles under his nose, then shoved those same fingers into the basket, grabbing a handful instead of only one.

The mother continued to pat and soothe, and she shook her head at Chance.

"Next time, just listen to his list," she said, turning away and hurrying toward the door. Over his mother's shoulder, the boy stuck his tongue out at Chance.

"Mommy, that was a *bad* Santa."

"I know, honey. We'll drive to see one in Helena tomorrow."

Chance watched as the doting mother carried her sniveling brat out the door, glad the kid was gone. All that fuss and the mother hadn't purchased so much as a packet of hand-warmers. When her darling baby grew up, his parents were going to regret the spoiling.

Shifting yet again, Chance attempted to settle himself into the uncomfortable chair and tossed the basket onto the table beside him.

"What do you mean? I need a refund."

Jenna's voice drew his attention. Feigning boredom, he closed his eyes and strained to hear the conversation, thankful no one else was nearby.

"I can refund everything but the clearance items.

Once you put those in layaway, they became yours. I can return the money you paid over the amount of those items, but I can't give you the full price. Minus the clearance, you've got a total of fifty dollars coming back to you."

"That's *it?* Look, I know I should've read the fine print, but I didn't, okay? Can't you make one exception? Something's come up..." She lowered her voice even more. "I really need the cash."

Chance got to his feet and onto his crutches without looking like too much of a one-legged loser. The moment he put the crutches in front of him and the rubber bottoms hit the floor, Jenna's head jerked toward him and a pinched look overtook her pretty features. Yeah, he felt the same way. Every time he'd seen her in town since Jeff's death he'd felt bad about what happened, even though every climber present—including him—had done all they could to save Jeff. There had been too much damage. "Is there a problem?"

There was no mistaking the hot flush of embarrassment or anger—maybe both?—that surged into Jenna's cheeks. Whatever was going on, she didn't want him involved. Not that he wanted to be. What did you say to a widow? Especially one he found himself thinking about more than he should?

"No," Jenna said with a firm shake of her head.

"She wants a full refund," Dooley, Chance's assistant manager, explained. "But she has clearance items in the layaway."

Jenna wouldn't make direct eye contact with him.

"Can I ask what's come up?"

Her chin lifted faster than a rocket. Her chest did, too. Through the opening of her thick winter coat, her breasts rose and fell beneath a brown turtleneck.

He'd always had a love-hate relationship with turtlenecks. Snug, they outlined a woman's body but at the same time they covered far too much. In this case, he was thankful she was covered. Considering the circumstances, *noticing* wasn't something he ought to be doing, since Jeff had been his friend.

"I don't owe you an explanation. I simply want a refund."

"Store policy is no refunds on clearance merchandise," he quoted. "So unless you can give me and Dooley a good explanation, we're going to have to stick to it."

That wasn't necessarily true. He could give Jenna or anyone else a refund if he so chose, but she'd piqued his curiosity, so the rule worked in his favor.

Inhaling, Jenna glanced at her receipt. He almost missed her wince and the way her fingers gripped the gloves in her hands.

"I need the layaway refunded because I lost my job at the school. The grant that paid my salary wasn't renewed. Happy?"

Happy? No, of course not. She was a single parent. A widow, no less. And it was seven weeks until Christmas. No kid deserved to wake up Christmas morning to find the space beneath the tree bare. "I'm sorry to hear that."

Jenna's blue-green eyes were rimmed in deep navy, and, gazing into them as he was, Chance was reminded of the ocean in the Caribbean where the water was so unique. But however pretty, there was no mistaking the resentment in them when she looked in his direction, and her chin lifted even more.

Chance knew a snub when he was on the receiving end of one. And even though he knew he'd regret what he was about to say, he resigned himself to doing the right thing.

"Boss?"

Chance had broken policy in the past and Dooley knew it. The McKennas always tried to help a struggling man—or woman—out. It was a trait Zane, his adoptive father, had lived by and one Chance tried to carry on. "Don't refund it."

"Losing my job isn't a good enough reason?" Jenna glared at him, her lips parted in anger, her gaze turning hard as stone.

"Not when you're hired."

She blinked. "Excuse me— *What?*"

"You need a job. I need responsible employees who'll show up and work when they're supposed to. Christmas gets busy and we're shorthanded thanks to me being off my feet." He lifted a crutch off the ground as proof. "I won't refund the layaway, but if you take the job, you'll earn a wage, plus I'll give you the employee discount on the entire purchase."

Dooley whistled long and low. "That's a good deal," he said to Jenna. "Especially on Big Green, there. I'd take it if I were you."

Confusion and distrust and more than a little bit of stubborn pride were etched into Jenna's face.

Under the circumstances, the best thing to do would be to give her the refund and send her on her way. In the end that wouldn't help her or her kids, though. As much as she tried to hide it, Jenna's expression revealed her desperation. She needed a job to put food on the table.

And in Jeff's memory, that was the least Chance could do.

"Thank you but…I can't accept."

That was not the answer he expected.

"Excuse me?" a woman said from the end of an aisle. "Could I get some help please?"

"Sure," Dooley called. "I'll be right there."

"Why not?" Chance demanded, attracting Jenna's attention before she could get mad at Dooley for abandoning them like a plague-laden ship.

She stared down at her hands, her fingers twisting her silver wedding band around and around.

"Jenna?"

"Do you really need me to spell it out?"

He readjusted his grip on the crutches and fought his frustration. No, he didn't need her to do that. But sometimes pride had to be set aside for common sense and this was one of those times. "Yeah, I'm thinking I do."

She swallowed audibly, as though she had to gather her courage—or repress her anger to a more manageable level. That was something he identified with, because when felt himself start to feel the pressure, he got in his truck and headed for rock.

"I cannot work for a man who holds no respect for life or health or—"

"No respect for *life?*" He knew how to respect life, knew how to enjoy it, too, and he resented her saying anything to the contrary.

"That's what I said. Look, I know you're being nice and offering me a job because of Jeff's death and the Rock Gods's part in it—"

"You make it sound like we shoved him off that cliff. Reality is, we didn't have any part of his death." They'd hauled ass from the scene to the rescue helicopter, done everything humanly possible to save him. If they hadn't, Jeff would have died at the bottom of the rock face instead of in the hospital bed. "Jeff knew the risks when he decided to jump. No one forced him to do it."

Her nostrils flared as she breathed.

"Jenna, there are a couple points here I think you're missing."

"Like what?"

He wondered why he was trying so hard to help her, but chalked it up to the fact it was Christmas, and Zane and Jeff would want him to help. Period. "There are very few jobs to be had right now. Are you really in a position to walk away from one? Do you really want to be the mom who canceled Christmas?"

Oh, yeah. He had her. Right there. He knew it by the way her expression softened and the tip of her nose turned red. No parent wanted to nix Christmas and, while she might not be at all happy about working for him, she would do it for her kids.

Spine stiff as a poker and shoulders squared, her gaze didn't quite meet his. "Well?" he asked.

"I'll take it. But only until I find something else."

Chance put himself in her shoes and tried not to take offense. He also knew he'd stand there all day if he waited on a thank you. "You start tomorrow. Be here as soon as the kids are in school."

CHAPTER TWO

"YOU'RE LEAVING US home *alone?*"

Jenna tried to ignore the knot of unease in her stomach. The question wasn't motivated by anger or fear. No, not her kid. Victoria's expression was one of calculated anticipation. *So* not a good sign. "No. After school, you are going to get off the bus, check in with Rachel at her shop and she will walk you here. Then you're going to get a snack, do your homework and fold your laundry. No TV until you're done. Got it? Rach will check on you frequently to make sure things are okay. You—" she gave them both a fierce stare "—are to do what she says and behave until I get home. I'm trusting you to act like the almost-eleven-year-olds you are."

"I'm in charge," Mark Jeffrey cried from the table.

"Nu-uh," Tori argued.

"Am, too. I called it first and I'm *the man*."

The schoolbooks stacked atop the scarred oak surface were higher than Mark Jeffrey's head. Her son was such a perfectionist. Nearly every day he'd finished his homework at school but would bring more home to complete the extra credit. "Tori, do you have homework?"

"Nope."

"Do, too," Mark Jeffrey muttered under his breath.

"Victoria Rose, do you have homework?" Jenna asked again.

Her daughter shrugged one bony shoulder. "Why

do I have to bring my books home, when Mark always brings his?"

"You can't use *my* books."

"Mom says we have to share."

"I'm the man of the house now and I say no."

There it was again. *Man of the house.* How many times did Jenna hear that in a day? She fought the urge to bang her head against the wall and turned to see Tori glaring at her brother.

"It only counts if you're a *man,* dork." Tori placed both hands on her slim hips. "Besides, I'm older, so *I'm* in charge."

The two began bickering with words like *meaner butt, pickle head* and *dork* flying out of their mouths until Jenna dropped the skillet on the stove and the racket restored order. "*I'm* in charge. Got it? I'm the parent and what I say goes." She used her best mommy voice. Until Jeff's death, it was a voice she hadn't had to call into duty that often. Now it was a daily, sometimes hourly, occurrence. "One more insult or comment or name and that person does *all* the dishes. Understood?"

"How long will we be here until you come home? Can't we just stay at Rachel's?"

If only they could. Having her best friend check in on them was one thing but she couldn't ask Rach for more. "No, you can't. Rachel has a business to run and her mother gets upset easily because of her Alzheimer's, so it's better if you stay here. Stick to the plan and behave and everything will be fine."

"But what about Thanksgiving break? Friday's our last day for a whole week. We have to stay here all day by ourselves? Can we have friends over?" Tori asked.

Oh, no. How could Jenna have forgotten Thanksgiving break?

She'd have to come up with another plan. Maybe Jeff's parents could watch the twins. She hated to ask but Karen usually took a week's vacation at both Thanksgiving and Christmas, so she'd be home... "No, no friends. Not when I'm not around to watch you."

Hiring a babysitter was not in her budget so Jeff's parents were probably her best bet. But what if they couldn't watch the twins? How did single parents *do* this?

"Mom, Tori said you got fired," Mark Jeffrey said. "Did you?"

Jenna stiffened in surprise and attempted to act casual while shooting her daughter a questioning look. She'd known word would get out, but so quickly? She had received the news after school on Friday and she'd spent Saturday and Sunday scouring the paper for a new job but had made a point to be discreet about it.

"You weren't at school today," Tori added.

"No, I wasn't. Where did you hear that I was fired?"

"Kenzie."

"MacKenzie shouldn't be gossiping. It's not nice."

"I know but... She said her mom said you were fired because you were shaggin' the janitor."

"What?"

"What's *shaggin'?*" Mark Jeffrey demanded, his gaze curious and way too perceptive.

Neither one of them knows what they're saying. Your response will dictate whether they drop the subject or it lives on in eternity, cycling around in those too-sharp brains. "Shagging isn't a very nice word for either of you to use. It has a meaning you're not old enough to understand, so I'd appreciate it if—"

"You mean, it's sex? You had *sex* with Mr. Henry?" Tori blanched before her cheeks flushed a bold, bright red.

Jenna vowed to more closely monitor who her children hung out with. But how was that possible when all of this was being said in school? "No, I most certainly did *not.*"

She pulled the last of the thawed beef out of the refrigerator and grabbed a knife, slicing it into chunks with a destructive glee she wasn't quite able to contain. She knew she had to have a more in-depth talk with the twins about the birds and bees, but it was another one of those topics she'd never expected to have to handle totally on her own. Other than getting Tori a book to help explain the changes beginning to take place in her body, they hadn't discussed sex. And Mark Jeffrey... She had planned to leave the boy's perspective entirely to Jeff.

Inhaling a steadying breath, she forced herself to focus. "Listen to me, because I'm only going to say this once. Mr. Henry is a friend, whose wife has been ill. Remember the lasagna I took to school last week? That was for Mr. Henry and his wife because she had surgery and couldn't cook. What MacKenzie's mother saw me doing was dropping off the food and leaving his office. *More important,* this proves that it's not nice to gossip. MacKenzie's mom obviously got the story wrong, and it's very hurtful to think someone is spreading rumors like that about me."

Tori looked more than a little relieved. "Because of Dad?"

"Yes, because of your dad, and because rumors like that would also hurt Mr. and Mrs. Henry. Gossip is rarely good, Tori. More often than not it simply hurts people."

"I know… Are we having hamburger *again?*" Tori asked when she stepped closer to the stove.

Jenna ignored the complaint and stayed on topic. "We're not done with our discussion. The one thing Kenzie's mother had right was that I was let go—not fired—from my job. I no longer work at the school, but I didn't mention it to you because I didn't want you to worry."

"Why'd they let you go?" Mark Jeffrey asked in a tone that revealed his distress. "Did you do something bad?"

"No, I didn't. But the school couldn't afford to pay me anymore and, as much as I like working there, I can't work for no pay."

Mark Jeffrey's eyes flared wider. "Are we going to have to move again?"

"Mom!" Tori cried. "Are we?"

Jenna found herself thankful to Chance, something she had never thought she would be. "No. No, we don't have to move, because I found a new job today. Everything is fine."

"What kind of job is it?" Mark Jeffrey asked.

She told them, and even though she rarely shopped at the McKenna store, both knew exactly where it was located, because they'd been there with their father.

"Done," Mark Jeffrey cried, slamming the cover closed hard enough to rock the table. He sent his sister a superior look. "Don't touch my book."

"Mark Jeffrey, if Tori has homework and doesn't have her stuff, she'll need to borrow yours."

"No."

"Excuse me?"

Mark Jeffrey had the emotional depth to blush at her scolding tone.

"Grandpa Les says I'm the man of the house." Mark Jeffrey shoved his glasses up with the back of his hand. "And I think Tori needs to stop being a baby and do her own work. She won't ever know how to do it if I always do it for her."

Always do it for her?

Jenna dropped the hacked meat into the skillet. Did she *want* to know what tactic her daughter used to convince Mark Jeffrey to do her work for her? "Victoria?"

"Mark Jeffrey doesn't do it *all.* Just sometimes when I don't want to."

"And why is that?"

"What? Why don't I want to? Or why does he do it?"

Jenna bit her tongue and counted to ten. She knew this was only a taste of what was to come in Tori's teenage years. "Take your pick."

Another shrug. Oh, how she was beginning to hate that gesture.

"I already know how to do it, so it's not like I'm stupid."

"You still have to do the work. The teachers assign it for a reason."

"That's what pickle—um, I mean, Mark Jeffrey says but he's only repeating what Mrs. Dunham says."

"Mrs. Dunham is a very good teacher. You were lucky to get into her class." Jenna stirred the meat a little too briskly and knocked some out of the pan. *Five-second rule.* She burned her fingers picking up the piece and putting it into the skillet, but she made it with one-point-five seconds to spare. "From now on, you're using your own books and I want to see your homework. Every night, Tori. No exceptions. Understood?"

"*I'll* make sure she does it." Mark Jeffrey nodded to

emphasize his statement. "'Cause I'm the man of the house," he said, drawing out the words in an obvious taunt to his sister.

Rolling her eyes at Mark Jeffrey, Tori refocused on Jenna with a pained stare but grudgingly nodded her understanding.

Jenna turned to her task and exhaled. She didn't want to argue about homework or gossip or attitude. She simply wanted a quiet evening, maybe a soak in the tub, so she could prepare herself to start working for Chance McKenna.

"Can I go now? I told Kenzie I'd call her."

Jenna performed a quick mental debate over questioning her children further about the homework issue. Mark Jeffrey was obviously still standing up to Tori, so maybe the matter was handled.

"No, you may not," she said, despite wanting to allow the phone call because she knew Tori would repeat the truth to MacKenzie, which would then make it to MacKenzie's mother. But Jenna couldn't put her need for retribution ahead of the need to correct her daughter's behavior. "That's your punishment for blackmailing your brother into doing your homework."

"But he was stupid enough to fall for it."

"No calls, Tori. Go feed Snickerdoodle and ask Mark Jeffrey *nicely* to borrow his book to finish your schoolwork, while I make dinner."

"But I want to watch TV. I'm tired and my favorite show is on."

She was tired? *She* wanted to watch television? "Not another word or I'll take the phone away for a week, not just an evening." Jenna lost what was left of her patience.

She opened the cabinet door to search for seasonings when she heard the distinct yet whispered sound of *pickle head* coming out of Tori's mouth as she passed Mark Jeffrey at the table.

Jenna saw red. "For that, you're doing dishes tonight, too."

"Fine! But if I'm in trouble already I might as well say it," Tori said, dumping a cup full of food in the dog's bowl. "He's a picklehead, picklehead, *picklehead!*"

"*Victoria Rose,* go to your room."

Fifteen minutes. Tori needed a fifteen-minute time-out. Once dinner was done, they could discuss the name-calling.

Sometimes Jenna felt as though she walked a tightrope with Tori and Mark Jeffrey on each end of her balancing bar. But even with Jeff's death behind her, she still had a long, long way to go before she reached the other side. Especially when Tori stomped up the stairs and slammed the door with enough force to rattle the glasses in the cupboard.

"Women," Mark Jeffrey said in a weary voice. "Tommy Colley says I don't stand a chance 'cause even the dog's a girl."

Hiding behind the cabinet door Jenna rested her head against the wood, torn between laughing and crying. Because *she* wanted to stomp up the stairs and flop on her bed and take a time-out.

And because she sure hoped Tommy Colley wasn't right.

THE NEXT MORNING, Chance waited for Jenna to arrive with more enthusiasm than was acceptable or appropriate, given the circumstances. He couldn't help it, though. He needed a distraction and she was most definitely it. He was tired of being stuck in the chair. Maybe if he'd stayed off his foot in the beginning the way he was supposed to... He hadn't and he couldn't turn back time, which meant he had another two to three weeks before the cast came off.

He needed something to occupy his mind that had nothing to do with Dooley farting or singing '80s hair-band music. Between working here during the day and sleeping in his one-room apartment in the back of the store every night, the walls were closing in on him. Sometimes a man had to get away, otherwise he risked losing it and doing something he couldn't take back.

Chance awkwardly lowered himself into the straight-backed chair and propped his crutches off to the side, dreading the evening hours when he had to don the hot, itchy Santa suit again.

In years past, his adoptive father would have worn the suit, or Dooley if Zane was too busy. But with Zane gone, it made sense for Chance to cowboy up and don the red, leaving the able-bodied Dooley free to help customers. Didn't make it any easier on the old ego, though. Chance hated sitting around all the time.

The glass double doors opened and Jenna paused to wipe her snow-soaked shoes on the weatherproof mat.

Sitting in this spot since November first had given Chance a lot of time to observe people and he'd noticed the care women took to wipe their feet, whereas the men tromped on in and didn't worry about the mess left behind.

Jenna took more care than most. Or maybe her lingering on the rug was due to nerves and her not wanting to work for him.

"Welcome."

The length of the wide entry aisle stretched between them. She stopped pawing the rug like a skittish horse, but nothing could disguise the look on her face when she squared her shoulders and fisted her gloved hands at her sides, all at the sound of his voice.

No, sir, she really didn't want to be there—which told him how rough things were financially. Hadn't Jeff taken any precautions? Taken out a life-insurance policy?

Chance was as addicted to climbing as any of the Rock Gods. But like him, most of the group didn't have kids. He had assumed that, because Jeff did, he would have taken more care to cover things like that—for Jenna's sake.

Her uniquely blue gaze locked on his and he felt a jolt all the way to his cast.

Even with her Rudolph-red nose and her hair scraped back from her face in some pilgrim-style bun, Jenna caught his attention the way few women ever had. But the ring on her finger was a constant reminder of who she was and what she had been through.

"Good morning," she said.

He smiled at her and wished doing so didn't make her frown immediately. "Mornin'. You can put your coat and purse in one of the lockers in back. I'll show you."

"No, no, don't get up. I'll find them."

She took off toward the rear of the store and he watched her go, his gaze straying to the sway of her hips and the curve of her ass. Nice.

Then she was out of sight, thanks to the swing door, and he realized what he was doing. That wasn't something a friend did to a buddy's wife—or a woman who made no bones about not liking him, how he spent his free time climbing or hanging with the Rock Gods.

Chance used the time until Jenna reappeared to lecture himself.

She might have been Jeff's wife but that didn't mean he wasn't curious about her. After work last night, Chance had swung by Carly's house and deliberately mentioned hiring Jenna to his gossip-knowing sister-in-law. Carly had given him the scoop about how Jenna had recently moved from her place outside town to a small home a few streets down from the sheriff's station.

Question was why had she moved? Had the house held too many memories of her life with Jeff? Or was it also a money issue? Chance didn't know her well enough to ask, but he wanted to.

"So, where do I start?" Jenna eyed him, her fingers knotted in front of her waist, her somewhat plain yet pretty features pinched.

Chance made a grab for his crutches.

"Don't worry, boss. I'll get her started," Dooley said, appearing at the end of an aisle. "Jenna, follow me."

And just like that, his distraction was gone, although his questions remained.

CHAPTER THREE

THE WOMEN IN THIS TOWN are idiots, Jenna decided later that same day.

A couple of hours before she was scheduled to leave work, Jenna watched as two women—a fortysomething mother and her twentysomething daughter from the looks of it—teetered into the store in ridiculous, four-inch heeled boots, spotted Chance and produced a camera, holding it out to Jenna to take their picture.

How old were they again?

"Hold the button halfway down to focus, then all the way down to snap the shot," the younger of the two instructed.

Jenna set aside the boxes of Christmas lights she was shelving and reluctantly accepted the hot-pink camera with a weak smile. She had work to do, her legs, feet and back ached from standing all day, and she didn't remember photography as being part of her job description. But with her Santa-coated employer watching, she couldn't refuse.

The younger of the two claimed Chance's good thigh, while Mama Bimbo carefully perched on the arm of the chair.

His arms full of ample hips and his face full of boobage, the duo flashed lipstick-coated smiles, while Chance's slate-colored gaze twinkled amid the bushy beard and faux-fur hat.

Typical man. He seemed to be enjoying himself, even if the entire situation made Jenna's skin crawl. She had grown up a missionary's kid in developing countries, used to huts and villages and more subtleties when it came to the interaction of the sexes. Not this blatant, in-your-face—*seriously*—flirting taking place on his lap.

Jeff had been a flirt, too. It seemed to be a quality shared among all the Rock Gods and climbers given their tendency to be confident people.

Jenna snapped the photo, wishing she had the nerve to screw it up. That was the problem with digital. It was too easy to check.

"Take pictures of us individually."

Just when she thought she was off the hook. The least they could do was say *please*.

Waiting while Mama Bimbo stood, Jenna watched Baby Bimbo lean in and give Santa Chance a kiss on the cheek.

"Oh, that looks so cute. Take it now," Mama cried.

Gritting her teeth, Jenna did as ordered. *Just part of the job, just part of the job.*

Just.

A.

Job.

"Take several so I'm sure to have a good one," the younger one said, latching on to Chance—er, Santa—like a leech. She continued to place teasing pecks on his cheek for each and every shot.

"Oh, that's just precious," Mama cried. "My turn. Move over, honey. Take lots of me, too."

Jenna decided then and there Christmas employees should get hazard pay for emotional trauma. She had work to do that did not involve grinding her teeth to nubs or feeling the need for a shower. She still had to sweep the floor, and Dooley was going to teach her how to cash out the register and all the other five-o'clock-store-closing things that had to be done.

"Did you take it?" Mama demanded.

Once more, Jenna snapped the photo as requested and handed off the camera like a hot potato when Baby Bimbo decided Jenna wasn't getting the right angle.

She could only imagine the things that poor camera had seen.

On her way to the closest bottle of hand sanitizer, Jenna heard Mama ask, "So, Santa baby, would you be interested in joining us a little later at the Honey? We're looking for some fun."

Mama B meant at the Wild Honey, the bar/honky-tonk hangout on the outskirts of town. Didn't they realize it was only Tuesday? Where did they go for fun on Friday nights?

If Chance said yes to those two, he would confirm her worst suspicions about him and the Rock Gods. The majority of them were single men known for partying hard once the climbs were over. Partying hard in general. That was another aspect she and Jeff had argued over during their marriage. Married men with children to raise didn't need to be partying with single men bent on getting in someone's pants, and Jenna had made it abundantly clear she wouldn't put up with a cheating man.

"Now, there's an invitation if I ever heard one. Some of my buddies said they'd stop in around closing. Maybe I'll see you there."

The mother-daughter duo's cleavage bounced up and down as they expressed their excitement over the possibility.

Jenna walked away in disgust and went back to stocking the shelves.

Her first day on the job and she wanted to strangle herself with the tinsel hanging from the ceiling.

CHANCE COULDN'T HELP but get a kick out of Jenna's behavior. Was she always so uptight? "It's safe now," he called out once the mother-daughter team had bought gifts for their boyfriends and exes and left. "You can stop hiding."

Jenna reappeared from behind the end cap of galvanized buckets. "I wasn't *hiding*."

He tugged the Santa beard down and scratched his itchy face. "Yeah, right. You acted like that camera was on fire."

She prickled like a porcupine and he used his hand to hide his grin. She saw it and stiffened some more.

"Come on, they were just having fun."

"You mean, *you* were having fun."

"Something wrong with that?"

She held the pricing gun in front of her as though she was ready to start shooting, her pink lips pursed. "Not at all. You are free to do whatever you like. Before I forget, you're three short on the Shake-n-Light Flashlights. They're not in the stockroom, either."

So she didn't want to talk to him unless they talked business? Had snapping a few photos gotten her panties in that much of a twist? "Someone probably walked off with them. That starts to happen more often this time of year."

The phone rang and Dooley hurried out of the back to answer it.

"Hey, Liam… Jenna? Yeah, she's here. Hang on." Dooley covered the mouthpiece with his hand. "Jenna,

it's for you. It's Liam—uh, Deputy McKenna. He's calling about your kids."

"What? Oh, *no*."

Jenna raced to the phone and Chance shoved himself out of the chair and snatched his crutches, hobbling
along after her.

"Hello? Yes, yes. What's wrong? Are they okay?"

The sound of his crutches marking every step
drowned out any opportunity he might have had to hear
some of the conversation taking place on Liam's end.

"Yes. Yes, of course. No, I—I'll be right there. Thank
you."

Whatever it was, it wasn't good. "Are they hurt?" he
asked the moment she pulled the phone away from her
ear.

"N-no. But I have to go. I'm sorry."

"Don't be. Get your keys. I'll drive you."

Jenna took a step and stopped to swing around and
look at him.

"I'm fine. You don't—"

"You're upset and shouldn't be behind the wheel.
Dooley's fine here. He can handle the last hour alone,"
he said. "I'm driving you."

"You're in a cast. And a Santa suit."

"Left foot," he said simply. "And some people think
the man in red is cool. You want to stand around and
argue or go? Liam can drop me off here later."

Jenna wanted to argue, he could see it on her face but
her fear over whatever had happened to her kids that
had Liam calling her on official police business won
the battle. She raced for her purse and belongings in
back while Chance murmured goodbye to Dooley and
set off for the door, knowing full well she'd probably
catch up to him before he made it to her truck.

Sure enough, Jenna arrived at the truck the same time he did. She grabbed his crutches to store and speed the process. "What happened?" he asked once he had the keys in the ignition.

"I don't know. Something about them playing in the street and someone reporting them. Just go. Please. I live on Oak Street."

Jenna pressed her palms to her temples and rubbed hard, and Chance saw how badly her hands were shaking. "But Liam told you to come home, not the hospital?"

"Yes."

"So they're fine," he said, driving along the main stretch of road toward the heart of town.

"I think so. He said they were but— I told them to stay *inside.*"

"They were alone? You didn't get a babysitter?" he asked, sliding her a look.

"Rachel—my neighbor—was supposed to be watching them but she has a business of her own to run and her mother to help. I thought they'd be fine. It's only an hour and a half and they're almost eleven. We *talked* about what they were to do when they got home."

He'd hot-wired his first car at eleven. Took it out and brought it back without his foster family catching him, too. The fact that Jenna had twins simply meant double the trouble. "I'm sure it's nothing major. Liam would've told you otherwise if that wasn't the case."

"I know. But I told them to stay *in the house.*"

Liam's car was parked along the street, lights on. Chance pulled into Jenna's driveway and had barely stopped when she opened her door and jumped out to hurry to the porch, where Liam and her kids stood.

Taking his time on the ice still coating her driveway,

Chance made it to the porch and ignored his brother's too-curious stare.

"What are you doing here?" Liam asked, his expression loosening its grimness for a moment.

"She was upset," he said simply. "Didn't think she ought to drive."

Jenna grabbed her kids and hugged them before setting them away from her, visibly checking them over for potential injuries, her face as pale as the snow in her yard.

"Are you all right?" she asked.

"Yeah. Who's Santa?" the girl asked.

Obviously she was no longer a believer. Chance winked at her anyway, but instead of the shy look and blush he usually got from girls her age, she stared at him as though he was a moron. Cute kid.

"Ms. Darlington, we have a problem here," Liam said, his tone turning official. "Is it true you left your children home alone?"

Jenna looked at the lowered heads of her children, seeming torn between wanting to throttle them and hug them tight without letting go.

The twins were bundled against the cold—proof of their exploits when they should have been behind the wide-open door.

He noticed the girl repeatedly shot glares in Liam's direction—no doubt blaming him for ruining their fun—while Jenna's son sniffed and looked as though he wanted to throw up. It was pretty easy to pick out the stronger personality of those two.

"My, um, neighbor was supposed to check on them," Jenna said. "Mark Jeffrey, are you sure you're all right? Tori?"

"Yeah, Mom," Tori said in a droll tone.

"I'm sorry," Mark Jeffrey whispered. A fresh set of sniffles came on quick and made his voice squeak.

Chance felt more than a twinge of pity for the kid. Mark Jeffrey was small for his age, obviously more sensitive than his sister—and an inch shorter than her, as well.

"Yeah, sorry," Tori dutifully repeated, looking anything but.

Inhaling as though to steady the storm brewing inside her, Jenna swallowed and faced Liam, who was making no pretense about sizing her up.

"Ma'am, are you referring to the neighbor who isn't home?"

"Rachel *left?*"

"She said she had an emergency delivery and she'd be right back," Mark Jeffrey said, his chin tucked tight to his chest.

"So you took that to mean you could play outside in the *street?*" she demanded.

"We were sledding and getting exercise. You tell us we watch too much television," Tori quipped.

Chance coughed. He had to in order to cover the laugh about to erupt from him. He must not have done a good enough job of it, though, because Liam and Jenna both glared at him.

"Deputy McKenna, I am so sorry for the trouble they've caused. It won't happen again."

"We're sorry, too," Mark Jeffrey quickly added, peeking at Liam before ducking his head once more.

"Ms. Darlington, like I said on the phone, we had a complaint from a neighbor who reported the children were playing in the street. It's a busy road and apparently one driver barely managed to get stopped in time to avoid hitting them."

"We didn't start off there, we just sorta slid there," Tori interjected.

"Are you going to take us to jail?" Mark Jeffrey asked.

"No, son, but your mom—"

"You're taking *our mom* to jail? No, it's not her fault!" Mark Jeffrey shot off the bench and plowed into Jenna, wrapping his arms around her waist and toppling her into Chance.

Thankfully his reflexes were quick and he shifted his weight to take the blow in time but still welcomed Liam's steadying grip keeping them all from tumbling down the steps.

"I'm sorry," Jenna said, turning to make sure Chance was okay.

"No problem."

"Dork," Tori muttered, rolling her eyes.

"Mark Jeffrey," Jenna said, forcing him to release his grip, "go inside and wash your face and get something to drink. Do it," she ordered calmly when it looked as though he'd balk—and bawl. Jenna gently nudged the boy toward the door. "Tori, you, too. No tormenting, either, young lady. Understood? I need to talk to the deputy and I need to do it in peace."

The kids tromped inside, snowy footprints left in their wake.

Jenna turned toward Liam and squared her shoulders. "I'm so sorry. I can't believe they did this. I thought they'd mind me and stay in the house. We discussed what they could do while I was gone, and trust me, playing in the street wasn't on the list. It won't happen again."

Liam readjusted his hat, but his expression didn't falter. He was still in full cop mode. "That's good to hear, but it's not that simple. Protocol is for me to call Children's Services when something like this happens."

Chance didn't think it possible for Jenna to pale any more but she did.

"*No,* you can't do that. Please, there's no reason to get them involved. It won't happen again. I promise."

"You can't make that promise."

"Liam, come on," Chance said, lowering his tone. "I heard Jenna call to check on them as soon as they were home from school, *and* I know she talked to the neighbor. She made arrangements for child care. You don't need to get CS involved. There's no reason to."

"This doesn't involve you," his brother said pointedly. "And they were nearly hit by a car," the deputy said. "I can't play favorites because she's working at the store."

"But it won't happen again," she insisted.

Chance took a step closer to his brother and lowered his voice. "I know situations like this get under your skin but she's not that kind of parent," he insisted softly. "One phone call to CS and Jenna will spend *months* trying to prove she's a good mother. You'd not only waste Jenna's time but CS's, as well."

The mere mention of Children's Services made his skin crawl. As a whole they were a great organization. Overworked, underpaid, understaffed, but the caseworkers were dedicated to making sure kids were cared for. But having been one of those kids ripped out of his life and shoved into the system, Chance wouldn't wish that on anyone.

"The kids can't be left home alone."

"Then they can get off the bus at the store and stay there until Jenna's shift is over."

"What?" she asked in obvious surprise. "I mean, yes.

Thank you. Only until I—I can make other arrangements, of course."

Chance could almost see the cogs and wheels turning in his brother's brain. "It's not a problem."

"Is that right?" Liam questioned with his best cop stare.

"Jeff was a friend," Chance continued. "The least I can do is help out his family. Like she said, it's only until she can make other arrangements."

The stare he received from Liam went on so long it seemed as though he was trying to figure out if aliens had taken possession of Chance. Maybe they had. God knew what he would do with two kids underfoot at the store.

"Fine. I'll agree to that. So long as child care is handled and nothing like this happens again, I'll let it slide. But I'd better not be called back." To Chance, he said, "And you'd better be right."

"I am."

Jenna held her clasped hands to her mouth in prayer position. "Thank you. Thank you *both.*"

"Ms. Darlington, go hug your kids, give them a lecture and have a good laugh," Liam said. "One look at the rig they put on the dog to pull the sled and I guarantee you won't be able to keep a straight face."

"Oh, poor Snickers," Jenna said. "Thank you, again, for not calling Children's Services."

Liam tipped his hat and nodded. "You're welcome. But find reliable child care."

"I will."

"Can you give me a lift back to the store?" Chance asked.

"Sure thing, Santa, but I should make you sit in the back."

Chance ignored the threat. "I'll be right there."

Liam strode down the steps as Chance lingered. "Don't take his attitude personally. He takes child neglect and abuse cases very seriously."

Jenna managed a weak smile. "Knowing that, how can I take it personally? That's a good thing. And I owe you an even bigger thank-you for your help in convincing him, even if it was for Jeff."

He descended the steps, careful of the ice.

"Chance?"

He twisted to face her, balanced carefully on his good leg and the crutches.

"You were taken by Children's Services?"

Memories flooded his brain. None of them good. Last time he'd seen his father, it was as he was slammed against the trunk of the car so the cops could cuff him. Children's Services had arrived minutes later. "My mother died when I was five. CS came to get me when I was six."

"I'm sorry. Your father died, too?"

"No. He's dead to me just the same. See you tomorrow at work, Jenna."

He made his way to Liam's cruiser and dropped into the front passenger seat. As they drove, the silence was broken only by the radio. When Chance couldn't take it anymore, he said, "She's a good mother."

"And you know this after she's worked for you one day?"

Yeah, that didn't sound so good, did it? "Come on, Liam, one look at her kids, and anyone can tell they're not neglected or abused. You can't put your past on them. Or Riley's," he said, referring to the abused foster kid Liam and his wife, Carly, were in the process of adopting.

"I'm not the only one with a past that gets in the way of things sometimes," Liam said. "Maybe I'll stop seeing calls like Jenna's as neglectful when you stop shoving your own family away and acting like you don't give a damn."

Chance welcomed the sight of the store as they rolled to a stop outside the entrance. He cursed the hassle of getting his crutches out and on solid ground.

"Chance," Liam called, before Chance could make his getaway, "don't *ever* interfere with a case again, otherwise I will put you in the backseat for obstruction."

Chance slammed the door shut. The comment was a reminder to control his temper—or wind up like his father.

CHAPTER FOUR

JENNA WATCHED Chance climb into the cruiser beside his brother but didn't feel the relief she should feel at them driving away. She lingered on the porch, well aware of the stares of her neighbors who were unable to hide their curiosity.

She and the kids had lived here only about three months and having the police stop by for a visit and *stay* until she showed up wasn't the way to make an impression.

Inhaling, she saw Rachel's delivery van slowly pull into her driveway across the street. Rachel hadn't been gone that long at all and, had the children stayed where they were told, nothing would have happened.

"Hey," Rachel called, waving. "I think I set a new delivery record. Everything okay?"

Jenna wrapped her arms around herself and forced herself to nod and wave. Rachel would feel horrible about the incident but Jenna could blame only herself. She'd known Rachel would pop in on the twins sporadically at best, timed around Rachel's work schedule, deliveries and caring for her mother. Jenna had hoped that would be enough, given the twins' age. Obviously it wasn't.

Later, after the kids were asleep, she would explain what happened to Rach. Maybe they could brainstorm child-care alternatives that didn't involve Chance—or duct tape.

"Mom?"

She didn't turn to face her daughter. "Tori, you don't want to talk to me right now. I need a minute."

"But...I brought you something."

She glanced over her shoulder to see Tori in the door, a mug cradled in both hands and a leery expression on her stubborn, too-pretty face. Proud mama or not, Jenna knew that in another couple of years she was going to be in big, big trouble between boys and teenage rebellion. Bigger than what she had faced tonight. *Jeff, I wasn't supposed to do this alone.*

"We made you some hot chocolate."

"*I* made it," Mark Jeffrey corrected.

"But I added the marshmallows," Tori said. "Just the way you like it. Are you coming inside?"

Tori gave a bright smile and Jenna knew they wouldn't leave her alone despite her request. "Where's Snickers?" she asked, instead of answering.

Tori's eyes flared wide. "Um, Snickers?"

At the sound of her name, Snickerdoodle came barreling down the stairs, dragging belts and sheets and the old sleigh bells Jenna had hung on the farmhouse door every winter for the past eight years before she'd had to sell the house after Jeff's death.

Deputy McKenna was right. One look and it took everything in Jenna to keep a straight face. The poor, ever-patient dog wore a headband of light-up antlers and a red plastic glowing nose attached to an elastic band. At the moment the nose was skewed to the right of Snickers's jaw like a giant pimple. "Oh, Snickers, what did they do to you?"

"You don't like it?" Tori asked. "I thought she looked cute."

"I'll take it off." Mark Jeffrey moved to do so.

"Oh, no, you don't," Jenna said, shaking her head. "Not until I get a picture. You two are getting in it, too. And remember, this is not a sign of approval or permission to have the police at my door, understood? I simply want proof for when I tell your children."

Jenna entered the house and walked into the kitchen to get her camera.

"She can't be *that* mad if she's taking pictures," Tori whispered.

"Shut up before you get us in more trouble."

"You shut up. Mom's mad, but Snickers has cute factor. Mom almost *smiled*."

"That's stupid."

"You're stupid."

"If we'd stayed *inside* and sledded down the stairs, no one would've seen us and we wouldn't be in trouble," Mark Jeffrey said in a superior, all-knowing tone.

Down the stairs? The old house they'd moved into had steep stairs that made her legs ache every time she climbed them. Not to mention the door at the bottom a scant two-and-a-half feet from the last tread.

There were some things parents just weren't meant to know.

Jenna kept her back to them and fiddled with the camera, trying not to imagine one of them slamming into the door at full speed. The image made her cringe.

The twins' stunt reminded her of when she and a few of the kids at an orphanage in Guam had climbed a hill with pieces of cardboard and sledded down—uncaring of the fast-moving stream below. The trick was to roll off the cardboard in the right spot.

No, the trick was knowing there are consequences. Life isn't all fun and games.

No, it wasn't. Jeff's death was the perfect example of that. Jeff was all about fun, but anytime she'd question what she and the twins would do if something happened to him, Jeff would brush off her concern.

For the twins' sake, she had to set the example Jeff hadn't been able to set himself. She had to give her children rules and routine, that sense of security that had been blown apart with their father's death and losing the house and all things familiar thanks to the debt Jeff's recklessness had created.

She had to get them to see that adventure was one thing, but they were responsible for their actions—because those actions *always* impacted other people. Deputy McKenna could have called Children's Services tonight. She could have been taken into custody for neglect. Lost her job. She and the kids could have been separated. All because the twins wanted to turn Snickers into a sled dog and play outside.

If she'd learned nothing else in her life, it was that the fun never quite lasted as long as the consequences. And one way or another she had to teach her children that.

"HEY," RACHEL SAID as soon as Jenna opened the door. "I've been meaning to call you all night to ask about your first day but I haven't stopped since I got home. I thought you'd come over as always but, since you didn't..." She held up a plate of muffins still warm from the oven. "How'd it go?"

"None of the neighbors filled you in?"

Rachel's eyebrows rose. "Oh, that doesn't sound good. What happened?"

Jenna moved so Rachel could come in from the cold, then led the way to the kitchen, noting that Rachel had made the trek across the street in her pj's, thick robe and snow boots. Jenna wanted to pull on her own pajamas and sink into bed to relieve the ache of being on her feet all day. More than that, though, she wanted her Rachel conversation fix.

"I got a call at work today—from the sheriff's department," she said, quickly relating the twins' stunt.

"Oh, Jenna, I am *so sorry.*"

"They're fine."

"But—"

"No buts. You are not to blame, Rach. I knew you'd be busy. I thought they'd be okay with periodic check-ins but obviously that wasn't the case."

"But if something had happened to them—"

"If something had happened, it would've been their fault—and mine—not yours."

Rachel lowered herself onto a stool and leaned against the scarred counter, worry visible on her bare face.

"I shouldn't have left them. I thought about denying the special delivery request but I didn't want to lose the sale and it was only to the edge of town. It's a wonder you're even talking to me."

"Stop it. I'm thankful things worked out like they did. But now I have to come up with child-care ideas or else attempt to work and watch the twins at the same time."

"I imagine it's hard enough to concentrate working with Chance McKenna around." Rachel had a gleam in her eyes.

From the first day Jenna had met Rachel at the elementary school during one of her deliveries, they'd hit it off and become friends. Not the close, we've-known-each-other-from-kindergarten type of friends but the kind that formed over similar tastes, similar problems—Jeff's death coincided with Rachel's husband moving out to be with another woman and Rachel's mother moving in due to health issues—and general life circumstances. Rachel was one of those people who was simply easy to talk to, about anything.

"Chance is not even on the radar," Jenna said bluntly.

"What? I don't believe you."

"It's true."

"How is that possible? Have you *seen* the man?"

She had. And true, he was gorgeous. But no man who played with the Rock Gods could ever be on her radar again.

Security. That was the word she used to approach life now. And any man okay with tossing himself off cliffs or free climbing without ropes or protective gear could not give her already broken family the security they needed. Period. "Yes, I have." She grabbed a couple of small plates and napkins so they could tear into the muffins. "I've also seen him in action and he's not my type."

"Explain how that's possible," Rachel ordered.

"Two women came into the store today—"

"That sounds like the beginning of a dirty joke."

Jenna laughed. "It certainly *looked* like the beginning of a dirty joke." She wondered if Chance had gone to the Wild Honey tonight and met up with the mother-daughter duo.

And if he had?

None of your business.

"So what's the punch line?"

"I think I was," she said, only half kidding. "I was

the lucky photographer who got to capture the special moments as they sat on Santa's lap—Chance being Santa—to have their pictures taken. You should've seen them. They were fawning over him, and Chance was eating it up."

"Most men would. And you sound jealous."

"Jealous?" Was that the word of the day? She was not jealous.

"Uh-oh. I struck a nerve?"

Not wanting to admit it and yet needing to get to the bottom of her emotional response, she sat on the stool opposite Rach's. "Chance said that, too. He said they were just having fun."

"Well, I can see his point. Wait. Let me finish," Rachel said when Jenna immediately opened her mouth to protest. "I probably would've been jealous, too. Not because of him but because I *miss* fun, and I don't doubt you do, too. Remember when our most important worry was about getting to a hair appointment on time or what we would wear?"

Jenna bit into the muffin and moaned at the delicious flavor.

"See? You're having a climax over a freaking muffin."

"Rachel!" Jenna struggled to chew and swallow, when all she could do was laugh. And feel sorry for her friend who carried so much on her shoulders. She should never have asked Rachel to watch the twins. "Forget Chance. How's your mom?" she asked when she finally got herself under control.

"The dementia is getting worse fast but she's in good spirits most of the time, so I'm trying to be thankful for that." Rachel finished off her muffin and reached for another, only to pause with her hand over them.

"What's wrong?" Jenna asked.

Rachel abandoned the muffins and grabbed her glass of milk instead. "I got the divorce papers today."

"Oh, Rach, I'm sorry." It seemed so petty to be complaining about those women and Chance when there were more important matters—like divorce papers and ill parents.

"I'm not. But it means I have to be date-ready—if I ever get to date again. With the shape Mom is in, what the guy would have to be willing to put up with... Well, I may be alone forever. You know what ticks me off the most?"

"That the man you loved, who you planned to spend the rest of your life with, screwed you over?" Jenna said, feeling every ounce of Rachel's pain. Jenna had been honest about Jeff's less-than-stellar employment history, their financial state and how her worry and warnings had gone unheeded. How he would come home from a climb, and swing her up into his arms, and because she was so thankful he was okay, she'd allow him to make her forget the worry. For a while.

Her comment earned a laugh from Rachel.

"Yep. That's the one." Rachel finished her milk and stood. "I'd better go. Oh, we didn't talk about childcare."

Jenna shook her head. "Don't worry about it. Seriously. It's covered for now and I'm almost positive Jeff's parents will take them over Thanksgiving break."

"What are you going to do if the Darlingtons can't watch them?"

"I have no idea. Take them to work and threaten them with duct tape, I guess."

CHAPTER FIVE

CHANCE RECOGNIZED TROUBLE when he saw it. And right now it was walking through the door in the form of miniature versions of Jeff and Jenna Darlington.

He frowned at the realization that as often as he'd seen the kids with Jeff in the store, he hadn't noticed how closely the kids resembled their parents.

Jenna's daughter was the spitting image of her mama, right down to the stubborn tilt of her pointy little chin. And the boy... Take off the glasses and bulk him up a bit and the kid was Jeff made over.

Staring at Mark Jeffrey, Chance suddenly wondered whether or not he looked like *his* biological father. All he really remembered from those early years was that his father had dark hair and was big, gruff. But weren't all fathers big and gruff to a small kid?

It freaked him out thinking about his biological father, about the possibility there were any of his father's traits inside him. He liked to consider himself his own man, not a replica of someone else. Especially not a murderer who hadn't cared enough about his young son to think twice before committing a crime that carried a life sentence.

"Hi, guys. How was school today?" Jenna asked, approaching them.

"Boring."

"Good. We learned about bridges and how they're

built," Mark Jeffrey replied. "And it was cool getting off the bus here."

"You can thank Mr. McKenna for that."

Jenna made the official introductions but kept them brief.

"Mr. McKenna is letting you sit over here with the camping equipment. Don't touch anything, got it? And the tent isn't to be played in. Keep yourselves busy by finishing up your homework."

Jenna's gaze narrowed entirely on the girl, Tori. "Did you bring your books?"

"Yeah, Mom. How long do we have to stay here?"

Jenna held up her hand, and surprisingly the kid immediately stopped talking. But, Chance noted, not arguing looked to be taking some effort.

"Absolutely no complaints allowed. You had an alternative and blew it, remember?"

Chance bit back a grin. Despite the words they'd exchanged and the tension between them, Liam had text-messaged a picture of the kids' *sled dog.*

He gave them a ten for originality.

"Mom, I'm hungry."

"Me, too," Tori said, glancing at the door.

The diner was in the middle of town—a pretty walk on a spring or summer day but a cold one in the winter. It was the main restaurant in town and Tori obviously debated the odds of escape.

Sometimes it took one ornery kid to recognize another.

"I brought snacks. They're on the table in the cooler, waiting for you. Clean up your mess when you're done and put it in the trash."

Jenna sounded like a drill sergeant, but he supposed after their adventure yesterday she had to crack the whip.

The kids tromped to the area Jenna had set up for them and listened while she added more to her list of instructions. The moment she walked away, however, the kids unloaded backpacks, shrugged off their coats and kicked off boots to make themselves at home, digging into the snacks with unabashed glee.

When Mark Jeffrey noticed Chance watching them, he shoved up his glasses and left a shiny purple trail on his cheek.

"You want one? They're peanut butter and jelly."

So he could see. "If you don't mind sharing."

Mark Jeffrey dug a sandwich out of the cooler and walked to where Chance sat.

"Thanks."

"You're welcome."

The plastic-wrapped sandwich was crustless—and shaped like a star. The extra length Jenna had gone to for her kids despite their behavior yesterday was sweet, and he found himself staring at the pointy little ends. It seemed like such a loving, parental thing to do.

What would it have been like to have a mom like Jenna growing up? A parent who cut off the crust and made sandwiches into shapes? The few foster homes he'd had were okay, but he'd never once received a star-shaped sandwich. Irrationally, that small, thoughtful gesture pissed him off because his father had destroyed the life they could have had.

It was more proof that while his adoptive brothers, Liam and Brad, were settling down and thinking about kids, Chance was right to steer clear of entanglements like parenthood. If he could get riled because of a sandwich, he was probably more like his father—who murdered a man in anger—than he cared to admit.

He needed to stick to what he knew and loved—

climbing. The sooner he was able to do it again, the better.

"What's the matter? Did I squish it?"

A laugh huffed out of his chest. "No, you didn't. It's fine. I was just admiring it. That's a mighty fine star."

"I guess. Mom always does that, even though we're not little kids anymore. She says we're special to her, so our sandwiches should be special, too."

Yeah, he could see Jenna doing that, saying that.

Mark Jeffrey leaned in a little closer, looking around all the while like a spy who didn't want to be caught divulging secrets. "Don't tell her, but Tori and me squish them up at school so the other kids don't see."

"Good thinking. Can't have anyone making fun."

"Nope. Do the little kids really believe you're Santa?"

"Don't I look like him?"

"I 'spose. How'd you break your leg?"

Out of the corner of his eye, Chance saw Tori leaving her books behind and sneaking closer to be a part of the conversation. "Actually, I broke my foot. I'd just finished climbing a mountain."

"Our dad fell climbing a mountain. He died," Mark Jeffrey said, his tone soft and sad.

Ah, man. Chance hadn't even thought of the impact of his statement, or memories the kids might have of Jeff and his death. "I know he did. I'm a member of the Rock Gods, too. I'm sorry about what happened to your dad."

"We miss him a lot."

"He was fun," Tori added softly. "He wouldn't have gotten mad about yesterday, either."

"He might've," Mark Jeffrey said with a shrug. "But if he hadn't died, we wouldn't have had to move, and then we could've played outside and no one would call the cops on us."

"Stupid neighbors." Tori rolled her eyes.

Chance looked around but didn't see Jenna anywhere in sight or hearing range. "So, uh, you moved to town to be closer to school?" The question wasn't exactly subtle or original but hopefully it would get the job done.

"No. Our house cost too much," Tori stated matter-of-factly, as only a kid could. "How did you break your foot? Did you fall like our dad?"

The twins obviously wanted to talk about Jeff. And surprisingly, Chance wanted to hear them. Maybe he could share some fun stories of his own, such as the time Jeff had come running out of the woods like a bat out of hell trying to escape a skunk.

To his knowledge, Jenna hadn't come on any of the Rock Gods's climbs, so she couldn't share that aspect of Jeff's life with their children. "Not exactly. I didn't fall during the climb. I was already finished and at my truck. It's kind of embarrassing, actually. I jumped out of the truck bed and landed wrong."

"You climbed a mountain but fell out of a *truck?*" Tori gave Chance a stare that made him feel like an idiot. Did women practice those looks from birth?

"Jumped out—but, yeah, pretty much."

"Have you done other cool stuff?"

"Does mountain biking and white-water rafting count?" he asked.

"Have you ever been in a rodeo?"

"A few of them."

The twins exchanged a quick glance, the interest on their faces unmistakable.

"You want to hear about those?"

"Yeah. What was it like?" Mark Jeffrey asked.

Chance shared some of the experiences he'd had competing in various rodeo events. From there, the stories changed to general stuff, like riding and roping and the tricks he'd learned to do.

"You *really* stood up when the horse was galloping?" Tori asked, appearing more than a little suspicious.

"I did."

"What kind of things did Dad do?" she asked.

Chance stared into the little girl's eyes and smiled. "He ever show you any pictures of when he climbed?"

"A few."

Chance pulled out his cell phone and tapped the screen to pull up the photos. He—or other people borrowing his camera—took tons of pictures, but he rarely downloaded them. Last count there were... fifteen-hundred-thirty-two images. He really had to download.

He scrolled through until he found some of a trip Jeff had gone on, and the twins gathered around the chair to see them.

"Oh, cool!" Tori said softly.

Chance glanced at Mark Jeffrey when the boy remained quiet. "Your dad was about halfway up the face in this shot and when he saw me he started acting like a monkey. You want to see some more?"

Mark Jeffrey nodded and swallowed.

"Yeah. Dad looks like he was having fun."

"He was, buddy. Your dad definitely knew how to have a good time."

"Mom put all of Dad's climbing pictures away. The only ones out now are the regular ones," Tori said.

One by one, he showed the pictures he had of Jeff and the Rock Gods together, telling the kids stories all the while. "This one was a really hard climb. You had to come at it from beneath that ledge there and—"

"What's going on here?"

Chance glanced up to see Jenna standing about ten feet away, her hands planted on her hips. He felt like a kid caught smoking in the john. "Just telling the kids some stories about Jeff and showing them pictures. You, uh, get finished in the back already?"

"Tori, Mark Jeffrey, homework. Now."

The kids scrambled, leaving Chance alone to face her wrath. And no doubt about it, Jenna was angry. Her eyes darkened and sparkled like stones under water.

"They wanted to know how I broke my foot." Her gaze dropped and he realized the sandwich was on his lap. "Mark Jeffrey gave it to me."

Chance winced, hearing himself. But the way Jenna was looking at him made him feel as though he was in the principal's office or facing his adoptive father for a *talk*. None of the lectures from his foster parents or the head of the boys' home where he'd met Brad and Liam had ever compared to one from Zane.

The thought of Zane struck a nerve of grief within Chance and he felt bad for showing the kids the pictures of Jeff. He'd wanted to help, not cause them more pain.

"Chance…" Jenna closed the distance between them, glancing over her shoulder once as though to make sure her kids were where she'd told them to go.

Jenna did *not* match the image he had of widows. Widows were generally matronly. Wrinkled. Dressed in old-woman clothes and sensible shoes, or else dressed like Tami last night at Wild Honey—desperate and on the make.

He still wanted to kick himself for going. After five minutes alone in his back room apartment, the silence had gotten to him. Some days all he wanted was the silence and peace that came with a good climb but Liam's lecture had Chance's thoughts churning in disquieting ways and he wasn't in the mood for his own company.

Today Jenna wore snug jeans tucked into those fake-fur-topped boots so popular with women. She had layers on top—something cream colored with a bit of lace peeking out from beneath her dark brown long-sleeved thermal T-shirt. Over those, she wore one of those puffy vests that hid as much as it revealed.

And for reasons he didn't want to acknowledge, that bit of lace made his gaze return there again and again. Did women—especially women like Jenna who seemed so quiet and contained—ever think about what the sight of that lace did to a man? Where it made his thoughts go? Mother of two or not, Jeff's *wife* or not, Chance's mind went there before he could stop it.

"Chance, I appreciate the job. And I *really* appreciate you letting the kids stay here after school until I can find a babysitter."

He wiped a hand over his face, Jenna's words registering but not sinking in, because when she came to a stop in front of him, he was almost eye level with that bit of lace. "No problem."

"But you need to know something." She dropped her voice to a seductive tone she probably intended to sound stern. "I do *not* appreciate you filling the twins' heads with stories about your irresponsible adventures or daredevil death wishes."

Wait a minute. *Daredevil* death *wishes?* He had absolutely no suicidal desires. Climbing was…*climbing.* The thrill, the challenge and, yeah, the adventure. Climbing was about the love of the outdoors. Man against nature, the elements. Hell, even physics. But daredevil death wishes?

"Given everything they've been through with losing their father, I think it's best."

The kids had said Jenna had removed Jeff's climbing pictures, now she didn't want them hearing stories of him. "You want them to forget him?"

"No, of course not. This is coming out wrong," she said with visible frustration. "I simply don't want them bothering you—or listening to stories about Jeff's antics with the Rock Gods. Your brother's trip to my house yesterday proved my children have enough wild ideas of their own without hearing more."

Chance narrowed his gaze on her and tried to keep his temper under control. Jenna was wrong. He had had the dad no one wanted their kid to emulate. He'd grown up in his father's shadow, constantly reminded by his foster parents of what a service they did to society by being willing to take him in given the violence of his past.

Jeff wasn't that man. And Jenna had no right to complain. "You're like that guy, aren't you? The one in that movie who talked about how dancing leads to sex. Sometimes, Jenna, it's just a dance. Your kids are smart. Give them credit for it."

"I do."

Chance held her gaze, daring her to look away. "Then if you believe they know better than to follow in their father's footsteps, why did you take down Jeff's climbing pictures?"

Already tense, she stiffened to the point of self-imploding. Even her face pinched. But it was the flash of hurt in her eyes that had him wishing he could retract the question.

He was getting involved with something that was none of his concern but he couldn't help himself. He knew better than anyone the shock of someone being in his life one day but gone the next. People coped the best way they knew how. Himself included.

"That is none of your business. You need to remember those are *my* children and I will decide what is best for them. No more stories. Am I clear?"

Chance held her gaze for a long moment. The line in the sand had been drawn and set in concrete. She couldn't be any clearer. Agree or not, a friend of Jeff's or not, he had no say in how she raised her kids. "As you wish."

"Thank you," she said stiffly.

"But I can't help but believe Jeff would have a different view on things."

"Yes, well, maybe he would," she said, seeming to make a point of glancing down at his cast. "But Jeff's not here, is he?"

CHAPTER SIX

JENNA MUTTERED to herself the entire way home.

She'd told Chance off. No, she'd told off her *boss*. The one who had stuck up for her yesterday and kept the sheriff's department out of her life.

Really? You couldn't just break up the conversation? Redirect and not make a big deal about it? The one job in town and you're risking it?

It was a wonder Chance hadn't fired her then and there. He probably would have if not for his friendship with Jeff. Even *that* made her resentful that the helping hand she'd received came from a Rock God.

Sometimes, Jenna, it's just a dance.

But it wasn't just a dance. That sentiment, that irresponsible, screw-the-consequences-so-long-as-you're-having-fun mentality, was the kind of thing she and Jeff had fought over during their marriage. Because as much as she liked to have fun, it didn't put food on the table.

She muttered mean things in her head as she unlocked the door and shoved it open for Tori and Mark Jeffrey to enter ahead of her. They had been quiet since the episode with Chance. Too quiet.

How much had they heard? Guilt stirred. Obviously they'd heard at least part of the conversation, which meant that, as much as she wanted to put it behind her, she couldn't. If she was going to remain true to her vow to teach her children right from wrong, the issue had to be addressed. It was one thing to talk so bluntly to Chance privately but to say what she had in front of the twins? About their father?

She needed a parenting guidebook. An instruction manual. *Something.* "Guys, listen, about what happened earlier with Mr. McKenna, and what I said about your dad not being here—"

"It's okay," Mark Jeffrey said. "We know what you mean, Mom."

Really? "Oh," she said, because right now she didn't have the energy to take the discussion deeper. "But I want you to know I should've handled that better. I owe Mr. McKenna an apology and I'll do it tomorrow. Right now I want you two to do your chores while I get dinner on. And take Snickers out for a walk."

"It's Mark Jeffrey's turn," Tori said quickly.

"I know." He heaved a pained sigh. "Come on, Snickers."

Mark Jeffrey retrieved the hated leash and fastened it to the dog's collar, leading her out the back door and into the yard.

Poor Snickers. Once she'd roamed free around their house in the country. So many changes in so little time. Was Chance right about Jeff? Was she moving too fast when it came to putting the accident behind them? Did the kids need more time for closure?

"Mom, can you sign this?"

"Leave whatever it is on the table and I'll do it after dinner."

"All you have to do is sign."

Warning bells went off in Jenna's head, drawing her from her thoughts. She dumped her purse and the mail on the counter, washed her hands and tried to find the last shred of patience she had within her. Really, after getting into so much trouble yesterday, was Tori going to attempt another stunt today? "What's it for?"

"Just an after-school thing. Want me to help with dinner?"

Considering her daughter didn't *like* school and was indicating she wanted to spend more time there, the knot in Jenna's stomach grew. "Sure. Get the potatoes, please."

Tori did as ordered, even going so far as to double-check that the cabinet door closed all the way.

"So, anyway, all you have to do is sign. A lot of the kids in my class are doing it and I can get a ride home with one of them."

"Home from where? School?"

"You wouldn't have to worry about me at all, or do anything."

Mark Jeffrey stomped his feet all the way across the deck before he and Snickers bounded into the house.

The pounding in her head increased but she soldiered on, pulling the thawed beef from the fridge. The one good thing about living in cattle country was the abundance of meat.

"It's not a big deal."

"Then why is it taking so long to ask?" Jenna countered.

"I told you to wait," Mark Jeffrey said to his sister. "Why'd you ask now?"

"Ask me *what?*"

"The traveling rodeo is coming," Mark Jeffrey said. "They have a Little Britches competition for kids our age and we all got a paper to sign up. I said you'd say no." His nose ran from the cold.

"Chance said he used to enter all the time."

"Mr. McKenna." Jenna turned to look at her children. Tori glared at her brother.

"You were supposed to let me tell her, dork."

"No name-calling. Tori, for that you get dishes again tonight."

Oh, if looks could kill. But Jenna prayed that the automatic discipline would one day put an end to the name-calling forever. Wasn't consistency supposed to be the key?

Consistency is great but dream on if you think it's gonna stop.

"So can I do it?" Tori asked.

"No." *No, no, no and* no. *That clear enough for you?*

"But, Mom, everybody in class is doing it. Mark Jeffrey wants to do it, too."

Say what? Jenna turned to stare at her son. *He* wanted to get on the back of a steer or a lamb or whatever animal they provided and hold on for dear life? "You?"

Mark Jeffrey looked as though she'd just punched him and pushed his glasses up his nose, a move that had gotten him picked on since kindergarten. "You don't think I can?"

Jenna fought for composure and the sense of mind to salvage something from the insensitive comment. "No, Mark Jeffrey, of course you could *do it* but—"

"Yes!" Tori cried.

"No," Jenna countered. "Do not put words in my mouth, young lady. I didn't give permission, I'm simply saying *if* I were to give permission—which I'm not—I have no doubt you could do it. Both of you."

The twins' expressions mirrored each other as they stared at Jenna. She was doing such a poor job of correcting her words.

"Mom, Kenzie and Jordan and Ericka and *everyone* is doing it. I'll be the only one not allowed."

"That's not true. Mark Jeffrey isn't allowed to participate, either."

"Why? It's safe, otherwise they wouldn't let kids sign up," Tori argued. "The school even excuses the days missed for the rodeo competitions. No school, Mom. You have to let us do it."

"I said no. I'm sorry, but neither of you is going to be in a rodeo. Don't ask me again," she ordered when she saw Tori about to protest.

Tori's face turned red with her anger. "Dad would've let us do it."

Jenna watched as Tori made a stomping dash for the stairs. Jenna sympathized with the floor. She was feeling stomped on, too, at the moment.

"We never get to do anything. You always say no. Dad would let us. I *hate* living here! I hate *you!*"

Tori's door slammed shut, her *I hate you* ringing in Jenna's head and weighing her down even more.

Seconds later, Tori's sobs drifted down through the vent above the kitchen window and Jenna's feelings of inadequacy increased.

She understood the twins wanting to do something their classmates were doing and she hated to disappoint them. They'd had enough disappointments in their young lives.

But safety wasn't the only concern Jenna had with letting them take part in such a program. Money was also an issue, time, travel, whatever equipment would be needed. And mixed up in that was the peer-pressure aspect. She wanted to counter that impulse in the twins to do something simply because their classmates were doing it. Jeff had always been that way. A spoiled only child, he constantly wanted to be part of the group and would try something new, no matter the risk.

"You don't think I could do it, do you?" Mark Jeffrey murmured.

The softly voiced question pierced her mother's heart. No, not him, too. Not now.

The meat began to sizzle and Jenna stared at the tiny bubbles, trying to find the words and right way to say them. She refused to focus on the fear that something might happen, that Mark Jeffrey or Tori would get hurt. That fear was there, close to the surface. Her own mother had died in a mudslide. How many people could say that?

Accidents happened all the time. She knew danger existed everywhere, in everything, so she didn't let fear control her decisions. But *why* take chances when there was no need? Why not be logical? Rational? "Mark Jeffrey, it's not that I don't think you can do it but—"

The sound of Snickers's leash dragging across the floor had her turning to see Snickers following Mark Jeffrey from the room. The sight reminded her of when he had carried a blanket as a toddler. Everywhere he went, the blanket had gone, too, dragging on the floor. "Baby, wait."

"I'm not a *baby*."

You will always *be my baby.* "I know that but—"

"But you don't think I could do it," he repeated softly. Unlike Tori's dramatic exit, Mark Jeffrey quietly unhooked and looped Snickers' leash on the hook by the door. Shoulders slumped, he left the kitchen with one last shove of his glasses.

Jenna watched him go. She clamped her hands over her mouth, and released a pent-up scream, thankful

Mark Jeffrey had switched on the television and cartoons drowned out the noise she made.

He had looked devastated by her lack of faith and his soft-spoken desolation hurt far worse than the slamming of Tori's door ever could.

Jenna had made the right decision. She'd stood her ground as a parent should. So why did it feel as though she was undermining her children's abilities every time she told them no?

CHAPTER SEVEN

"GET IN HERE," Rachel ordered the moment she opened the door and saw Jenna standing on the other side a little after ten that evening. "I can't wait to hear about your day. What happened?"

"I'm not sure you really want to know." Maybe coming over wasn't such a good idea, since Liam had warned her not to leave the kids home alone. But if she stayed in the house and listened to the wind blowing or the water dripping in the sink, she might lose what was left of her mind. The kids were asleep and, to be safe, she'd grabbed Mark's walkie-talkies, duct-taped the talk button on one to act as a transmitter and carried the other in her coat pocket. If either of her kids moved, she'd hear it.

"You're kidding, right? By saying that it means today was better than I thought it would be. Am I right?"

"It was something, all right."

Rachel shut the door and Jenna headed toward the kitchen, which faced the street and gave Jenna full view of her house.

Rachel's florist business was separated from her home by a connecting hallway and two doors, but despite that, the house always smelled like flowers, scented candles and homemade goodness. And BEN-GAY, Jenna added as they walked by the chair where Rachel's elderly mother spent most of her day.

"Sit down. Chocolate or raspberry?"

"Ice cream? None for me. It's too cold out."

"How about some hot chocolate then? Or tea?"

Jenna shook her head again.

"Something stronger? 'Cause you know I got it."

"Tempting, but no." The last thing she needed was alcohol on her breath if by chance Deputy McKenna decided to do a drive-by and caught her crossing the street.

"Oh, honey. Start talking."

Jenna dropped onto a stool and shrugged off her coat but pulled the walkie-talkie out of her pocket to set it on the counter. Rachel raised her eyebrows high. "My version of a tween monitor," she said wryly.

"Gotcha," Rachel said, nodding. "So what happened?"

"Well, first, I kind of lost it and got into a fight with Chance. Then I came home and got into another fight with the kids because, despite having the *police* on my doorstep yesterday, today they want to sign up for the *rodeo*." She buried her face in her hands and rubbed hard to ease the tension making her left eye twitch. "What am I going to do if Chance fires me?"

"Wouldn't he have done that today if he was going to?"

"Maybe. I don't know. The kids were there watching so who knows."

"And what was the fight with Chance about?"

She winced, peeking out from beneath her fingers. "I *ordered* Chance to stop telling my kids about his and Jeff's daredevil death wishes."

"Harsh."

"Yeah. I don't know what I was thinking. Chance

was talking to the kids, being nice. But I opened my mouth and out came the words."

"Because?"

She closed her eyes and pictured the scene in her mind, the way the kids were practically draped over Chance's shoulder—the way they used to do when their father was alive. "I walked up to them, and I heard Chance regaling the twins with this story and I...saw red. It was the kind of thing Jeff used to do before—" She was getting angry all over again.

"Before he jumped off a cliff and killed himself in the process," Rachel said. "You really see that much likeness between Jeff and Chance?"

"In Rock God attitude? Yes. But as much as I don't want to be working for Chance or any of the other Rock Gods, Rach, I *need* this job. Why did I open my mouth?"

"Jenna, it's perfectly understandable that you have strong feelings about what happened, not only to you but especially to your kids. Go in tomorrow and apologize to Chance before he can open his mouth and fire you. It'll be fine."

Fine? Highly doubtful. "I will. I mean, I know I have to apologize. It's just awkward."

"He's really pressing your buttons," Rachel said, a curious expression on her face. "Interesting."

Jenna lifted her head and immediately shook it in denial at the expression Rachel wore. "No. No, it's not *interesting,*" she drawled. "It's irritating in the extreme."

"What was the story about?" Rachel asked.

Jenna smoothed her finger over the rough edge of one of her nails, barely managing to resist the urge to pick at it. "Jeff climbing, what else? What kind of a mother am I that I don't want the kids to hear stories about their own father?"

"You know the answer to that. Why are you doubting yourself?"

Yeah, she did know the answer. Jeff's stupid stunt while climbing had killed him and her children had had a hard time handling it. How could telling them stories glorifying his actions help? "You should've seen them," she said softly. "Chance had pictures of Jeff on his phone and the kids were huddled around him looking at them. Tori was smiling like…like I haven't seen her smile in a long time. Sometimes I wonder if we can get through the day without arguing over something. If I do anything right."

"You are the mother of almost teenagers. You need to remember they've got a lot of hormone issues going on right now in preparation for the big show. You can't take it personally."

Jenna moved toward the window to stare at her house. Beneath the bright light of the moon, it looked dull and rundown. Like her?

Maybe she was jealous of those women in the store as Rachel had said. Jealous because Jenna missed the fun side of herself that had been buried beneath the weight of adulthood and widowhood and parenthood.

She leaned her forehead against the cold glass. "Should I display Jeff's climbing pictures again?"

"Do you want to?"

That wasn't an easy question to answer. Jeff and climbing went together, yet every time she had looked at those pictures she was reminded of how he'd died. And she got angry again. Acceptance was the last stage of grief but the books described the stages as a circle, with the person shifting between the emotions for a long period of time. "No. The family pictures are out. I think it's enough."

"Then don't. And as far as Chance goes, just apologize. I'm sure he'll understand."

Yeah, right. What man wanted a woman to talk about her feelings? Chance had been very understanding given the situation with the twins and her schedule. She couldn't fault him there. But how long would it be before Chance's tolerance for Jeff's seemingly embittered wife ran out when she wouldn't accept the Rock Gods' stupid philosophy on life?

Worse still, how awful was it that when she'd stepped close enough to see that the picture on the screen showed Chance and Jeff together, it had been Chance's expression she was drawn to? Her gaze had immediately focused on Chance, not her husband. How could she even think about another man so soon after Jeff's death? Despite her anger at his carelessness, even looking at another man—let alone another Rock God—had felt like a betrayal to Jeff's memory, his life and their vows. "I should go. It's late."

"But you just got here."

"I know but I'm really tired," she said, feeling the stress of her day in the weariness hitting her now that she'd slowed down.

"Jenna, are you okay?"

"Yeah," she said quickly. "I need to find another job so I can put Jeff and the Rock Gods behind me. That's all. I'll see you tomorrow," she said as she gathered up her belongings.

Rachel followed her to the door.

"Try to get some sleep and give it time," Rachel said. "Everything will work out. It always does."

Jenna tromped her way through the snow and slush

to her house. As she entered a tall shadow moved causing her to gasp and jump back.

"M-M-Mom?"

Her heart thumped so hard in her chest, Jenna had to remind herself to breathe. "Mark Jeffrey, what are you doing up?"

Her son emerged from the stairwell, carrying his baseball bat, Snickers at his side.

"I heard a—a noise."

It took a moment for the words to sink in, and she realized her makeshift monitoring system hadn't worked. "So you came down to investigate it? Did you go to my room to tell me you heard this noise?"

"No. I didn't want to wake you in case it was just a noise."

She knew without a doubt he was on that *man of the house* thing again. Why, why, why was this such an issue with him? "Come here," she ordered, moving toward the couch to sit. Her trembling legs needed a break.

One of the selling points of choosing this house over the other she'd looked at was that this one was located so close to the police station. The real-estate agent had given her the statistics and crimes were nearly nonexistent here, whereas the isolated area where they'd lived with Jeff had been seeing more and more thefts and break-ins. "Sit."

Snickers immediately planted her hiney but Mark Jeffrey carefully walked across the floor. Was he wearing a pair of Tori's old cleats? What was he going to do? Hit them with the bat and then kick them?

Finally Mark Jeffrey lowered himself onto the couch beside her, and she winced at the sound the cleats made scraping across the carpet.

She bent and quickly removed the shoes. "Mark Jeffrey, we need to get something straight and I need you to hear me. I realize you are growing up but right now you are *ten years old.*"

"Almost eleven."

"Yes, well, almost eleven isn't an adult man yet, and you do not need to be wandering the house with a baseball bat. What if someone had actually broken in here? Most likely it would've been a man bigger and meaner than you, who would've taken the bat and maybe even used it against *you.* Your job isn't to protect us. That's *my* job as a parent. And if you ever hear another noise that scares you enough to get out of bed, you come to my room and wake me. And if—*if*—someone is in the house, you call 911 and you hide. Is that understood?"

Mark Jeffrey nodded but she could tell his ego had taken another beating due to her words. "Honey, you are going to be a wonderful young man."

"No, I'm not," he said, his voice growing thick. "You don't think I can do anything. You don't think I'm big enough *or* strong enough."

"I don't want you to feel like you have to grow up before it's necessary. You're only a child once. I want you to *be* a child while you can."

"I wish Dad was here. Then I'd know what to do."

Mark Jeffrey rarely voiced his thoughts on his father's death. He'd talked of being the man of the house, yes, but usually it was Tori saying she wanted Jeff back, not Mark Jeffrey. "I wish he was here, too. But what do you mean, you don't know what to do? Honey, you don't have to do anything."

"But I'm supposed to be a boy."

"You are a boy," she said, unable to keep from smiling.

"Mom, the other day in class I called something lavender instead of purple. *Lavender.* All the boys made fun."

She hugged him tight and buried her smile in his hair. "Is that why you want to do the rodeo?"

Mark Jeffrey shrugged and wiped a hand under his nose. "It's just sometimes I think if Dad were here, things would be different. And if he'd really loved us, he wouldn't have done stuff like that and…died."

Jenna pulled Mark Jeffrey closer, his pain too much for her mother's heart to deal with because she knew *exactly* how Mark Jeffrey felt. Her childhood insecurities of not being enough, of not being as special as the indigent children her parents had dedicated their lives to caring for, tried to surface but Jenna stomped them down. She would not foist her own insecurities on her children. "Mark Jeffrey, your daddy loved you. So much. But he wasn't always good with…" She struggled to find the words, the sincerity she needed. "He wasn't always good at expressing his feelings. But I know for a fact he wouldn't ever want you to doubt his love."

She needed to remember that in regard to herself, too. Jeff had loved her. And she'd loved him. But like Mark Jeffrey, sometimes she couldn't help but wonder…

One of the things that had first attracted her to Jeff was his sense of adventure. At twenty-two and out of college, he'd seemed glamorous and worldly, confident, all very appealing to a seventeen-year-old girl.

But Jeff hadn't expected her to get pregnant any more than she had and while he'd done the "right thing" and married her, and while they'd loved each other and created a life together, she'd often wondered if Jeff seeking more aggressive thrills wasn't his outlet from the responsibilities of marriage and family.

But it had taken both of them to create the twins, not

just her. The pregnancy had disrupted both their lives, not just Jeff's. And while she wouldn't change what happened because it meant she wouldn't have the child in her arms and the one asleep upstairs, she'd often wondered what would have happened if she and Jeff had simply gone their separate ways when his climbing vacation in India had ended.

She had planned to go to college, become a linguist. Where would she be now if she had? How would her life be different? Once upon a time, before her mother's death, she'd dreamed of traveling to the finer countries of the world. But reality had a way of waking a girl from her dreams. "It's late. You should be in bed."

"I love you, Mom."

She squeezed Mark Jeffrey tight. Her life had taken an unexpected turn but she wouldn't change it for the world. "I love you, too."

CHAPTER EIGHT

CHANCE WENT TO physical therapy the next day. By the time he'd completed his session, he was as worn out as an old man after a big church dinner.

Sitting around was making him weak. He was used to challenging himself and pushing his body to the limits. Doing so this year had resulted in a series of injuries that not only curtailed his climbing, but it also earned his brothers' wrath because he wasn't able to pitch in at the Circle M Ranch the way he normally did.

Liam was more forgiving, because as a cop his priority wasn't the ranch left to them upon Zane's death. Liam's focus was on his new bride, and completing the expansion of Carly's little house in town because their foster child's adoption was almost final.

Brad, on the other hand, Chance's older adopted brother, ran the Circle M for the entire family, but he still counted on Liam and Chance to carry their weight during the busy seasons. This year, both he and Liam had slacked off, leaving the brunt of it to Brad.

Chance had missed branding season due to a concussion and broken ribs, and more recently, the fracture in his foot had kept him from participating in the roundup and sale of the herd. To say Brad wasn't pleased was laughable.

It was true Chance wasn't able to help out much but that wasn't what had Brad stomping around like a bull.

His upcoming wedding to Gabriella, Zane's biological daughter, was at fault for that. Somehow the small intimate wedding had evolved to include a guest list of two hundred, a world-famous chef and the transformation of a barn into the Christmas-themed winter wonderland wedding Gabriella wanted. Brad didn't have the heart—or the balls—to deny her.

Chance shoved himself onto his good foot and grabbed his crutches to go to the refrigerator in the corner of the storage room they used as a break area. He spied Jenna hurrying past the office door on some mission, going ninety miles an hour the way she had ever since she'd arrived. Watching her wore him out even more, their disagreement weighing heavily on his mind.

When he made it to the fridge Jenna stood at her locker and he took the opportunity for what it was—a chance to look her over, guard down. Yeah, having her around wasn't a hardship.

"I know what you're going to say," she said, her back to him. "But can I say something first? I should've come to talk to you first thing, but you seemed busy. I didn't want to disturb you."

He couldn't wait to hear this. He'd given her a job, tried to help her because it was the right thing to do. He didn't need her jumping down his throat over every little thing. He balanced himself and waited. "I'm all ears."

"I owe you an apology for yesterday."

Jenna still didn't look directly at him, and it appeared as though she was chewing rocks and swallowing lemons. She reminded him of a rubber band pulled taut, ready to snap. He could relate—he'd felt the same way quite a few times. Felt that way right now, as a matter of fact. Honestly, he didn't like the way she treated him as though he was immature and irresponsible and didn't have the sense to take care of himself.

Just like dear old Dad.

He shoved the thought away. He could control his temper. He knew when he needed to let off a little steam and the best way to do that. So, no. *Not* like his father.

"You're my employer and for that reason alone, I should have approached the matter of my kids with more respect," she said, her speech sounding very well rehearsed. "I've already talked to them about my behavior toward you. How it was...rude."

He noticed she didn't exactly say she was sorry, only that she should have been more tactful and respectful when reprimanding him. The awareness of the difference took him back a few years to when he'd issued those type of apologies to Zane when he'd screwed up and done something wrong—such as taking off to climb without leaving a note of where he was going or how long he'd be gone. But Chance also remembered how his adoptive father had always accepted his excuse and let the matter end. "Apology accepted."

"Chance, I know the only reason I'm here is because you and Jeff were friends. I also know I've given you more than enough reasons to fire me for insubordination. But...my children have been through too much already. I said what I did because I don't want them so dazzled by your stories they have unrealistic dreams or expectations."

She really ought to have stopped with her apology.

"Aren't kids supposed to have dreams?"

"Of course they are. But that's different than wanting to do ridiculously dangerous things for the heck of it and letting someone else be responsible for the consequences. I'm trying to teach them they can have fun, full lives without chasing adrenaline rushes the way their father did and you… You talked to them about standing *up* on a galloping horse, knowing they want to take part in that rodeo."

Yeah, maybe he shouldn't have told them that one.

Chance planted his good foot at an angle and settled his weight more comfortably against the lockers. "I'll be more careful what I say to them, but I competed in the Little Britches competition a few times when I lived in the boys' home. It's a respected organization and well managed."

"Maybe it is but the answer is still no."

"Why? If the twins were allowed to do it and spent their time practicing and competing, you might not have my deputy brother showing up at your door because they're bored," he pointed out, trying again to sway her, because the kids had seemed really pumped about the rodeo. The same way he got excited about tackling a new climb. Didn't Jenna see the need there?

She closed her eyes briefly and wet her lower lip, and he told himself he did not notice the action—even while his mind committed the flick of her tongue to permanent memory.

Okay, so maybe he had noticed Jenna over the years. But the ring on her finger, Jeff's friendship and the fact Chance wasn't a man who trespassed had kept him from paying too much attention.

But now?

She's still Jeff's widow.

And if he was having this much trouble keeping his mind off her, it had to mean he'd been cooped up too long.

"Because that's my decision and it's final." She

yanked on the bag stuck inside her locker, her frustration visible and reminding him once more of that rubber band.

"If you reconsider, I could arrange for them to practice at the Circle M, even transport them back and forth from the ranch." He wasn't sure where the offer had come from or why he was making it but there it was.

"That's very generous of you but no. Thank you."

He told himself to accept her decision and walk away, but something held him in place. "Jenna, have you ever considered the possibility that the twins are acting out because you're keeping such a tight grip on them? Maybe if you loosened the reins a little—"

The moment her mouth dropped open, he knew he'd stepped on a land mine.

"*Excuse* me? That is the second time you've said something like that to me and I resent it. You don't even know me. And since when did you become a parent? Last I heard, you weren't. Or has that changed?"

He'd be the first to admit he knew nothing about parenting and didn't want to learn anytime soon. But he did know what it was like to be a kid determined to test boundaries. "No, I'm not a parent, but anyone with eyes can see there's an issue."

"Yeah, there is—their father *died*." She grabbed her lunch and stalked to the table, settling herself in one of the padded folding chairs with a not-so-subtle sigh of disgust and get-away-from-me attitude that attracted him the way every adrenaline-filled stunt he'd chased since childhood. Someone had once told him he'd make a good firefighter because he ran toward trouble rather than away from it. This was definitely one of those occasions.

Rattling the plastic thermal bag like she wanted to

rip it in two, she said, "You know, it was hard enough being the person who always sucked the joy out of Jeff's fun. In the end, his death proved I was right to worry. Life isn't a joyride and I'd be an irresponsible parent if I let my children grow up thinking it is."

He hobbled to the chair beside her and sat, despite the fact she was coiled up tighter than a snake. With one arm propped on the table and one hand on the back of her chair, he faced her and tried again. "Jenna, nothing is that black-and-white. Is that what you want for them? To teach them to be too frightened to challenge themselves or have a little fun while they do it?"

Her gaze fastened on the tattoo inked on the inside of his wrist. Beneath *Embrace the Rush* was the number VI. Before she could ask what it meant, he shifted so that the textured surface of the table pulled his sleeve down to cover it. "They're *kids*. They wouldn't be riding anything aggressive."

"Any animal frightened and angry enough to buck is aggressive," she said.

She ignored him and took out a plastic-wrapped sandwich, this one with crust and minus the fancy shape, a thermos and a bag of carrot sticks.

No chips for her. No cookies, either. Man, but she really didn't have any fun, did she? "They're baby animals, not full grown. And the kids barely get jostled around. It's a good time they'd really enjoy."

"No."

Something about her tone made him hesitate and then he wanted to smack himself for not realizing. Jenna had come into the store that first day to cancel her layaway due to monetary issues. Why hadn't he considered that? "Is it the entry fee? I can arrange for it to be waived."

They donated feed, tack and other supplies to most

of the rodeos when they came into the area. It was a good business expense that doubled as advertisement. It wouldn't hurt for them to cover two specific entry fees, as well. He'd pay it out of his pocket if he had to. *For Jeff.*

About to take a bite of her sandwich, Jenna paused and lowered it. "This is supposed to be my lunch break. Can we change the subject, please?"

"Aw, now that's way too polite a response for the looks flickering across your face. Say what you like to me," he urged, leaning closer. Close enough to smell her perfume—the scent soft and simple and sweet. He wasn't sure why he was torturing himself but maybe he deserved it for lusting after Jeff's widow.

Several seconds passed before she inhaled and turned to meet his gaze full-on. The moment she did, he had to force himself to remain where he was. Sitting so close to her was not a good idea.

"Okay, fine. What's wrong with it? That's the statement of a man who has job security in a family-owned business, who drives a reliable, company-owned truck and who has no commitments to significant others like a wife or child. What's wrong with it is that even if the entry fee is waived, there are other concerns. The twins could get *hurt,* which means I'd have to take care of them, pay the doctor bills *and* try to keep my job and a roof over our heads while doing it. By saying no, I give us all security. You—Jeff and the Rock Gods—you never think beyond the moment. But what about long term?"

"What do you mean?"

"Chance, you carry the obligation of running this business for your family. Did you ever think that maybe—just maybe—you ought to play it a little safer?" she said, sliding a pointed glance toward his broken foot.

Jenna's words reinforced the guilt he felt at putting the load of the ranch work on Brad and the store work on Dooley, however briefly. He mulled that argument over but it didn't sway him. "You're teaching them to never take risks, when risks can be rewarding."

"They can be," she said slowly. "But what if you died doing something you didn't *need* to be doing? You don't think that would be a waste of life? One that would devastate your family like it did mine?"

He rubbed his hand along his jaw before squeezing the back of his neck, not really comfortable with the subject of death itself. He didn't like dwelling on things like that. When it happened, it happened, ready or not. Jeff's death last year and Zane's this past summer were proof of that. "At least I'd die a happy man, doing what I love to do. And I know for damned sure Jeff felt the same way."

His answer was automatic. One as practiced as the pseudo-apology she'd given him earlier. Zane, Brad and Liam had all voiced that same question over the years and that was the answer Chance had always given them. At least he'd die happy. Somehow saying it to Jenna seemed wrong.

With a look of disgust and hurt and condemnation all rolled into one, she shoved her sandwich away and fiddled with the bag of carrot sticks.

"Sweetheart, all I'm saying is that your kids have to learn to take on challenges and the sooner they learn, the better."

Her gaze narrowed on him, searching too deep for comfort. "You don't think they've been *challenged* this past year?"

Ah, man. He was the last person who should be doling out advice. The tattoo on his arm seemed to throb and burn, reminding him of that fact.

The VI imprinted beneath the script on his arm was an ever-present visual of the sixth commandment—*Thou shalt not kill.* It was a reminder of his roots, his past. Everything he'd lost at such a young age due to his father letting a rush of anger destroy them in one life-defining moment.

With every stretch of his arm, he was reminded not to give in to the anger he felt. He'd grown up a sick, scrawny kid getting picked on because of his size and quick fire temper. Time and again he'd gotten into trouble, and had heard the refrain he was on the same path as his father.

"I'm saying everyone needs an outlet," he said simply, unable to share more.

The night he'd first met Zane, Chance had lost himself in his anger and taken Brad and Liam along for the ride. But rather than killing someone, the three of them had torn their way through Zane's property, destroying everything in their path, messing up fields, taking down fences. For a terrifying moment that night, he'd embraced the rage he knew he'd inherited from his biological father.

Zane had hoped Chance's interests would be in ranching like Brad, or law enforcement like Liam, but Chance had always been drawn to physical challenges, especially once he'd grown out of scrawny and into his muscles.

But even though Zane had worried every time Chance scaled rock, his adoptive father had encouraged him to channel his anger and frustration into something productive rather than self-destructive. "Like you said, the kids have been through a lot. I thought they could use a way to let off some steam."

That said, Chance stood and grabbed his crutches.

"I was a missionary kid," Jenna said abruptly. "If we were to compare, I'll bet I have more travel experience than you, it simply happened at a younger age."

Chance paused before he sat again. "I can't quite see you as a world traveler."

She held up her hand and began to lift her fingers as she named countries. By the time she was finished, she'd outtraveled him three times over. "Where are your parents now?"

"My father is in Haiti. He's a doctor. And my mother is buried in India. You said your mother died when you were five. Mine died when I was seventeen. She was an engineer."

"I'm sorry," he said, meaning it.

"Me, too. I understand acting out because of grief. Losing her changed everything. My father rededicated himself to the work he and my mother were involved in. But I didn't need a doctor, I needed him to be my *parent*."

He stared into her eyes, wondering how she'd feel if she knew they had that in common? "How did she die?"

"We had lived in India for three months, then the worst rains in recorded history sent mudslides careening down the mountains into the villages."

He couldn't hide his surprise. "You were in a mudslide?"

"No," she said uneasily, standing and walking over to the barred window facing the delivery ramp. "I'd snuck away from my studies to go to the city with a friend. But getting back, we saw the destruction. My father looked like a mud zombie when we finally found him in the tent they were using for a hospital."

"And your mother?" he asked softly.

"We found her four days later. The point is," she said as she faced him, "I know what you're saying. But I disagree with your opinion on what my children need. After my mother died, all I wanted was to feel secure again and know everything would be okay."

He thought of lying in bed at the first foster home he'd been taken to the night of his father's arrest. How he'd felt about what he'd seen. How he'd pulled the blanket so tight around his shoulders his fingers had gone numb. His father may have been big and gruff, but he'd never abused him, so he hadn't known his father was capable of that kind of violence. All Chance had wanted was to go home.

"I know we never have a guarantee of safety in this world, but I *can* do my best to give my children security. It comes by establishing a routine, having rules and sticking to them and staying focused on what's really important. I can stand here and say my mother died helping thousands of people but Jeff died because he was so into *embracing the rush* that he didn't *think* before he leaped." She shook her head. "I'm sure the competition is wonderful and fun, but we don't need another disruption or disaster in our lives. Right now, all we need is to be a family."

He thought of Liam's words to him in the cruiser the afternoon at Jenna's house and scowled. Jenna and his brothers had more in common than he liked.

"My parents placed helping those people before the needs of their own child. I probably sound selfish. I know there are plenty of people who would argue for the greater good but I will always put my kids first. I've been the responsible parent in their lives from the moment they were born because *someone* had to be while Jeff was thrill-seeking. And despite our different views on the subject of the Rock Gods, I believe it's my job as a mother to steer the twins *away* from Jeff's impulsiveness. I loved Jeff, but I don't want the twins to grow up and be like him."

Her soft-spoken words had the impact of a lightning strike. Jenna's father had been able to focus on his work following the death of his wife. But Chance had been left with a man overwhelmed by grief and filled with anger, spiraling so out of control he'd killed a schoolmate's father with his bare hands while Chance watched from the backseat of the car parked outside a bar.

He'd woken up to the sound of his father's shouts, the sight of his face as he began to hit the man.

In a world filled with violence and disaster and chaos, how could Jenna deny the twins any moments of joy they might experience?

"I guess I'm one of them," he said. "Because the way I see it, Jeff died doing what he loved. So did your mother. Can you really fault them for that?"

Jenna walked to the table and began to gather the contents of her lunch. "I should've known you wouldn't understand."

"Jenna, come on." He grasped her arm. She sat on the edge of the seat, ready to spring away, so he didn't let go. "You believe you're doing what's best for them."

A disgruntled laugh huffed out of her chest. "You have nerve."

"I do, thanks in part to those competitions. They taught me self-confidence and gave me a sense of worth I didn't have because I didn't have a father around to teach me those things. Sweetheart, can you sit there and tell me those are things Mark Jeffrey and Tori don't need, especially now?"

Jenna straightened and shifted away from him, the warmth of her gone and only the slightest hint of her perfume remaining. "Given your situation, I can see how the rodeo may have helped you, but it's not the same for Tori and Mark Jeffery."

"You sure about that?"

That pointy chin of hers lifted a couple of notches, but she couldn't quite meet his gaze. "Maybe the competitions helped you gain confidence as a boy but what about now? You think the term *adrenaline junkie* is a joke? There's a reason it exists, and you and all the rest of the Rock Gods are perfect examples."

"A little adrenaline keeps the blood pumping."

She pulled her arm away and went back to gathering her lunch, her entire body rigid as she stood. "Yeah, well, while you're off doing all the things the Rock Gods do, you're missing the good stuff."

His temper simmered at a low boil. "I'm not missing anything."

She shoved her sack in her locker and swung to face him, eyes sparkling, skin glowing. More beautiful than he'd ever seen her look, despite the fact she was pissed at him and him at her. How was it possible to be so drawn to a woman so opposite in all he believed in?

Ask Jeff.

"No, you aren't, are you? Because you have nothing to miss. And that's sad because there *is* so much more. But sadder still is that the scale always tips and it will eventually tip for every member of the *reckless* Rock Gods. Even you. A broken foot is nothing but a *warning*. Over the years, Jeff broke ribs and ankles and

wrists, arms, his collarbone. I can't even count the con-
cussions."

He wanted to squirm beneath the intensity of her
stare—beneath the truth he saw in her eyes. How many
times had Zane said the same thing? That it was only
a matter of time before Chance's luck ran out? How
many times had Zane asked him why he had the nerve
to dare God?

"He said those were all part of the *fun*. The thrill of
the rush," Jenna said with a heartbreaking smile. "But
you know what he missed? The first steps, the first
words, the first smiles. The first home run. When Jeff
fell, do you think he embraced the rush, or did he regret taking his life for granted? Maybe what I'm about
to say makes me a horrible wife and a huge bitch, but if
there's *any* justice in this world I hope that in that split
second of time, he finally understood what he could
have been a part of if he'd put *us* first."

Jenna gave him one last lingering look and walked
toward the swing door, shoving her way into the front.

He remained in the chair, her words ringing in his
ears with deafening intensity.

He scraped his palms over his face and sighed. For
a moment when she'd talked about all those firsts her
expression had lit up with a mother's love, softened,
despite her upset.

Jenna was strong, resilient. Loving and stubborn.
Sexy.

And for a brief second he'd allowed himself to pretend he was the one with her, experiencing all those
moments.

Truth was, he'd never had that kind of relationship
with anyone in his life. And thanks to the monster sleeping within him, he never would.

Climbing came first.

It was the only thing that kept the rage away and guaranteed he didn't turn into his father.

CHAPTER NINE

"I CAN'T BELIEVE I did it *again*," Jenna said that evening as she helped Rachel change the remaining Thanksgiving flower displays to the pre-made Christmas ones. She carried a table arrangement bedecked with orange, green and yellow fall ribbon, multi-color pumpkins and a glass candle holder to the sale display at the front of the store. "Or that you've marked this down so much."

"You want it? Take it. Seriously," Rachel ordered when Jenna opened her mouth to protest. "I owe you for not keeping a better eye on the kids last week. I should've packed them into the car and taken them with me. It's seventy-five percent off for regular customers, but for you? It's free. If you don't take it and it doesn't sell, it could get ruined in storage."

The beautiful arrangement was too pretty to set on the markdown table. Or in storage. "Will you let me pay you later? I was thinking of giving it to Karen. She won't let me bring any food for Thanksgiving so…"

"That's fine. Don't think anything of it. Back to our discussion. I think the question is why the man is so capable of getting under your skin? Is there something you're not telling me?" Rachel led the way through the floral and gift shop to retrieve more of the markdowns.

Jenna refused to admit her awareness of Chance's… attractiveness. "No."

"So nothing has happened between you two since you started working there?"

"No!" Jenna said. "Rach, Jeff's been gone only a year."

"*Over* a year."

"It doesn't matter if it's been twenty years," she said, shaking her head. "Nothing has happened and nothing is going to. Not with Chance McKenna."

"Okay, fine, but what about someone else? That thing about being in mourning a certain amount of time is from the dark ages. You're young and beautiful—why should you wait?"

She could think of about a million and one reasons. "Now's not a good time, you know that."

"You can't put dating off forever. You need to get out there and have some fun."

Jenna grabbed another arrangement. "Yeah, I can see asking Jeff's parents to babysit while I date. That'll go over well."

"But they've been great, haven't they?" Rachel asked.

Jenna stepped back from the markdown table and watched as Rachel performed her magic of turning a mishmash of items into a beautiful display. "Yes, they have, but they wouldn't handle *that* well. Karen hasn't even touched Jeff's room since he went away to college. Everything is exactly the way it was then."

"Parents aren't supposed to bury their children," Rachel said, tilting her head and angling a flower just so. "I'm not saying for you to go out and jump into something serious but what would a date or two hurt?"

"Uh…you want to repeat that and take your own advice?" Jenna couldn't imagine dating again. Technically, she'd never actually gone on a date. She and Jeff had sort of hung out together in a group of friends at first and when they'd gotten to a point where they couldn't do what they wanted to do in front of a crowd, they had found ways to be alone. But "go to dinner and a movie" dating? Never.

"I have Mom to think of," Rachel said.

"And I have twins."

"It's not the same and you know it. As much as it hurts to say it, the twins act older than my mom most days. You're not changing diapers or dealing with dementia, just mood swings—and I don't have a very willing babysitter."

"The approval for an aide still hasn't come through?"

"They say I'm next on the list for review but not yet, no. Believe me, you'll probably hear me shouting from the rooftops when it happens." Rachel flashed Jenna a downcast look. "I sound horrible, don't I?"

"You sound like a stressed sole caregiver. I get stressed out and I have Jeff's parents to help me. You don't have anyone. Parents aren't supposed to bury their children anymore than children are supposed to tend to their parents the way you do with your mom."

"Definitely true," Rachel agreed. "But we're getting off track again. Do you still feel that strongly about Jeff that dating seems wrong?"

Jenna handed Rachel one of the smaller arrangements left on the floor from earlier. "I don't know. It just feels strange, even talking about it."

"Well, for what it's worth, they say men begin the hunt much sooner than women, so you shouldn't feel bad about it."

"I don't. I mean, I know Jeff wouldn't be upset about it because he wouldn't want or expect me to be alone forever."

"So what's holding you back?"

A grin pulled at Jenna's lips. "If I say fear, you'll smack me, won't you?"

"Anyone who can tell her boss off is not the timid type."

"No, I'm not. But I've never been with anyone but Jeff. I'm not sure I'd even know what to do."

"Oh, wow. You're practically a virgin."

She nudged Rachel with her knee and knocked her off balance. Rachel simply righted herself and laughed.

"Don't make fun. I'm the mother of two, who was married for ten years, so I know I don't qualify for that title. But I wonder what the kids will think, what Jeff's parents will think. I'm not even sure what *I* think about dating again."

Who would she date? She didn't want to date losers or perverts and there were plenty of them in the dating world. How did a single mom go about dating? What were the rules?

Maybe the first rule ought to be to have some fun first. Make some GNO—girls' night out—plans with Rachel and her other girlfriends and get out of the house instead of sitting at home whenever Jeff's parents had the kids. Once she was used to doing that, maybe then she could tackle dating. "It would be fun to get out."

"See?"

"But I'm not in a hurry. I'm perfectly fine with baby steps."

"Honey, the moment you started working for one of North Star's most eligible bachelors, you jumped over baby steps into a full-out dash."

"Chance McKenna is not date material. Not for me, anyway."

"Exactly. But who better to break the ice with than a man you know you could never get serious about?"

"That is such twisted logic I can't even wrap my brain around it," she said with a wry laugh. Granted, Chance was gorgeous but... Yeah, she'd been down that road.

"Well, *technically,* you don't have to wrap your brain around anything," Rachel said with an ornery waggle of her carefully plucked eyebrows.

"Have you forgotten Chance and Jeff were *friends?*"

"Jenna, that doesn't mean you and Chance can't be friends, too."

Jenna rolled her eyes and gathered up the last of the items meant for the sale table display. "You scare me sometimes, you know that? Chance and I can't have a conversation that doesn't end in a disagreement. The idea of getting together as anything *other* than friends is crazy."

"Yeah, well, you said you wanted to have some fun, so maybe it's time you let your *crazy* out."

Yeah, right. The last time that had happened, she'd wound up pregnant—and married—at seventeen.

HAVING WORKED AT THE school since the twins entered kindergarten, the usual Saturday mornings at the Darlington house were sleepy and slow.

But this morning had been a frantic dash to get the twins up, fed and out the door before she wound up late for work. That wouldn't be a good way to finish out her first turbulent week on the job.

Jenna hadn't seen much of Chance since their discussion in the break room on Thursday. On Friday, Chance attended distributor meetings in Helena, while she and Dooley minded the store. Chance returned about a half hour before her shift ended that evening but he'd gone straight to his office, much to the twins' disappointment and her relief.

Given her emotional response to him every time she was within speaking distance, keeping a professional distance was best, no matter Rachel's opinion to the contrary.

Dragging bags and pillows and a few toys from home, Jenna hauled the twins into the store so Jeff's parents could pick them up and keep them for Thanksgiving break, freeing Jenna to work without worrying what her children were up to whenever her back was turned. Frankly, she was looking forward to the reprieve. Her son and daughter's moping silence was getting to her. Almost-eleven-year-olds were not silent. Tori was still upset over not being allowed to participate in the rodeo, and Mark Jeffrey had been quiet ever since admitting he knew what lavender was. Was she worried about her offspring?

Definitely. And maybe a bit of space between them would help Jenna put things into perspective and possibly come up with a solution or two.

She poked her head into the aisle to see the twins at the camping table and chairs awaiting their grandparents' arrival.

Tori doodled on her paper instead of completing the book report she was supposed to be working on. Nothing unusual in that. But even Mark Jeffrey's usual zest for learning was nonexistent. He propped his chin on his fist and stared into space despite the open book in front of him, a tiny frown pulling his eyebrows low.

Jenna still shuddered to think of what could have happened if someone had actually broken into their home and her son had attempted to face them on his own. Mark Jeffrey was trying so hard to be the man of the house; but she knew her child, and that was too much pressure for him. He needed to spend more time with other boys his age. Be a kid.

Maybe she should reconsider letting him attend the upcoming Scout trip?

She'd found the flyer in his backpack this morning but Mark Jeffrey hadn't said anything about wanting to go. And rappelling was one of the activities on the trip.

Given Mark Jeffrey's statement about Jeff climbing, maybe Mark Jeffrey truly had no interest.

She went back to work but the tedious chore of stocking and straightening the shelf didn't keep her mind from spinning.

Mark Jeffrey's demeanor had changed since Jeff's death. And it was more than sullenness that could be attributed to grief. For years before Jeff's death, she'd sensed his absences were making Mark Jeffrey feel ignored or neglected. Given his age, he'd been content with spending time with her while his dad was away. Now it seemed as though Mark Jeffrey had begun to compare himself to his father—and found himself lacking.

How could she combat that? Was she compounding the problem? Damaging his self-esteem even more? Instilling doubt in his abilities when he was already struggling?

Was Chance right?

She'd known being a parent would be hard but when she was young and in love she'd never thought she'd be doing it alone.

She slammed another box on the shelf.

"Easy there, slugger. Something wrong?"

Chance stood a few feet away, looking ruggedly

handsome, crutches and all. It wasn't fair. Guys like him... What was it about them that drew women? Drew *her* attention and notice despite their obvious night versus day views on very important topics?

Men like Chance and her husband and all the other rugged, hard-hewn outdoorsy types needed to come with a warning label. *Broken hearts guaranteed.* "Nope, just didn't know my own strength."

Chance was handsome, yes, but she wasn't some teenaged girl looking for a hot guy. And definitely not a hot, thrill-seeker. When the time came and she got serious about a man, she wanted someone with substance and sustainability. Not another man trying to find himself in an adrenaline rush.

She lowered her gaze to the cart holding the items to be stocked and wound up taking note of the way Chance's faded blue jeans were ripped ankle to knee up one side to allow for the black cast. Yeah, nothing appealing about *that*. She'd been there, done that and was still paying off the hospital bills. So long as she kept that thought foremost in her mind, she had no worries about giving into the wrong type of guy.

"You sure?"

She found her gaze focused on the burgundy-and-gray plaid, flannel shirt, open across his broad chest atop a gray T-shirt the exact same color as his eyes. Smoky eyes. "Positive."

Concentrating on her task, she managed to place the next box on the shelf a little less forcefully. "Did you need something?"

"Grandma!"

Jenna blinked, but she didn't move. Facing Jeff's parents took some doing.

Jeff's mother desperately wanted to hold on to the

past, to Jeff and the kids, the way their family used to
be, whereas Jenna found herself wanting to go in the
opposite direction. To put it behind her and move on.
She wanted more space and fewer reminders of how
she and the kids hadn't been important enough for Jeff
to make them a priority. "Jeff's parents are keeping
the kids over Thanksgiving break," she explained to
Chance. "They've come to pick them up. It'll just take
a few minutes to send them off."

"Not a problem."

Jenna smoothed her hands over her jeans and tried
to paste a welcoming smile on her lips as she made her
way to the front of the store, vaguely aware that Chance
followed her. "Karen, Les. Thanks for picking them up.
You're right on time."

Jeff's parents had the twins wrapped in their arms
and were showering them with kisses. Kisses that
brought smiles and a few laughs. Last time she'd tried
to kiss the kids in public, she'd been shot down.

"Happy to do it. Chance," Les greeted with a dip of
his balding head. "How's that foot?"

"Healing, thanks. Good to see you both again. It's
been a while."

An awkward silence followed Chance's statement
and Jenna quickly realized the last time Chance had
probably seen Jeff's parents was at their son's funeral.

"Can we go now?" Tori said. "I'm tired of sitting
around here." She slid Jenna a glare.

"Gather up your project and take it with you, since
you didn't finish it," Jenna ordered. "Karen, they both
have a book report and display poster to make. Please
don't let them put it off all week or we'll be up half the
night before school next Monday."

"Homework?" Les said with a playful groan, patting

Mark Jeffrey roughly on the back. "Don't those teachers know it's a holiday?"

"Les, you're going to give him the hiccups. Stop
that," Karen scolded. "You two kiss your mother goodbye and get your things. Are you hungry? Your grand-
dad and I thought we'd take you to eat at the diner before
we see a movie."

"Yes!" Mark Jeffrey said, giving the air a fist pump.

"We haven't been to the movies in *forever,*" Tori
added.

Jenna tried not to be embarrassed but both Les and
Karen glanced at her as though the kids had said she
starved them.

They hadn't been to the movies because she couldn't
afford it. Simple as that. Working at the school had been
a blessing but it had barely covered their expenses. Any
extra cash—of which there was very little—went into
savings for emergencies. And she had plenty of those.
Broken water heaters, colds, vet visits.

Jenna hated that money issues meant she'd become
the no-fun parent, while the twins' friends and Les
and Karen were the ones who treated them. Or rather
spoiled them.

Jeff's parents were good people, nice people, but
they were lax and indulgent. With Jeff, and now with
the twins. With Jeff gone, Karen and Les focused too
much attention on their only grandchildren, and over-
indulged them at every opportunity. "Have fun. And
don't forget the teacher grades on neatness and detail.
She'll be able to tell if you throw those reports together
at the last minute. Work on them a little bit every day."

"We'll do our best," Karen said. "Come on, babies,
are you ready? We should get going."

While Les held out his hand to shake Chance's, Mark

Jeffrey glanced over his shoulder to where his sister stood reluctantly gathering her project items. Mark Jeffrey put his head down and moved to Jenna for a hug.

"Love you, Mom."

Sweet baby boy. "I love you, too. Have fun."

Tori bypassed Jenna and walked straight to her grandparents. "Bye, Mom."

Les normally didn't notice slights or the contexts of conversation so she wasn't surprised he didn't see the significance of Tori's slam. But Karen? Not only did she notice, she even made a pitying face. Yet she said not a word to correct Tori's behavior.

As the group left, Jenna hugged her arms around her front and bit her lower lip until pain demanded she stop.

The only word to describe her relationship with her in-laws was *awkward.* She wasn't sure how to behave around them now because her grief over losing her husband had changed to survival mode to keep herself and the twins afloat financially, while the Darlingtons' grief seemed to remain unchanged. But how could she fix it when she felt as though they were the ones who needed to catch up?

She pressed a hand to her forehead and rubbed away the tension. She had a really bad feeling about sending the twins off this weekend with this stress between them, but maybe a few days' break was what they needed. Time to decompress? "Oh, crap."

"What?" Chance asked. "Did they forget something?"

She shook her head and barely managed to stifle a moan. She'd been so busy doing laundry and packing she'd forgotten to talk to them about not mentioning to their grandparents that the police had come to the house.

"I forgot to tell the kids not to mention your brother's house call," she said simply. And now it was too late. "I can only imagine what Karen will have to say when she hears about it."

Chance's smile brought out a reluctant one of her own.

"Chance, you got a minute?" Frank Deemer asked from where he stood at a shelf of Christmas lights.

"Sure thing, Frank. Excuse me," he said to Jenna, his warm gaze holding hers for a second longer before he turned away.

Jenna pushed her worry aside and returned to work, marvelling at the fact she and Chance had actually had a conversation that hadn't ended in a fight.

A half hour before closing, she grabbed the push broom and began her daily clean up. A couple of men entered and made their way deeper into the store.

"Yeah, I'm just in the area for a visit. My wife's family told her it had been too long," the man said. "I told her to go have fun. I can't break tradition now. I *always* climb on Thanksgiving."

The second man stopped by the bags of salt, while the climber continued to the section of climbing equipment.

"Well, good luck. You're going to need it with that storm on its way," the second man said, hefting the salt onto his shoulder. "Chance, ring me up so I can get out of here before the wife overcooks my dinner."

"Sure thing, Hal."

Chance quickly punched some buttons on the register and gave the customer his total, the two of them chatting about the upcoming snow and predicted accumulations. In a minute flat the transaction was done.

Chance had a certain ease when it came to dealing

with customers and running the store. Jeff had been good at his job as a car salesman, but it had merely been one of many jobs over the years. The reasons varied—his employers not being pleased when Jeff took too much time off to climb, his numerous injuries restricting his ability to work, his boredom—but the result was always the same. He'd be unemployed long enough for them to burn through most of their meager savings or get a different job at a lower salary.

"Storm's only an overnighter," the first man said from the aisle. "It'll be gone by noon."

"Ah, that's not what the weather reports are saying, but you sound like a man who enjoys a challenge," Chance said. "Where you headed?"

"Granite Peak. You climb it?"

"Several times. Piece of cake."

Jenna looked up in surprise. *Piece of cake?* Granite Peak was where Jeff had died and one of the most challenging climbs in the area. It definitely wasn't a cakewalk.

"Wait, what'd you say?" the climber said. "My buddy said that's the climb I wanted."

She discreetly watched them as she flipped the push broom the other way and began walking slowly across the floor, avoiding Chance and the customer by several yards but well able to hear the conversation since the customer's voice carried like a bullhorn.

"It's a good climb in summer, maybe, but you'll spend all your time just trying to access it."

"Oh, man, don't tell me that." The climber shook his head, hands on his hips. "Okay, so where would you go?"

Chance shrugged. "Everybody has their own preferences."

"Dude, give it to me straight. Where's the challenge?"

Making a face as though he was reluctant to give in and share a secret, Chance motioned the climber toward the framed map on the wall behind the register. "Best climb this time of year is right here."

Jenna squinted to see where Chance pointed and her mouth fell open in surprise. *What?*

"How high?"

"Not as high as Granite Peak but I thought you wanted a challenge? There are a couple of great walls here. The approach is a challenge, with lots of twists and turns, but the roads are decent so you won't spend your time digging out of drifts. You'll get several climbs out of a trip here. You won't have to see the wife's family until it's time to say goodbye."

The man laughed at Chance's comment and continued to stare at the map. "That's what I'm talking about."

Jenna didn't bother trying to be discreet anymore. The climber's back was to her and she raised an eyebrow high—which Chance ignored.

"So that's the place? Hellgate Gulch?"

"Doesn't get its name for nothing."

The guy looked down at Chance's cast. "Thanks, man. You've talked me into it. I'd ask you to go along but looks like you're out of commission for a while."

Chance tugged on his ear, a habit she noticed he was prone to slip into when he was stuck in an uncomfortable situation like having to confront the Jones boys about slipping tobacco into their pockets or Mrs. Merriweather's request for Chance to pick a couple of things out for her husband who had been dead for nearly twenty years.

"Yeah," he said, nodding. "That I am."

Spying a box Dooley had forgotten to break down, she set the broom aside and ripped the box apart while the man grabbed rope and carabiners—the metal rings used as connectors—along with a map to Hellgate Gulch and the favored rock faces there.

Once the climber was gone, Jenna ambled to where Chance stood by the register, her mind spinning with what had transpired. "You sent him to Hellgate?"

"There are some nice climbs there."

"But nothing as challenging as Granite Peak."

Chance's gray eyes held a glint of humor. "The guys who brag the most have the weakest skills. It's a given. And if I've learned anything over the years, it's that telling a man he can't or shouldn't do something is a surefire way of guaranteeing he tries."

Meaning what? Was he speaking from experience? "I see."

Like it or not Chance's gesture of conning the climber struck her as…sweet. So sweet she wondered what Jeff would have said to the man in the same situation.

"It's not a big deal. Actually, it's pretty selfish," Chance added.

"How so?"

"I did it to save my friends and family some time and effort. It's a safer climb, and there will be others at Hellgate. The guy can team up with some of them and talk their ears off."

"But how does that save your friends and family time?"

"He'd be out of his league at Granite Peak and, with the weather right now, there won't be as many people around. So when he got himself into trouble, Liam would be called out on search and rescue. So would

Carly's father and stepmother. The Rock Gods, too, since we know the area so well."

It made sense that Liam and the sheriff would be called in to help as law enforcement. And Rissa Taggert volunteered her helicopter to help with search and rescue several times a year when a camper or child wandered off and got lost. But the rest of them? "Jeff was never *called out* for search and rescue. When did the Rock Gods start doing that?"

This time there was no mistaking the way Chance's gaze shifted away from her. "After Jeff died. The guys talked about it and thought it was time. A few of us were trained as EMTs, as well. It seemed like the thing to do."

She was torn between gratitude that Chance and his friends had taken it upon themselves to assume such a role in honor of Jeff and feeling way more than she should for a man she shouldn't be feeling anything for at all.

As silly as it sounded, she liked fighting with Chance better than how she felt right now. Arguing was easier. Way easier than looking at one of the Rock Gods and admiring him. "You probably saved that man's life."

"Don't give me too much credit, Jenna. I don't want to spend Thanksgiving searching for a moron."

"But isn't it all about the challenge?" she said, trying to lighten the moment and distract herself from how Chance looked leaning his hips against the counter to take the weight off his broken foot, a lock of his longish, sun-streaked hair falling over his forehead.

She was completely unprepared for the way Chance's gaze warmed and slid over her. Her body felt stripped of its defenses, instantly alert. All from a look?

The moment was broken when Chance shifted. "I

have somewhere I need to be. Dooley will show you how to lock up."

Jenna watched him hobble toward the back room, unable to come to terms with whatever had happened.

Maybe she'd judged Chance inaccurately. Maybe his healthy zest for life wasn't as irresponsible or self-serving as she'd presumed. But he was a Rock God. And that, she mused, wasn't healthy at all.

But combined with the look he'd given her?

Pure and total danger.

CHAPTER TEN

THE WEEKEND PASSED much too quickly. After leaving the store on Saturday, Jenna picked up groceries and went home, then made her almost nightly trip to Rachel's where she sat on a stool in the floral shop, handing her flowers or wire cutters or foam like a surgeon's assistant, while they kept up a steady dialog about life issues large and small.

On Sunday, she overslept and wound up in front of the television with her cereal bowl, channel surfing until it was too late to consider attending church. When Jeff was alive, their church appearances had been sporadic at best but since his death, she'd rarely gone. Her reluctance wasn't because she blamed God for Jeff's impulsiveness but rather how she felt under the scrutiny of some of the members. It was almost as though so long as she was married she was acceptable, but now that she was a widow something had changed.

Rachel said it was her age and marital status more than anything. Now she was competition. Jenna got a kick out of that theory. Who else was in the running? She came complete with two hormonal almost teens, a farting dog and a broken-down house. Plus she shaved her legs only if she felt like it.

She puttered the rest of the day, finishing some of those tasks she usually had no time for. Monday and Tuesday went by in a blink of an eye because the store was busy selling all the items needed for the upcoming Turkey Shoot. Instead of live animals, contestants shot at turkey-shaped targets spaced at challenging distances, which meant a lot of ammo went out the door. The winner received bragging rights, a frozen turkey from Frank's Grocery and slew of other prizes—some of them cash, making Jenna wish she was a better shot.

Finally it was Wednesday, and because it was the day before a holiday, McKenna Feed closed early. Yet it was nearing seven o'clock and Jenna was still working.

She sat back on her heels and stretched out the kinks in her back. Done. Finally.

Dooley had been scheduled to stay after closing to prepare the store for Black Friday but his wife had called with an emergency. In a bid to earn some extra cash, Jenna had volunteered to cover for Dooley rather than return to her empty house.

Maybe she'd even tuck away the extra cash for the girls' night out she hoped to plan once the holidays were over and everyone wasn't so busy.

A quick call at closing had Rachel using the spare key to take Snickers for a walk, and without the kids home to entertain the dog, Jenna knew Snickers would spend the evening snoozing on the couch she wasn't supposed to lay on.

The way Jenna saw it, even the dog should have some rest and relaxation considering all she'd been through in recent months.

Jenna cleaned up the boxes and trash, checked the new prices in the registers one more time to make sure they had been entered correctly and headed for her locker. Humming in tune to the music playing over the storewide sound system, she pushed through the swing door and stumbled to a halt, gasping when she realized she wasn't alone.

"Sorry," Chance said, pulling his keys from the rear entrance. "I didn't mean to scare you."

She was startled, yes, but considering Chance was dressed in his Santa suit and carrying a takeout bag from the diner, scared was pushing it.

"What are you still doing here? Where's Dooley?"

"He had an emergency and couldn't finish the prep for Friday, so I volunteered. The baby and his wife both have a virus and he went home to take care of them. Where were you?" She indicated the suit.

Chance pulled off his hat and beard. "The old folks' home."

Seriously? "That's...very nice of you."

"Zane always did it. I'm trying to keep up the tradition," Chance said with a shrug.

He walked deeper into the back room and she noticed something about him was different. "What happened to your crutches?"

"Ah, they're history," he said, flashing her a pleased grin. "I had an appointment this afternoon and he finally had mercy on me and changed my cast out for a boot."

"That's great," she said, even as she wondered how long it would be before Chance wound up right back on the crutches.

"Yeah, it is. Hey, Porter packed up a ton of food. He likes it when I show up at the diner in the suit. Good for business. You hungry? There's no way I can eat all of this."

Dinner? With him? "Oh, no, I should get going. I finished the inventory sheet Dooley was working on and all the new Christmas arrivals are unboxed, shelved and plugged into the system. We're all ready for Friday morning."

"Great. But if you've been here all afternoon it sounds to me like you deserve a break. Come on, you stayed when Dooley couldn't. If you hadn't, I'd be up all night doing it myself. The least I can do is provide dinner. What are you going to do, go home and watch TV?"

Was he kidding? What single mother got to do that? There was always a mountain of lists to tackle. Not only the typical mom jobs but the stuff Jeff would have been responsible for, too.

More than anything, she was leery because this was a little too cozy and her defenses weren't as strong as she needed them to be. He'd left that afternoon to go to a nursing home? Voluntarily?

Just wait until you tell Rachel that.

Tradition or not, what Chance had done was noble and kind and the act drew her in despite the ever-present awareness of who Chance was when he wasn't injured. Maybe they had gotten along a little better lately, but it was only because they didn't talk about climbing or the Rock Gods. She wasn't that woman, wasn't the *type* of woman swayed by a few good deeds or pretty words spoken by a handsome man. "Actually, I was going to… wash my hair," she quipped.

Chance winced. "Ow."

She laughed and shook her head. "Thank you, but I really should go."

"I'll bet you didn't bring lunch and haven't had anything to eat since breakfast, have you? You've got to eat, Jenna."

She hadn't, because she'd planned to get off around

noon and go home. And she was hungry. But...dinner with Chance?

"Give me a couple minutes to change out of this suit and we can share it," he said, walking toward the door marked Private.

She'd noticed the door numerous times and meant to ask Dooley what was behind it but it had slipped her mind time and again.

Chance produced another key and motioned for her to follow him inside. She paused on the threshold to see a large, one-room apartment that was very well equipped with a kitchenette and stacked laundry, a couch, massive television that took up a big portion of the wall, and a dresser and bed. He lived here? How did she not know that?

"Start digging into that and make yourself at home. I'll be out in a second."

Chance left the sack on the counter and grabbed clothes off the bed before he disappeared through another door, presumably a bathroom.

She eyed the food and felt like Eve when presented with the apple. She really should go but Jenna was so hungry she was starting to shake a bit. Would dinner hurt considering it smelled wonderful and was made? She wouldn't have to think about what to eat.

"I got a movie earlier when I was out," Chance called through the door. "It's not a chick flick but it's a new release and there's lots of action."

The door opened abruptly and he strode toward her, clad in snug jeans faded in the right places, and in the act of smoothing a faded shirt over the hard-hewn ridges of his six-pack.

She looked away but not in time. And not before realizing she'd forgotten to breathe.

"Don't be shy. Dig in," he ordered, joining her in the kitchenette.

It was tempting. *So* tempting. The twins being gone since Saturday had given her a nice break but the house was really starting to feel empty. "I should go."

"Oh, man. Blackberry cobbler. I owe Porter big. Have you ever had his cobbler?"

She had. And maybe if Chance hadn't said *cobbler* she could have stayed strong, ignored her stomach and refused.

Darn it, she hated her sweet tooth. It had gotten the best of her on more than one occasion, as her jeans would attest. "It does smell good."

"Plenty for both of us."

Did he have to open the container to show her? "Maybe I'll stay. But only for a little while."

For the cobbler, not the guy standing there grinning like the *snake* who'd tempted Eve.

She didn't allow herself to pay too much attention to the masculine awareness and flirtatiousness she saw in Chance's eyes. The smugness that said he'd caught *her* looking when he'd stepped outside the bathroom.

This was what she'd been afraid of when it came to dating again. Not that she was thinking of Chance that way, because she *wasn't.* Just that she didn't know how to act. As much as she'd seen of native villages and cultures as a child, this was a whole other world she didn't know how to navigate.

But if she'd learned nothing else from her brief encounters with Jeff's climbing buddies over the years, it was that none of them lacked confidence and flirting came as natural to them as blinking. Something she couldn't allow herself to forget.

Making herself a plate, Jenna edged toward the coffee table, focusing one-hundred percent of her attention on putting some distance between them. He didn't have a table or chairs and, since he'd mentioned watching a movie...

She settled herself on the floor between the couch and the coffee table, and waited for Chance to join her. "I didn't realize you actually live here."

Then it hit her. Would Chance sit on the couch? Or beside her on the floor?

"Yeah. I wanted my own space and it made more sense than driving back and forth to the ranch every day," he said, limping across the room on the boot.

Couch? Floor? Couch? Floor?

She released the breath she didn't know she held when he chose the couch. Why was she so nervous?

Since Chance was settled, she finally took a bite of food and closed her eyes in bliss. Oh, she was *hungry*.

"Glad you stayed?" he said, a teasing note to his voice.

Pretending not to be embarrassed, she shrugged. "I didn't realize I was so hungry until I smelled it."

His husky laughter brought out more of the flush she hoped he didn't notice.

"I'll tell you a little secret if you don't spread it around. Show up at the diner at the end of the day and Porter will load you up with leftovers fit for a king."

Oh, wow. Good to know. Considering her financial state, she might have to start doing that. Porter wouldn't know what hit him when the twins smiled at him.

"Want me to get the movie started?"

Jenna took another bite and watched while Chance moved to the television and inserted the DVD in the system housed in a small cabinet below it. Despite her lack of funds, she liked movies, too. It was her favorite way to veg out and relax. But she couldn't remember the last movie she'd seen that wasn't either a cartoon or by Disney.

Teasers for upcoming releases rolled with a blast of the speakers. Thankfully Chance had invested some money in a sound system that drowned out all need for conversation.

While she watched, Jenna downed the food. Everything was delicious and the cobbler—it was so good she had to fight the urge to lick the container.

By the time she was done, Chance was also finished eating and engrossed in the movie. Should she leave now? She waited awhile longer, starting to relax a bit more once she realized it was simply dinner and a movie and Chance wasn't going to invite her to snuggle up with him on the couch.

Other than making himself comfortable and stretching his injured foot out on the end of the coffee table, Chance sat sprawled in what she'd always considered a *guy* pose—his arm along the back of the leather cushion, taking up a lot of room. He was a fairly tall man, who had a tendency to take up a lot of room no matter what.

Another ten minutes passed. Twenty more. During the biggest of the action scenes when things were exploding and the hero and the damsel in distress were on the run, Jenna finally sank into the couch and got comfortable. She needed to go home but she hated the thought of leaving the warmth of the back room for the cold outside. And the movie was good.

Forty-five minutes later, the ending credits rolled. The story line wasn't surprising. Good triumphed over evil, the guy got the girl into bed with a blaze of action-packed passion that faded to black—but not before Jenna became really uncomfortable, because she watched the scene with Chance. And suddenly she *really* had to leave. "I should get home. Thanks for dinner."

"Yeah, no problem. Thanks for the company. Dooley's usually eaten everything in sight by now. I still have enough for breakfast and maybe even lunch."

"But tomorrow is Thanksgiving. Aren't you going to the ranch to eat with your family?" she asked, standing.

"Maybe. Probably," he corrected.

*O*kay. Obviously he wasn't sure. But why wasn't he?

They were both awkward during the cleanup process. Finally it was taken care of and she left the apartment to grab her stuff from her locker.

Very much aware of Chance's presence behind her, she put on her scarf and coat and tried to ignore her suddenly trembling hands.

At the rear entrance, Chance muttered something under his breath.

"What?"

He pointed at the window. "It's really coming down out there. Let me get my coat and keys. I'll drive you."

"Why?" she asked, opening the door but seeing nothing unusual for a Montana winter.

"Because I want to make sure you make it home safely."

She glanced up at Chance in surprise and tried hard not to be touched by the gesture. "It's not far. I'll be fine." Inanely nervous, she wet her lips, only to hear him swear under his breath. "What?"

"Nothing." He reached out and snagged the collar of her coat, tugging on it gently.

"Oh, thanks," she said when the collar righted itself from its turned-in position. But Chance didn't let go.

His gray gaze locked on hers, so intense she would have sworn the blowing wind outside somehow sucked all the air from the room.

"Jenna…"

Pulse pounding in her ears, she watched as Chance lowered his head. And even though her mind screamed at her to pull away, her feet refused to move.

His lips brushed over hers and the mixed taste of blackberry cobbler and vanilla ice cream registered, along with the vague but daunting fact that this should not be happening.

Chance used his hold on her coat to draw her close, until she was flush against the hard, lean length of his body. A rough, hungry sound exited his chest and he took a step back, still holding her, and shut the door.

It was the quiet sound of the metal latch scraping into place that brought her to her senses. Her hands were wedged between them and she pushed him away, unable to fathom what had come over her to let Chance kiss her that way. She stared at him, well able to recognize the shock stealing over his expression, because it matched what she felt inside.

"I have to go."

"Jenna, wait. Just give me a second. I'll drive you home."

"You've done enough," she said, yanking the door open.

She should have known this would happen. Dinner and movie. Could she be that naive?

The cold bitter wind cooled the heat in her face and brought much needed clarity. There was a reason why the snake was a snake. She knew better than to get sucked into the vortex that was Chance McKenna. Like so many members of the Rock Gods, he had a reputation when it came to climbing—and women. What kind of man kissed his friend's wife?

What kind of wife kisses her deceased husband's friend?

"Call me when you get home. Let me know you made it okay," he called.

She ignored him, pretended not to hear him. *Same difference.*

"Fine, I'll call you!"

She didn't acknowledge that, either. Jenna braced herself against the gusting wind and hurried toward her old truck as fast as she could, careful of the patches of ice. Locked inside the vehicle, she jabbed the key into the ignition and thanked God when the engine caught.

That did *not* happen.

Thoughts racing, she drove down the street toward home, grateful the thick snow provided an excuse to crawl at a snail's pace, because she didn't have the brainpower required to navigate at a faster speed.

It took her four times the normal amount of time to complete the drive. She was so relieved to see her porch light gleaming on the new fallen snow, she sat in the rapidly cooling vehicle and watched the snow dive from the sky like little kamikaze balls of fluff. Sat until the cold seeped into her layers of clothing and brought her out of her trance with a shiver that reached her bones.

So you liked it. It means you're healthy. Ready to date again, like Rachel says.

Jenna mentally stomped on the voice of her inner bad girl, so ready with lame excuses. She wasn't seventeen anymore. She was too old to let her hormones get the best of her.

The phone was ringing when she unlocked the door.

It could be Les and Karen or, much more unlikely, the twins, but she knew who it was—Chance.

His kiss flashed through her mind and brought a tingle to her lips as she reluctantly picked up the phone and said hello.

"It's about time. Jenna, are you okay?" Chance asked.

"I'm fine. I drove slow."

"That's not what I meant."

She knew what he meant. "Don't do it again and we'll be fine."

A long, weighty silence filled the phone line. "Happy Thanksgiving."

Happy Thanksgiving? That's it?

She hesitated a full second in sheer disbelief before she rolled her eyes and hung up on him.

Chance McKenna had kissed her.

And, Lord help her, for a brief moment, she'd *liked* it.

CHAPTER ELEVEN

THANKSGIVING WAS A SOMBER occasion at the Circle M. Chance wandered the house and took in those gathered, a strong tug of loneliness hitting him hard. Zane may have been his adoptive father but the man had understood where Chance came from and he hadn't judged him the way some of his foster families had.

No one measured up to Zane's presence in his or his brothers' lives and that made it that much harder to stomach Zane's passing, even though it had been several months since he had died in the accident that had pinned him beneath a tractor.

Since their very first year in Zane's life and living beneath his roof, Thanksgiving day consisted of a turkey shoot in the morning, dinner with all the trimmings and all four of them—or three in recent years if Liam pulled duty—in front of the television watching the games and shootin' the breeze.

Last night when Jenna had reminded him it was Thanksgiving, he still hadn't made up his mind about showing up today. Doing so had taken some effort on his part, and he couldn't help but wish his foot was healed so he could have had an excuse to be somewhere else.

Like the climber in the store?

His sense of unease wasn't helped by the fact that they'd gained Charlie, the ranch foreman and Liam's recently discovered biological father. To Chance, it was another hard-hitting reminder of the monster of a man rotting in a prison cell. Why was someone like his father alive after what he'd done, while Zane was dead? Where was the justice in that?

"Would you listen to them?" Liam said with a smile, his ear cocked toward the doorway where Gabriella and Carly's feminine laughter filtered in.

Chance couldn't help but shake his head at his brother's sappy expression. Married only a few months to the sheriff's daughter, Chance had never seen Liam so happy. Brad, either, for that matter, despite the chaos of the wedding plans driving his typically quiet, backward brother crazy.

"I think there's less noise out in the hen house," Brad added, a smile lacing his words. "It's nice, though, isn't it? That they get along so well."

Chance frowned, immediately picturing Jenna in the kitchen with the women. The image stopped him cold because he was still kicking himself for kissing her, and before he could stop it, a soft curse flew from his lips.

"What's up with you?" Liam demanded.

"Nothing." He could picture Jenna there all he wanted, but it wasn't going to happen for a lot of reasons. Jenna was Jeff's widow. He and Jeff had been *friends.* Buddies didn't kiss each other's girl. And then there was the climbing.

Being out of commission since Labor Day weekend had more than proven Chance wasn't ready to give up his adventures. Why else was he pushing himself so hard in physical therapy? It wasn't to stay home and twiddle his thumbs. Even if he and Jenna somehow moved beyond Jeff's presence in their lives, after everything Jenna had been through, Chance's friendship with the Rock Gods would always be an issue.

Jenna considered climbing an irresponsible activity for any man with a family and if he got involved with her, that's exactly what he would have. A family. Jeff's family, who had already endured one loss. Jenna and the twins, Jeff's parents—they all factored into the equation and Chance couldn't let himself forget it. They didn't need more upset in their lives and it stood to reason that every time he went for a climb all of those bad feelings and memories would return. The same way they did for him every time the news flashed someone's mug shot and he felt an instant jab of shame. Until Zane had adopted him and changed his name, an awful lot of people had known him as the murderer's kid.

"Everything okay at the store?" Brad asked when Chance remained quiet.

"Yeah, fine. The place practically runs itself."

Brad grunted. "When you're there, maybe."

The pained statement drew a chuckle from the other men and a wry smile from Chance. Brad wasn't a sociable guy and hated anything that took him off the ranch and required him to deal with humans instead of animals.

But it was true. The business was virtually maintenance free with loyal employees like Dooley, and now the ever-conscientious Jenna following fast on his heels. There were a few day-to-day operating issues that crept up but nothing major. Nothing to hold Chance there for long, especially not once the cast came off and winter really set in. Maybe he and a few of the guys could head south into Utah or Nevada to some favorite climbs there.

"Are they always so noisy?" he asked, hoping to get the subject off him.

"Usually." Brad lifted his glass of iced tea and drained the contents.

"What's got you looking so down in the mouth?" Liam asked.

Everyone turned to Chance once more.

Charlie sat forward in his chair to grab a handful of nuts from a nearby bowl. "You get some bad news about that foot of yours?"

"No, my doc says it's healing nicely. I'll be able to lose the boot in a couple more weeks. Should be back to normal real soon."

Chance shifted his attention to Liam and found his brother rubbing his chin. The moment Chance made the mistake of making eye contact, he knew he wasn't hiding the fact that he wasn't comfortable being here but how did you tell that to the people who shared your last name? He should've made an excuse to show up later, right when the food was being served.

Or claimed to have Dooley's virus and not shown up at all.

"Wouldn't have anything to do with your pretty new hire, would it?" Liam asked.

Something in his expression must have given him away, because his brothers exchanged a look. Chance ran a hand through his hair and decided to come clean. "If I admit I screwed up, will you stop staring at me? You're giving me the creeps."

"Fix it," Brad said with a groan. "Whatever you did, make it right. I'm not driving all the way to town to fill in at the store again."

Chance brushed some peanut shell dust off his pant

leg, giving it way more attention than it needed. "It's fine. I apologized."

"Apologized for what?" Liam demanded. He was always the guy who got straight to the point.

"Kissing her."

"You kissed Jenna Darlington?" Brad asked, his eyebrows shooting up in surprise.

"It won't happen again."

"Why not? Because you didn't like it or because she didn't?" Liam said.

All three of the men waited like teenage girls wanting to hear the latest gossip, and Chance thought about getting up and walking out right then.

"Whoo-hoo, she didn't!" Charlie practically crowed.

"Shot down," Brad said, his tone incredulous.

"That had to be a first." Liam's expression held no sympathy at all.

Chance ground his teeth. "I've been shot down before."

"Doesn't happen often," Brad said, sliding a knowing look toward Liam. "I like her. We need to make her job permanent. Give her a raise, too."

"What'd she do when you planted one on her?" Charlie asked.

Chance inhaled and resigned himself to a long afternoon. The moment the last bite of pumpkin pie was in his belly, he was out of there. "It was an accident."

Brad laughed. "I know I'm not the smoothest when it comes to women but how do you kiss a woman by *accident*?"

You don't. And dreaming about her and waking up hard and uncomfortable wasn't any fun, either.

"I meant it shouldn't have happened. She's Jeff's widow."

"Deflection," Liam said, smirking. "That doesn't answer how she responded. It's a dead giveaway."

"She ordered me not to do it again and hung up. It's fine."

"Doesn't mean we're out of the woods. She could slap us with a sexual harassment suit," Liam warned. "Everyone knows Jenna was let go from the school. If she's hard up for money, she might try to see what would happen with a lawsuit."

"She wouldn't do that," Chance said, knowing in his gut he was right.

"And you know that because?" Liam asked, still thinking like a cop.

Because Jenna was too kind, too considerate of other people and the impact that would have on everyone. Maybe if he'd been a jerk about kissing her and not taken no for an answer, but that wasn't what happened. "Because she wouldn't. I'll apologize again if it makes you feel better. I'll handle it."

"Just don't handle her," Liam warned.

"Dinner!" The call came from the kitchen, rescuing Chance.

They got to their feet, but Charlie remained seated.

"Aren't you coming?" Liam asked.

A wary expression crossed Charlie's face. "Maybe."

"What's holding you up?" Brad asked, rubbing his hands together like a starving man.

Charlie scratched his head. "Just had something occur to me is all. Those are two fine girls you boys have in there but did either one of you make sure they knew how to cook a turkey?"

Chance stopped and looked to find Liam and Brad regarding each other with expressions of horror.

Yeah, Thanksgiving wasn't going to be the same without Zane.

"SHE MEANS WELL."

Jenna looked up from the magazine she flipped through and found Les regarding her from the doorway of the weatherproofed sunroom. This room was colder than any other in the house but it was quieter because of it.

The kids were playing video games in Jeff's old bedroom and, since Karen liked to prepare the Thanksgiving meal all herself, Jenna had escaped here to gather her temper and her nerves.

Her whirling thoughts about Chance and the kiss were about to drive her insane, so it wasn't surprising that she'd lost her cool with Karen. The kids had been there since Saturday evening. In all that time, Karen couldn't make Tori spend *a little* time on her report?

"If you say so," she said in response to Les's comment. "Who's winning?"

"It's just pre-game right now. They talk about the same thing fifty ways to Sunday before they ever get started. Want me to turn on the gas logs?"

"No. I kind of like being snuggled under the blanket. It was your grandmother's, correct?" she asked, her thoughts fixated on what had happened last night. She felt so…guilty. And why should she feel guilty when he was the one who'd kissed her?

Maybe so, but you were the one having the couch or floor debate.

If only Rachel was in town. She had left yesterday morning to drive her mother to Helena to spend Thanksgiving with her mother's elderly brother. They wouldn't return until late tonight, which meant Jenna had spent last night tossing and turning and berating herself about the humongous mistake of kissing Chance McKenna.

Les walked over to the mantel to turn the logs on anyway. That done, he pointed to a frame.

"That's her picture, right there. She was a strong woman. Her grandmother was one of the first women to settle in the area as a girl, even held captive by the Indians for a while until the army rescued her."

"You have quite the family history in Montana."

"So do you." Les nodded as though to confirm his words. "Doesn't take long to build a history once you put down roots, and you've lived here how long now? Ten years?"

"Almost eleven," she said, unable to believe how fast the time had flown by. When Jeff had told her where he originated she'd thought of the Wild West state she'd seen depicted in movies. And, oh, how it had appealed to her adventurous side despite the shock of her pregnancy and hasty marriage before they'd left India and her father behind. But now...

You can't accuse Jeff and the Rock Gods of running and then turn around and do it yourself.

Jenna drew her knees up beneath the blanket and tried not to think about kissing another man while her father-in-law, one of the sweetest men she'd ever met, stood before her staring into the flames. But how could she not think about it when it had gotten to her so quickly?

She felt insanely naive. And crazy. But she hadn't expected that type of reaction.

"Jenna, it upset Karen when you mentioned looking for a job in Helena."

"I know. I shouldn't have brought it up today," she said, meaning it. But she'd be lying if she said the urge wasn't there, luring her to act.

She'd stopped to get gas for the drive and picked up one of the monstrously thick newspapers with the Black Friday sales ads. A too-sharp turn had sent much of the paper careening off the seats onto the floor, and the remaining section listed the job postings for Helena.

The thought had come out of nowhere, but once it had made an appearance... Why not broaden her search outside North Star? When she was the twins' age she'd moved over a dozen times, lived all over the world thanks to her parents' careers aiding developing countries. But while Jenna didn't want that extreme instability for her children, a move to Helena might improve their livelihood, so how could she not at least consider it? "All I did was mention expanding my horizons, Les."

"And then you got upset about Tori's book report."

"One has nothing to do with the other. There simply aren't a lot of good paying jobs in North Star."

"If things are that tough, you could always move in here. You know we'd be happy to help you out."

"No. Absolutely not." She gave Les a stare that dared him to argue. "You know that would never work."

Les moved toward her, his worn house slippers silent on the carpeted floor, and sat on the arm of a nearby chair. "Yeah, well, like I said. Karen means well and the offer stands."

"Thank you. Les, you have to admit Karen lets the twins take advantage."

"You've never let them get by with something?"

"Of course I have. But look at this from my point of view, will you? When the twins are here and I ask *one* simple thing, would it hurt Karen to back me up? Does she have to make things more difficult?"

"Sometimes we have to overlook a person's flaws for love and no other reason. Kind of like you and Jeff. You made allowances for him, same as he did for you."

It was true but where did Karen get off—

"Jeff's birthday is in two weeks."

"Yes, I—I know." But it was a lie. She'd been so busy working and pondering *the kiss* that she'd actually forgotten Jeff's birthday was coming up. What kind of wife was that? Did the kids remember?

"There was a little snow on the ground, some in the air. Last year, Karen was too numb to do much of anything but go through the motions but this year…I think it's hitting her extra hard."

She set the magazine aside, guilt riding her. Rachel was right. No parent should ever have to bury a child. Given Jenna's feelings of guilt about one simple kiss with Chance, how could she downplay Karen's love for her son? "I can't imagine losing a child, no matter the age. I'll try to be more patient with her about that. But what am I supposed to do, Les? I tell the twins no and she says yes. I establish clear rules and she allows the kids to break them, then she gives me this look like she's helpless to correct them when she's *not*. Les, I lost him, too. I lost my husband and my coparent, and I get tired of always being the bad guy. Having someone back me up in making the twins mind me would be a nice break every now and again."

"I never thought of it that way but I'll talk to her. I hear what you're saying, Jenna."

"Thank you." Jenna stared into Les's wrinkle-lined eyes, so like his son's and grandson's.

Les could talk until he was blue in the face, but Jenna

knew Karen would never change. She didn't understand how her actions now impacted the twins' future. But Jenna did—because she'd married the result. She'd fallen for Jeff's unbridled, I-deserve-everything-I-can-have spirit. She'd loved his impulsiveness and spontaneity—until there were two more mouths to feed and diapers to buy and kids to raise and Jeff left her to do it, while he continued to play.

His trip to India had been courtesy of the remaining balance of the college fund he didn't use to attend graduate school. Instead he'd traveled from mountain to mountain, country to country, until one day he'd fallen and, bleeding, had landed in her father's little medical clinic.

He'd smiled at her, flirted with her and the rest was a fast-forward example of exactly how dangerous and dazzling a Rock God could be. *Something to remember.*

"Too bad the McKenna job is seasonal. I've always thought they were good people. Zane really turned those boys around."

She'd heard bits and pieces of the story from numerous sources over the years, tidbits of information dropped into the conversation from Jeff and at work whenever the Rock Gods were mentioned. Small towns knew everything. But that didn't mean there weren't details missing. "How old were they when Zane McKenna adopted them?"

"Well, Karen would be able to tell you for certain, because she remembers things like that. But if I recall right, they were all around fourteen or fifteen. Full of spit and fire, those boys, and more trouble than they were worth to a lot of people."

"I can imagine." She couldn't handle her twins, much less three boys from difficult circumstances and questionable backgrounds. So what had Chance's life been like before he went into foster care and the boys' home? He'd said his mother had died, but when Jenna'd asked if his father had died...

No. But he's dead to me just the same.

Jeff had had a good life, she knew that, but her husband had still had issues with responsibility and authority. A kid like Chance? A child so bitter toward his father? Was that why he tried so hard to climb? To rise above whatever it was that had happened?

"Folks thought Zane had lost his mind," Les said. "He did well by them, though, and they turned out to be good men. I wish... Well, I guess I can say it now. With Jeff being our only child, we spoiled him too much. We're partly to blame for why he chased a good time until he couldn't chase it anymore."

Jenna blinked at Les in surprise. In the time since Jeff's death, she'd never once heard either of Jeff's parents breathe a word of criticism against their son. But right then she recognized that Les at least had an inkling of Jeff's flaws. Maybe with his behavior as a cautionary tale, Les could convince Karen to not make the same mistake with her grandchildren. "I don't want Jeff's impulsiveness to carry over to the twins," she said softly, to be clear.

Jeff's father nodded his understanding. "Neither do I, hon. Neither do I."

"Dinner's ready!" Tori called.

"Come on," Les said, standing. "Let's eat before the game starts."

Jenna shoved the homemade quilt aside and accepted Les's extended hand. Together they made their way to the kitchen.

Leaning close along the way, he whispered, "My

wife might not always be the most agreeable woman, but she's a mighty fine cook."

Jenna laughed, wondering if he had always been a glass half-full kind of guy or if living with Karen had forced him to adopt that way of thinking. "That she is," she said, patting his arm and smiling at him. "The food will be wonderful today."

CHAPTER TWELVE

HAVING OPENED THE DOORS of McKenna Feed at five o'clock that morning, Jenna slurped her third cup of coffee by nine and waved goodbye to Rachel, who wore a garish Christmas sweater that lit up and played a Christmas carol.

Jenna had been surprised to see Rachel out and about but Rachel had said she'd returned from Thanksgiving dinner to find a message on her answering machine approving her request for a Home Health aide who would arrive at seven sharp. She had, and Rachel had immediately made her escape for some much-needed retail therapy. Apparently the feed store's metal wire came in handy in her shop, especially when purchased at a discount.

Jenna turned her head this way and that in an effort to relieve the tension in her shoulders. So far she, Dooley and Chance had been so busy with customers they'd barely said hello but after another sleepless night because she'd dreamed of kissing Chance, she knew the situation had to be addressed before she collapsed from exhaustion.

Ever since Jeff's death, it seemed she'd been running on adrenaline, caffeine and sheer grit. Adding sleepless nights in might send her over the edge into the *crazy* Rachel had referred to—not at all acceptable under any circumstances.

Find a new kind of normal, that's what the self-help book had said. And for her? No version of normal included Chance McKenna.

She finished helping another customer, then grabbed a cart, snagging misplaced items to reshelve and ignored the annoying Christmas tunes. What would she say to Chance when she had the opportunity?

Chance was probably used to the women he took into his apartment being receptive to his advances. But until he'd fixed her collar, she hadn't gotten the impression that he was out to score. When he'd asked her to stay, he'd seemed...lonely. Like her. But not interested.

And this bothers you?

No, definitely not. She didn't want him interested. But she'd be lying if she said kissing him hadn't stirred something deep within her she found highly disturbing. She was a single mother of rambunctious twins. No matter how much she tried to psych herself up for dating, she wasn't sure she was ready. And if she was, what about sex? If the magazines were right, that's all men were interested in, whereas a good night to her was uninterrupted sleep and no sign of vomit, human or canine.

"We're out of the early bird flashlights. If anyone asks say you're sorry and point them over there," Dooley said, lifting his hand and indicating the endcap where the more expensive flashlights were displayed. "I posted a sign."

She gave him a nod and her best fake, cheery, good-morning smile. "Will do."

"When you finish that restocking, go help Chance. He's ringing people up as fast as he can but there's still a line. You're a lot quicker on the cash register. He said he'd bag as you total."

"Okay, great." *Great?* The last thing she wanted to do was be stuck behind the counter with Chance. There was barely enough room for one person, much less two.

A new song blasted out of the speakers above her head as she glanced at the checkout counter and the man behind it. Chance was dressed in faded jeans and a black sweater. Really. Couldn't the man tone it down a notch?

"YOU CAN'T AVOID me forever, you know," Chance said later, once the crowd of customers had thinned a bit.

He hobbled along after Jenna, moving much faster now that his crutches were gone. But for such a small woman, she was quick and, short of breaking into a lame-ass hopping jog, he couldn't keep up with her.

"I'm not avoiding you."

Yeah, then why was he staring at her back?

Jenna headed toward the break room and since her shift was over he followed her, using it for the opportunity it was to settle things. "Jenna?"

She stopped in front of her locker and squared her shoulders before she turned to face him. She'd worn layers again today, at least three, the third one being a thick flannel shirt she left open over the other two.

"We can pretend it never happened if you want to."

"Good. That's exactly what I want. Even if you weren't my employer, I'm not interested in getting involved with anyone right now. It's too soon."

His instincts said to let the comment slide but he was curious all the same. "Anyone? Or me?"

"Chance, I don't want to get into another argument with you. We both agreed it's best forgotten."

It was best forgotten. So why couldn't he? "Jeff

would never expect you to be a nun the rest of your life. He'd want you to move on and have some fun."

"I realize that, but do you really think he'd want me to move on with you?" she said, her tone derisive. "Somehow I doubt that."

He stomped down the guilt he felt at her words and chose to look at it from another angle. "He'd know I'd look out for you, however long we were together."

Shock stole over her features but it was nothing compared to the shock he felt that he'd said the words aloud. When he'd followed her into the back room he'd had no intention of doing anything more than apologizing and settling the matter; but when he'd opened his mouth, the wrong words had come out.

He wasn't a guy who did commitment or long-term. Working as much as he did, then climbing the rest of the time didn't leave a lot of room for dating or relationships.

His friendships with women typically lasted as long as the woman was willing to put up with him, but he made sure to spell things out ahead of time so wires didn't get crossed. Once the woman realized he worked hard, played hard, and she had to fit into the mix where she could, she usually moved on to someone else.

"However long we're together," she repeated, sarcasm lacing her tone. "Such a typical Rock God response. Never plan too far ahead because you don't know where you might be—or if you'll be alive."

He didn't like the smart-ass side of her, especially not when he was trying…what? "You know what I meant."

"Yes, I do, unfortunately."

"Look, I wasn't planning to kiss you. It happened. But now that it did, I can't say I wouldn't mind it happening again."

"I am not some Rock God *rally girl,* who goes from climber to climber."

"I never thought you were." He was making a mess of this but she wasn't making it any easier. "Jenna, I'm trying to figure this out, just like you."

"There's nothing to figure out," she said, insistent. "I'm not seeing or dating or sleeping with a Rock God ever again. *Ever.* What kind of *name* is that anyway? You think because you climb a few mountains you have the right to call yourselves gods?"

"I didn't come up with the name, sweetheart. And why are you getting so worked up about it if you don't care if it ever happens again?"

A strange expression flickered over her face. Embarrassment and…guilt?

"I'm not getting worked up."

"You are. Did you like it when we kissed?" he asked softly, hope flaring high and hot inside him when she avoided his gaze. He moved closer to her. "Jenna, did you wonder what it would have been like if we'd done more than kiss?"

A fiery blush surged up her neck and into her face, and seeing her response put a whole other spin on things.

He might not date much but he knew enough about women to figure out she wasn't upset because of her feelings toward Jeff but because he'd kissed her and… she'd liked it?

"I can't believe you'd even suggest— *No.* Of course not." Something about the way she said the words made him question their authenticity.

"There are plenty of women in this town. Go kiss one of them. You were Jeff's friend. I was his *wife.* Isn't that enough to end this now?"

It was. It should be. But he took another step forward anyway. "Jenna…"

"Back off, Chance. I mean it."

When a woman said no, he took it to mean no. Period. He retreated, hands up. "Your decision." He moved toward the swing door even though it was the last thing he wanted to do.

Because now all he could think about was how it had felt to kiss her and how Jenna was denying both of them because of her loyalty to Jeff—something Chance should probably feel more of.

He should have left well enough alone. Jenna was upset, and he had all sorts of inappropriate thoughts going through his head. None of them doable. He blamed his interest in Jenna on the time he'd spent with Brad and Liam and their families yesterday. He'd never once thought about settling down but watching the couples interact had gotten him thinking about things. Such as what Jenna had said about firsts and how he didn't want to wind up like Charlie, broken down, alone, with more than his share of regrets.

Carly and Gabriella were both smart, beautiful women and there had been a lot of teasing and flirtation going on, making him doubly aware of his solitude. Before he'd known it was happening, he'd started pondering the possibilities, picturing Jenna there with them, because he knew she'd fit nicely into the mix.

But he had to get that image out of his head. And as soon as the boot came off…

Instead of spending Christmas watching his brothers leer at their wives and ignoring his desire for Jenna, he needed space. Distance.

He had to find a climb. Focus on the details of it and

taking off for a while. In fact, he'd start planning his trip now.

He needed a distraction from the woman who was supposed to have been his distraction.

"RACH?" JENNA SAID SOFTLY when she got a good look at her friend. "Are you okay?"

Rachel's cheeks were wet with tears she hastily wiped away. "Hey. What are you doing here? Is it five already?"

Jenna stepped into the prep room in back of Rachel's shop, taking in her friend's attempts to pretend she hadn't been crying. "No, I got off early today because I went in for the morning madness. What's wrong? Did something happen?"

"Oh, you know me. I cry at commercials."

Jenna pulled out a stool at the long counter covered in flowers and sat. "Those swags are beautiful. For a wedding?"

"Yeah, yeah. Actually, it's for Brad McKenna and Gabriella Thompson. Wait, watch," Rachel said, snagging the cord attached to the garland and plugging it into the closest electrical outlet. "What do you think?"

"Rach, that is gorgeous. I think you've outdone yourself." The swag was filled with tiny twinkling white lights, winter white silk flowers and berries and glittering twigs topped with ribbon.

"I hope so. Especially since I'm making twenty-two of them to fill the top of the barn."

"The bride will love them. Now tell me why you were cry— Wait, a barn? They're getting married in a *barn?* In winter?"

"Trust me, it's not your typical barn—never housed animals, only been used for storage. You could park a couple planes in there and still have room for more. It will be heated and all decked out. You can go with me when I take these out there to set up. In fact, I insist. Brad wanted to use local people as much as possible, so I lucked into getting most of the flower order. Talk about a boon for business."

"That's great."

"Yeah, but I could use an assistant on this job if you're interested. I'll pay," she said, dangling the word like a carrot.

"Consider it done." She'd been Rachel's assistant several times in the past for the bigger jobs she'd contracted. This close to Christmas, every little bit of cash she could earn would help. "So, why the tears?"

"Oh, it's fine. Mom had another spell."

"It must have been a bad one," she said, hating the fact that it had happened today when Rachel had finally managed to get some time on her own.

Rachel nodded and sniffled, her eyes glittering with a fresh onset she managed to blink away. "She was fine, having a good day with the nurse. Everything was perfect. When I got home, I realized I'd been so busy shopping I forgot one errand, and Mom was having such a good day, I decided to take her with me. It was great. But when we got home, she got out of the car and started throwing a fit, pointing at the house and screaming."

"Oh, Rach, I'm so sorry."

"Me, too. I got her inside and gave her something the doctor prescribed to calm her but I had to come out here and keep busy."

"Did you call her doctor?"

"Yeah. Dr. Walsh said— He said, given her progression, I should consider putting her in a home. She'd hate that, but I don't know what else to do. She's getting worse, and I can't watch her and run a business at the same time. And if I don't work, we're both going to be out in the street."

"That would never happen. We wouldn't allow it," Jenna said reassuringly. She'd never considered herself lucky that her mother had passed away so suddenly but wasn't it better than slowly losing oneself the way Rachel's mother was? Having such a poor quality of life?

"But a home?" Rachel said. "She's still so young."

"It happens, though. You need to give yourself credit for being there for her."

"I know. But I wish I could do more. She hasn't been the same since Dad died. It's like her guilt completely overtook her."

"What do you mean?"

Rachel bent over the swag, her expression thoughtful and contemplative. "Mom and Dad had big plans. They talked about going to Europe and the Grand Canyon, Hawaii. Dad wanted to travel so badly but Mom always made excuses. She put him off and put him off with the promise of 'one day.' But that day never came and then...he was gone. I know she felt guilty because she kept Dad from fulfilling his dreams. And I know it doesn't do any good to think this way but sometimes I can't help but think during her lucid moments that Mom *knows* if Dad was still here instead of her, he wouldn't have let anything stop him. He would've taken those trips."

"And she feels guilty for being the one alive? Oh, Rachel."

"I know. It's bad, isn't it?"

"I'm sorry." Jenna knew she sounded like a broken record but what else could she say? "Do you need me to get you something? Have you eaten since you've been home?"

"No, I'm fine. I just need some time to come to terms with things. I've always known life wasn't easy but this past year I never thought it would be this hard."

"What are you going to do?"

"I'll call the doctor tomorrow and see if I can set things up for sometime in January. I don't want to do it before then. I want her to have one last Christmas at home."

"She'll like that, and so will you." She would have loved one last Christmas with her mother. People would cherish things more if they knew what the future held or how things could change in a blink of the eye.

"Yeah, and now that's enough of that," Rachel said firmly. "Let's talk about you and how you're not going to get asked on many dates wearing this wedding ring."

"Oh, no. Not tonight, Rach, okay? My nondating status doesn't matter after a day like you've had."

Rachel's gaze narrowed on her face and Jenna knew the moment she was busted.

"Did something happen?" Rachel asked, grabbing a flower to place in the swag.

Jenna picked up the glue gun and squeezed a bit into the spot Rachel indicated, the system an old one after four months and quite a few late-night chat sessions. "Sort of. Chance, um, kissed me."

Rachel let out such a squee of happiness Jenna felt her face flush.

"Stop it. You're going to scare the neighbors and that is *not* a happy dance kind of thing."

"Of course it is. Don't you remember what I said? Who better to be your hump guy than a man you won't fall for? Hubba-hubba. Oh, hand me those pinecones.

No, the flocked ones. Yeah. So how was it? Good? I bet it was good. He looks like a good kisser." Rachel scrunched up her nose as she grinned. "Was it good?"

"You are insane."

"Honey, at this point my sex life can only be lived through you. Let me have my moment. Was there tongue?"

Jenna dropped the glue gun onto the counter and buried her face in her hands.

"There was. *Oh,* that is *fantastic.* The next question is what did he *do* with his tongue?"

"Stop. Stop, stop, stop," Jenna said, laughing but mortified. Growing up she'd never had anyone to talk to about these types of things. But if this was what it was like growing up with a BFF and having sleepovers and GNOs, she could only imagine the fun. "You need to be the one dating, not me. And as far as Chance goes, it will *never* happen again because I told him it *couldn't.*"

Rachel looked horrified by the news. "What? No, no, no, you tell the gorgeous man *to* kiss you again. Not to stop." She waved a rose in the air like a magic wand. "Take it back."

"Will you please be serious? I'm glad this has you smiling again, but Chance is my boss. And he was one of Jeff's friends. It's not right."

"Jenna, you can't hold on to a man that's not here. That's exactly what my mother's done for the last *twelve* years and look where it's gotten her."

Jenna rolled her wedding band around her finger as Rachel's words sank in. That wasn't how she wanted to live her life at all. But where did she go from here?

CHAPTER THIRTEEN

JENNA WAS GLAD to note that over the next week Chance made a point of not being alone with her. Busy as they were at the store, it wasn't that hard to do.

That didn't mean she didn't catch him watching her sometimes, though, with a look in his eyes that wasn't hard to interpret.

Tori tried to talk to Chance about the rodeo a time or two, but Chance changed the subject or else made an excuse to end the conversation. Several times during the week she also heard Chance talking to Dooley about planning a big climb for when the protective boot came off. Apparently Nevada and Utah were possibilities and several of the Rock Gods had already agreed to go.

Whatever. If climbing was more important than Chance's life, he wasn't as smart as she thought he was.

"Mom, I can't breathe."

Jenna forced herself to release her grip on Mark Jeffrey and pasted a smile on her face. She wasn't sure how the time leading up to this Scout event had flown by so quickly but between working, homework and mountains of chores, here it was, the first Saturday of December. And even though she had this particular Saturday off, she found herself in the McKenna Feed parking lot, waiting while the last of the Scout troop kids arrived for their big outing. "Sorry," she said.

"I'll be okay, Mom. I promise I won't get hurt."

His words pierced her heart and she wanted to tell Mark Jeffrey not to make promises he couldn't keep, but he was so sensitive to comments that she didn't dare. "Just remember what I said."

"I will. No horsing around, no throwing rocks, no sword fighting with sticks…"

Jenna nodded, urging him to continue the list to make sure he remembered it all. She'd debated long and hard about this trip, but belonging to the Scouts had done a lot to bring Mark Jeffrey out of his shell. Still, it had taken last night's phone call from the troop leader to convince her. So now the big problem was breaking the news to Tori that Mark Jeffrey was taking part in the outing.

Her daughter was asleep at home under Rachel's watchful presence, but when Tori awoke and discovered her brother gone, Jenna knew an epic battle would erupt over not being allowed to participate in the rodeo. But as Jenna had explained to Mark Jeffrey, she knew his troop leader and trusted him, and the man had assured her the hike, first-aid training and lesson in rappelling were part of the wilderness awareness lessons they needed to learn. He'd been sensitive to Mark Jeffrey's loss, and hers, and assured her that every possible safety measure would be taken.

"Mom, they're getting ready to *leave*."

The knot in her stomach twisted into a pretzel. "Okay, okay. Just promise me—"

"*Mom,* come on, I'll be fine."

"Hey, Mark Jeffrey," Chance said with a smile. "I think they're ready to go. Why don't you say goodbye to your mom and join the other boys? I need to talk to her before we take off."

Before we *take off?* "You're going?" What kind of trip was this? What kind of chaperone would Chance be on impressionable boys?

Mark Jeffrey wrapped his arms around her waist, squeezed for all of two seconds, then bolted. "Bye, Mom."

"Mark Jeffrey—"

"Let him go," Chance whispered. "Don't embarrass him in front of his friends."

"I wouldn't do that."

"You think they haven't noticed you two hiding over here behind your truck? You've barely let go of the kid since you pulled in."

"I'll go make an excuse."

"Jenna." Chance caught her arm and held on, smiling a gentle, too sexy grin that did unthinkable things to her insides. She tugged free of his hold and tried to be discreet as she peeked around the cab of the truck to where the boys gathered.

Not a one of them stood still. They jumped and gestured, each of them trying to outdo the other. Mark Jeffrey was right in the middle, watching it all and smiling but not really participating. Still, being a part of the group put such joy on his face it made Jenna's heart hurt. "He'll be okay," she whispered, wishing she could convince herself. Hard to do when it was the first event of this nature Mark Jeffrey had been on since his father's death.

"Yeah, he will. I'll keep an eye out for him."

"I didn't realize you were going," she said, barely managing to contain her upset. Did they allow *any*one to go on these trips?

"It's last minute. Jason's climbing assistant came

down with that virus that's going around and none of the dads climb. He asked if I could lend a hand."

"But you can barely walk."

Apparently catching on to what she was doing and where her attention was focused, Chance nudged her back a step, until her shoulders were pressed against the passenger door of the truck and she couldn't crane her head to see the troop.

"I walk just fine. Mark Jeffrey will be okay, and you need to relax. It's a quarter-mile hike and I'll keep an extra-close eye on him."

"Like you did Jeff?" she said, before she could stop herself.

Chance's jaw firmed to the point of stone and she felt an instant twinge of remorse. That was low. "I'm sorry. Really. That was uncalled for and totally untrue. The doctors at the hospital told me how you all worked to get Jeff to the airlift. I didn't mean it, I'm—" she inhaled, then sighed "—nervous."

"It doesn't show."

That comment garnered a wry laugh from her, and she glanced at him and tried to maintain her composure given the way Chance looked at her with sympathy, despite her verbal slam. "This is the first trip like this," she explained. "Mark Jeffrey joined Scouts right before Jeff's death and I'm not sure how he'll respond to today."

She watched as Chance's gaze shifted to the direction of the group before he gave her a grim-faced nod. "I'll keep that in mind. Don't worry, he won't have to do anything he doesn't want to."

"I know." She closed her eyes, gathering her scattered emotions as she leaned against the truck. "Chance, despite what I said, I know you'd never let anything happen to any of those kids, not just mine." She gave a weak smile, hoping to undo the damage done by her earlier words.

Chance lifted his hand and stroked her hair away from her cheek, the tenderness of the move surprising her considering their strained awkwardness all week. The sudden shift in the air between them putting her senses on high alert.

"I didn't expect to see you today," he said softly. "Mark Jeffrey said yesterday that you weren't letting him go."

Welcoming the safer subject, she shrugged. "Mark Jeffrey needs this trip. I'm not so dense that I don't see his need for time with other boys, and when Jason called last night, I changed my mind."

"I'm glad. It looks like they're loading up. I'll see you tonight when we get back."

That sounded too intimate, too familiar.

Jeff's response to anything family oriented that required his attention was always *later*. That left her sitting at home, waiting on him to return. "Maybe. Will, um, Dooley be all right running the store alone? Is that what you wanted to talk to me about?"

"Tim's working," he said, referring to the teenager who came after school. "He should be okay. I only said that to get you to let go of Mark Jeffrey."

"Yo, Chance. Moving out," Jason called.

"Try not to worry yourself sick," Chance said.

Jenna watched as Chance walked away in his limping stride, his weatherproof boot looking thick and ungainly even though Chance still made wearing it seem masculinely graceful.

She studied his broad shoulders, the way the wind lifted the longest strands of hair brushing his collar from beneath his hat. And because he was leaving and taking her son with him, she had to have the last word.

"Chance!" She waited until he turned to face her. "Don't let anything happen to him."

His expression softened with understanding before he winked at her and grinned. "Enjoy your day off. I'll bring Mark Jeffrey home when we get back."

He hurried toward the group, while Jenna tried to stem the flutter in her stomach caused by his words.

CHANCE TOOK THE REAR of the meandering line of kids, since he had to be more careful of his footing. They made their way along the trail to River's Edge and The Rock, the air filled with the sound of the boys jabbering about everything from football to ranching to their Christmas lists. In between, they concentrated on their surroundings, pointing out birds and trees and strange-looking rocks that resembled other things.

Mark Jeffrey walked with the other boys at first but when the boys separated into twos along the path, Mark Jeffrey fell back to Chance's side and the gap between the group and Jenna's son lengthened.

"Hey," Chance said, careful to keep his voice low, "you could run up by the kid in front and buddy up."

Mark Jeffrey pushed his glasses up his nose for the thousandth time of the morning. "No, thanks. I'll stay here and keep you company. You're slow. I don't want you to be left behind."

Chance chuckled. "That I am. And I appreciate your concern. I'm glad your mom changed her mind and you got to come."

"Yeah. Me, too." Despite his ready agreement, right now Mark Jeffrey didn't look so sure he was happy to be there.

"You know, sometimes you have to jump in there and act like you belong until you do. It works, trust me. I had to do that a lot when I was your age."

Mark Jeffrey stared at the boys ahead and frowned but he made no move to test Chance's advice or comment on it.

"Don't you go to school with any of them? Have classes together?"

"Yeah but…it's okay," Mark Jeffrey said with a shrug. "I'll stay here."

"Suit yourself."

"Do you like my mom?"

Chance was so surprised by the question he shot a glance at Mark Jeffrey and got the distinct feeling he'd been busted. "What was that?"

"I saw you by the truck. You looked like those actors on TV, right before they kiss." Mark Jeffrey scrunched his nose up as though to hold his glasses in place. If he kept that up the kid would look like a wizened old man before he turned twenty.

"I came back to get you for Jason, but I didn't want to interrupt."

Chance nearly choked on the spit in his mouth. Had the other boys said something? Was that why the kid was hanging back?

"You should know I'm pretty sure she hasn't kissed anyone since my dad died."

He wasn't surprised by the bit of news, but it took all Chance could do not to laugh at the fact he was having this conversation with Jenna's son. "Thanks for telling me."

"So do you like her?" Mark Jeffrey's gaze reminded Chance of a gun-toting father watching for his daughter's date to arrive and he knew he needed to speak with care.

"Your mom and I are friends, but it's complicated, so I'd advise you not to mention this conversation with your mother or anyone else."

"She'd be embarrassed?"

"Probably so."

"Sometimes I hear her crying at night after me and Tori go to bed."

This was not information Mark Jeffrey was meant to share—not that Chance was about to correct the boy. "Yeah?"

"Yeah. I don't think it's because she misses my dad, though. Just so you know."

"I'll remember that. Why do you think she cries?"

"'Cause she's mad. It's usually after she has to pay bills or something. Dad had a lot of hospital bills and there's always a big stack of 'em every month. Sometimes they call and leave messages, too."

Chance held his tongue, getting a mental image he wasn't happy to see. All this time he'd assumed Jenna's reasons for not getting involved were entirely because of her prejudice against the Rock Gods and losing her husband the way she had. He'd never considered the other aspects of their climb-at-will lifestyle. He'd known Jeff had switched jobs a lot but what about life insurance? Why hadn't Jeff taken care of them and left his grieving family enough to get back on their feet?

"I shouldn't have come."

Mark Jeffrey's statement pulled Chance from his thoughts. "Why not?"

The boy tucked his head down. "Because I know it made Mom worry a lot and now Tori will be mad because we still can't be in the rodeo but I get to do this."

"I'm sure they'll both be fine."

Mark Jeffrey bent and picked up a rock, drew his arm back to launch it off the path into the trees but suddenly stopped.

"Try hitting that big boulder over there," Chance urged. "The one that looks like a big turtle shell."

"No, that's okay." Mark Jeffrey dropped the rock.

"Hey, you never know if you'll make it or not until you try."

"I can't. I'm not so good at it and Mom said no throwing rocks."

Chance stared at the boy, wondering if Jenna knew what she asked. Every red-blooded male knew the thrill of rock throwing. How could she expect the kid not to be a kid?

"My dad could throw really far. He could climb really high, too."

And every boy compared himself to his father. Over the years, it seemed as though no matter how hard he tried not to compare, someone else wound up doing it for him. Now Mark Jeffrey was doing the same.

It was yet another example of why Jenna was right to push Chance away. She wasn't without baggage, and hers had hearts and minds and feelings only beginning to explode inside them. Once they hit puberty, the twins' emotions would be all over the place and he didn't have the right to insert himself into their lives, only to walk away after they got attached. He was drawn to Jenna, wanted her, but he couldn't give her or her family what they needed.

Even with Jenna off-limits, there was no reason he couldn't spend some time with Mark Jeffrey on days like today on Jeff's behalf. He owed it to his friend.

Ahead of them, the troop leader had called a break

and the boys were digging into their backpacks for snacks and drinks. "You thirsty?"

"No."

"Then come on. For the next five minutes it's you and me and rock throwing. Just this once, what your mom doesn't know won't hurt her. This is our secret, okay? No tattlin' on me. Deal?"

"She'll be mad."

"Only if you tell her. Now, you know how to throw a knuckle ball?"

Mark Jeffrey shook his head.

"Then I'd say it's about time you learned."

CHAPTER FOURTEEN

"So now I get to be in the rodeo, right?" Tori demanded two minutes after Jenna had returned from dropping Mark Jeffrey off.

Tori was still dressed in her pajamas, and one side of her hair stuck up where she'd climbed out of bed to stumble to the couch and fall asleep again while watching TV with Rachel. Rachel was able to be there, since the aide was at her house again this morning.

Tori followed Jenna into the kitchen and searched for breakfast.

"I do, right, Mom?" Tori asked again.

Jenna braced herself for the drama. "No, you don't get to be in the rodeo."

In the process of getting her breakfast, Tori's spoon hit her bowl with a sharp clatter.

"That's not fair. Climbing is *dangerous*. How many times have you told us that? Rappelling is the same thing."

"Tori—"

"That's *not* fair!"

"Tori, mind your tone and listen to me," Jenna ordered, struggling to control her own temper. There were times when Tori's peevish attitude sliced through her like a knife, shredding the last of her nerves and now was one of those times. She'd sent her son off to spend the day in the wilderness with Chance and even though she knew—she *knew*—Chance would keep his word and watch over Mark Jeffrey, it didn't keep her from wanting to go after them.

The grief counselor had said wanting to keep her loved ones close was normal and would abate in time but how could that possibly apply to her kids?

"Mom."

She found her recipe book. Sometimes when all else failed, cookies soothed the savage beast. "I thought we could do something fun today. Just the two of us, together. Wouldn't that be a whole lot more fun than arguing over the stupid rodeo?" The moment the word came out of her mouth, Jenna regretted it.

"It's not *stupid!* Just because you don't like it, doesn't mean that it is."

"You're right." She held up her hands in surrender. "I'm very sorry. That was a poor choice of words on my part and I apologize. The rodeo is not stupid, however, I refuse to allow you to take part in it, and arguing with me isn't going to change my mind."

"But you let Mark Jeffrey go on his stupid field trip."

And it wasn't fair, yeah, she got it. "I know you don't understand this, but Mark Jeffrey needs to spend some time with other boys, with men who can show him how to do guy things."

"He spent last week with Grandpa."

Jenna could tell by the expression on Tori's face that she was digging herself a deeper hole in which to crawl. "I know that, but Grandpa is getting up there in years and Mark Jeffrey needs to be with boys his age, and their dads."

Tori crossed her arms over her chest. Her lower lip trembled and her eyes sparkled with tears as she glared at Jenna. "What about me? Don't you think I miss Dad, too? You always stand up for Mark Jeffrey. You always let him do stuff but I don't get to. You always tell me no. Why?"

Tori was right. Jenna did find herself encouraging Mark Jeffrey more than Tori, but only because Tori needed so *little* encouragement. It wasn't fair but how did you explain to a child the difference in risks? In personalities? No way would Tori ever see beyond *fair*. "How many times a day do you say you miss your dad?"

"I don't know. A lot, I guess."

"Exactly. Tori, you talk about missing Dad but your brother doesn't and he needs to. It's…how people heal after they lose someone they love."

"They talk about stuff like that in the Scouts?"

"Honestly? I don't know. Maybe. Mark Jeffrey's leader knows what happened to your dad, so if he sees that Mark Jeffrey is sad today when they do their exercises, I'm sure he'll try to help."

"And that's why you let him go even though they're rappelling?"

"Rappelling was only one of the exercises. Besides, Mark Jeffrey will be wearing safety equipment and they're practicing on rocks the two of you would normally jump off playing King of the World."

"Oh. I guess that's all right then."

Wow, such a concession. "I really would like to do something fun. After I make cookies, why don't we go get a tree to decorate tonight after Mark Jeffrey gets home? Or we could get the Christmas lights out of the garage for the outside the house."

"That's not fun, that's work."

"Okay, fine. Aside from signing up for the rodeo," she said specifically to thwart a new round, "what would you like to do?"

"Mark Jeffrey is doing fun stuff. Today's Brooke's birthday party. Remember? Did you get a present for her?"

Jenna had a little bit of money saved up and had hoped to get a Christmas tree. Something to brighten things and make their new house feel like home. Did it have to go toward a birthday present for a girl Tori was upset with for one reason or another half the school year? "I thought you were mad at her."

Tori shrugged. "Fine, I'll stay home. Brooke will probably get a cell phone for her birthday anyway."

That was what Tori wanted for Christmas but Jenna couldn't afford it. *She* didn't even have a cell phone. "Go get the mixer and set it up for me, please."

Tori pulled the heavy mixer from beneath the counter, setting it on top.

"Now what?"

"Now you eat your breakfast and then wash your hands to help," she said, preparing for round two.

"If I help, I want to make those lily cookies that have strawberry stuff in them."

"Okay."

"Really?" Tori asked.

"Why not?" It made Jenna feel good that they were getting a few hours of quality time together. "Hurry up and eat so we can start baking."

"Cool. Those are my favorite. This will be fun, Mom."

Yeah, it would. "You're not mad you have to stay home?"

"It's okay. I'll just say you wouldn't let me."

Jenna grabbed a few more items, her mind turning that bit of information over several times. "Tori, have you picked fights with me to get into trouble so you wouldn't have to do things you didn't want to do?"

Head down, Tori stared into her cereal bowl.

"Tori?"

"Maybe. Just sometimes. Is that okay?"

Jenna almost laughed. Was it okay to pick a fight, when all she had to do was be honest? "How about we talk about that while we bake these cookies?"

"THERE YOU GO. Keep easing down," Chance said, watching Mark Jeffrey lower himself over the boulder. "Perfect. Stop and hang."

Mark Jeffrey did as ordered. He held on to the ropes with both hands so he lifted one of his coat-padded shoulders and leaned his head down to shove his glasses up his nose. Poor kid. Jenna needed to buy him some contacts as soon as she could afford it and the kid could handle the responsibility of them.

"This is so cool. I'm doing it!"

Chance smiled at the pride in Mark Jeffrey's voice. The kid struggled to find his place amongst the group, with the more boisterous boys talking over anything Mark Jeffrey had to say. But over the course of the morning he'd emerged a little at a time, growing more confident with every task the group had learned to perform. And while a couple of the kids had balked once they had to step over the edge of the rock, Mark Jeffrey took to it with his father's passion. "Keep going. Remember what to do next?"

Mark Jeffrey slowly loosened his grip, bent his knees and bounced as he lowered himself the rest of the way over the rock. His foot skidded a little when he made contact with the ground but Mark Jeffrey quickly righted himself. "Great job, Mark Jeffrey. Very well done."

Jenna's son beamed like a light switch flipped on inside of him. The sight made Chance feel a kind of pride he'd never felt before. The kind that came by helping someone achieve something big.

Out of nowhere came an image of a man stepping away from him. Chance remembered tightening his grip on the bat in his hand, the grit of dirt in his mouth from where the wind blew around the ball field, his mother calling out his name from behind the plate, telling him he could do it. His father threw the ball, he swung the bat, made contact. And then he was lifted up and spun around in the air until everything was topsy-turvy when he was back on his feet.

Chance blinked and came out of the memory-induced daze, the boys' chatter and Jason's instructions to the boy lowering himself over the boulder drawing him back to the present. He wasn't sure where the memory had been hiding all these years but it certainly didn't match the ones that came later.

Forcing himself to focus on the task at hand, he watched the next kid come down, and couldn't help thinking that six-year-olds weren't meant to learn how to spell *killer* and *murderer* before *dog* and *cat*.

"Chance, you ready?" Jason called out.

"Yeah, send the next one down."

An hour and seven more kids later, the rappelling lesson was over and it was time for lunch. Chance scooted over and made room for Mark Jeffrey to sit beside him on a downed log. "You were a natural up there. Did your dad show you how?"

Mark Jeffrey slurped his juice box. "No. He didn't

like taking me. I just watched Jason and listened to what you said to do."

Chance frowned. There was no reason Jeff shouldn't have had the honor of this first, but Chance was glad to have had it himself. "You did well. Your dad would be proud of you, too, Mark Jeffrey."

About to take a bite of his sandwich, Mark Jeffrey lowered it onto his lap. "Can I tell you something?"

"Sure."

"But a secret? Like throwing the rocks?"

Chance glanced around when Mark Jeffrey did, noting the other boys' whereabouts. Jason caught Chance's eye and mouthed the word *problem?* and Chance discreetly shook his head. "Yep." He wasn't sure what he'd do if Mark Jeffrey's secret was anything major but for now the boy needed to talk.

"I don't like being called Mark Jeffrey."

Okay. The kid obviously thought it was a big deal, whereas Chance didn't. What was the problem? "You'd rather be called after your dad? Jeff?"

The kid shook his head. "No. I'm not him. I just want to be me."

Chance smiled at the logic. Made sense to him. "You being…?"

"Mark. It's an okay name, right?"

"I think so. Why don't you say something to your mom? Ask her to call you Mark instead?"

His questions sparked a round of fidgeting and glasses-pushing from Mark Jeff—*Mark*. No doubt about it—the boy wasn't comfortable.

"She probably wants to call me Mark Jeffrey. She has since I was born and it was my dad's name, just the first and middle names switched."

"Ah, I see. But the thing is, I think, more than anything, your mom wants you to be happy. If calling you Mark makes you happy, she'd be okay with that."

"You don't think she'd be mad? Or my dad? What if he's, you know, listening?" Mark said, lowering his voice. "I don't want him to be sad."

Chance sat surrounded by the beauty of Montana, the light snow on the ground, the breeze in the trees, a sky so blue—complete with white fluffy clouds—it looked as though someone had just finished painting it. "I think your dad knows you better than you think. He'd want you to be happy, too, and if he is listening, then he just heard you say you don't want him to be sad about it, right? So there you go."

In the distance, an eagle took flight and Chance welcomed the distraction. "Hey, look over there."

"That's cool."

"I'll tell you something else that's cool. Something someone once told me. See, I always thought kids with parents had it made."

"You didn't have parents?"

Since the truth wasn't exactly an easy answer, he stuck to facts. "Not for a lot of years. I lived in a home with a bunch of other boys. But one day I was adopted and Zane—my new dad—said something to me I'll never forget. Zane didn't do a lot of hugging like your mom does, but one day I did something really wrong and ticked him off. I don't remember ever seeing Zane that mad but instead of smacking me or something, he walked up to me, gave me a bear hug and told me parents don't love their kids because they have to, they love them because they can't help themselves. Your mom loves you more than any mom I've ever known. That's why she's so protective all the time and why you have to cut her some slack, because all the stuff she does is because she loves you."

"She does love me a lot. And Tori."

Chance nodded his agreement, liking that Mark was so confident in his mother's love. "Exactly. She won't be mad, Mark. If anything, I think she'll wonder why you haven't told her before now."

"Do you think maybe you could tell her?" Mark gave Chance a sheepish look. "I don't want to hurt her feelings."

Put on the spot, Chance faltered but only for a second. The kid was asking for help. What else could he do but say yes? "I'd be happy to bring it up for you, but she'll probably want to talk to you about it."

"I know," he said with a sigh. "Women sure like to talk a lot, don't they?"

JENNA WIPED HER HANDS on a kitchen towel and hurried toward the front door to open it. "Rach, where have you— Chance?"

One side of his mouth lifted in a lopsided grin. "Expecting someone else?"

Definitely. She'd let Mark Jeffrey go to the movies with Jake Rowland and his boys, and a friend of Tori's had called and invited her over for a sleepover. After their baking session this afternoon in which they'd managed to get along, Jenna figured the sleepover was a nice treat. "My neighbor."

"Ah, the MIA babysitter." He looked rugged and sexy and all sorts of adjectives that disrupted her equilibrium. "You going to let me in?"

Not unless she had to. "What are you doing here?"

Jenna glanced over Chance's shoulder, thankful that most of her neighbors had shut their curtains for the night. But that didn't mean they weren't peeking out of them.

If she invited him inside or someone saw him leaving, it wouldn't look good. And while she didn't care what people thought of her, she did care what impact that sort of gossip might have on her kids. It sounded old-fashioned but in small towns and quiet neighborhoods, a woman had to be careful. She didn't doubt the gossips were already talking about how Chance had hired her, so she certainly didn't want to give them fodder as to why. And after her supposed affair with Mr. Henry the janitor… "Chance, I'm not sure why you're here but you shouldn't have come. Surely whatever it is can wait until Monday morning."

He leaned his shoulder against the frame and propped his injured foot to the side as though he could—and would—stand there all night.

"No. It's not about work at all. I promised Mark I'd talk to you about something and since I knew he would be with the Rowlands, I thought now might be a good time. Is Tori upstairs? This is kind of private."

Private? "What's wrong? What happened?"

Apparently losing patience, he gently grasped her elbows and squeezed past her in the doorway. She got a whiff of his cologne and soap and the outdoors as he walked by.

"Close the door, Jenna."

Glaring at his back, she complied but didn't move from her position. He strolled into her living room with his hobbling stride, his broad shoulders taking up too much space, his gaze seemingly inspecting every inch.

She tried to see her home through his eyes. The house was small, old, the carpet worn but clean, the walls a light beige with white trim she'd painstakingly painted to brighten things up. Magazines and books were stacked on and under the coffee table, the dust bunnies temporarily conquered.

"No tree?"

Who cared about whether or not she had a tree? "Not yet."

"Your house looks nice."

She didn't bother to say thank you. "What about Mark Jeffrey?" She hoped to speed Chance up then send him on his way. "When he called to get permission, he said he had fun and he seemed fine. Did something happen?"

"No, he had a blast. It took him a while to warm up to the other boys but toward the end I don't think I've ever seen a happier kid."

Instead of the joy Chance's words should have brought, once again her heart squeezed at the thought. She was thrilled Mark Jeffrey had had a good time. It made the anxiety she'd carried with her throughout the day worthwhile. But it hurt that her son hadn't been that happy at home in ages. "That's good."

Chance smiled, the lines around his mouth giving him a craggy, sexy appearance she'd always found so attractive on men.

And like it or not, her heart fisted a little more for an entirely different reason.

"Yeah, it is. We hiked and rappelled. And, I suppose I should tell you we threw rocks," he said.

The last time Mark Jeffrey had thrown a rock his aim had been so bad the rock had flown sideways and hit Jenna in the head.

"He told me you said he wasn't allowed."

"But you let him do it anyway?"

"Jenna, you're cutting the boy off at the knees. Don't

worry, I taught him how to do it right. It didn't take me long to figure out why you told him not to throw rocks around the kids," he said, smiling. "But the kid's got a heck of an arm on him when he throws straight and by the end of today, he was."

"Really?" Chance chuckled at her surprise and she flushed. "I mean, that's wonderful." And all because of a day spent with Chance and the other Scouts.

"He was really pleased with himself, so don't give him a hard time about it, okay? It's supposed to be our secret but I figure at some point he's gonna own up to it because you told him not to. He's honest to a fault."

"Yes, he is." And she wouldn't change that characteristic for the world. If Mark Jeffrey did something wrong he always told on himself, while Tori remained sneaky and silent. "Is that what you needed to tell me?"

His expression grew serious and a flutter of anxiety hit her hard. "Do I need to sit down for this?"

"Up to you."

Jenna perched on the very edge of the couch.

"Once we got going and Mark Jeffrey felt comfortable, he wanted to get something off his chest. For such a quiet guy, he has a lot to say. A lot he's been keeping pent up inside him because he doesn't want to hurt you."

Chance's statement cut to the quick. "He could never hurt me."

"You're hurt right now. I can see it in your expression, because he told me and not you."

She opened her mouth to deny it but couldn't. Yes, she was hurt. How could she not be? She was Mark Jeffrey's *mother,* while Chance was...just a guy.

Like his father.

Chance tugged off the knit cap he wore. His hair was

mussed beneath it and the urge to protest him being the one Mark Jeffrey confided in was almost overcome by the compulsion to smooth the strands. She made a fist, her nails biting into her palm.

How could she even think that at a time like this?

"I'm sure you listen, but you're still his mom and he doesn't feel like he can tell you everything, that he's not supposed to."

"That's ridiculous."

"Is it?"

"Tell me what he said."

"He doesn't want to be called Mark Jeffrey any-more."

"Excuse me?" She stood and started to pace. Where was this coming from? Mark Jeffrey had never breathed a word to that effect.

Chance unzipped his jacket and tossed it aside.

She wanted to tell him to get his things and leave, but she couldn't. She had to know what else Mark Jeffrey had said, *why* he'd said it.

"Look, Jenna, he's gone through a lot for his age and is more mature than his friends because of it. Smarter than they are, too, which doesn't help a lot in this situation. He knows you've had a hard time dealing with things, with the bills. He's heard you crying."

No.

"He doesn't want to add to what you're already dealing with and he's trying to be the man—"

"Of the house," she whispered. Chance's words had landed like blows, hard and fast. "Did he say why he didn't want to be called Mark Jeffrey?"

"He said he wants to be himself, which is just Mark. That's what he wants to be called. Mark."

"I see." But she didn't see. How had the subject even

come up? Why would Mark Jeffrey share such a thing with Chance and not with her? Why did her son feel like he had to *be* anyone but himself? "He actually told you that?"

She was so tired. Tired of being the sole breadwinner, tired of being mom and dad *both,* tired of the bills and the worry and the anger, because it wasn't supposed to be this way.

Her son couldn't talk to her, her daughter's mercurial moods changed as swiftly as spring weather, and Jenna didn't have the energy to fight anymore. She felt frozen and numb from too many debilitating blows.

Chance closed the distance between them, the look in his eyes intense. She held up a hand to ward him off but it didn't work. Her hand landed flat on his chest, the warmth and muscles and man beneath firm to the touch.

"Come here."

"I'm fine."

"You don't look it."

Because she *wasn't.*

Head down, arms stiff, she let Chance embrace her and, even though her mind screamed to distance herself fast, she didn't. Couldn't.

In that moment, just for a moment, she needed someone to lean on, a shoulder to bear the weight she struggled to carry.

Why hadn't Mark Jeff—*Mark* come to her?

"Stop overthinking it, Jenna."

"How can I not?" The words rasped out of her throat over the lump she refused to acknowledge.

"You're getting yourself worked up over nothing." His hands ran up and down her back in gentle strokes that eased some of the tension. "He wasn't sure how to tell you, so he asked if I could."

"But he should have come to *me*. He should have known he could talk to me about how he felt. About *anything*."

"Give him some credit for being a kid who has already realized his mom is human. How many kids his age would recognize what you're dealing with, much less have taken your feelings into account?"

Chance's hand shifted, began massaging the back of her neck, the base of her scalp. She nearly moaned aloud in response when the impossibly tight muscles loosened and no matter how much she knew she ought to move away, she couldn't. *Just a little while longer.* "I thought I did fairly well in front of them."

"You're a fantastic mom, Jenna. He just didn't know how you'd feel about him wanting to drop his father's first name. I think he's worried about what his grandparents will think, too."

She moaned aloud this time. "They won't like it."

Suddenly aware that she breathed Chance in with every inhalation, she lifted her head. What was she doing? Talk about giving mixed signals. "Thank you for telling me."

He slid his fingers into her hair and tipped her head back. She'd be lying if she said the curiosity wasn't there. The need to see if that one kiss was really as good as it had seemed. It had been so long since she'd been held. Made to feel like a woman. Beautiful and desirable.

Chance was danger and excitement. That ornery, sexy, make-me-hot kind of guy so very few women would even consider turning down.

A flash of heat burst to life inside her, spurred on

from the emotions she tried so hard to keep in check. The anger and frustration and loneliness, that need to feel cherished. That somewhat frantic, intimate, carnal awareness of what could happen when two consenting adults were in an empty house with no children or witnesses.

But he was also the man who could break her, once and for all. And that scared her enough to make her step away. "You should go."

A lengthy silence followed, and neither of them moved. The moment lasted long enough for her body to urge her to kiss him again. The thought alone quickened her heart and made breathing more difficult.

Finally Chance grabbed his coat and left, the door closing with a quiet click.

She dropped onto the couch. The cold of the house seeped into her and the emptiness of her life threatened to overwhelm her. Yet she knew it was nothing compared to the pain she'd feel if she let herself get involved with Chance, only to lose him to the same fate as Jeff.

Smarter, wiser. A more secure future for your family. You can't travel this road again.

Her gaze fastened on the glint of silver metal encircling her finger. If she'd needed proof that she was ready for the next step—whatever it was—what had *almost* happened with Chance was it. After Jeff's death, she'd wondered when it would be time to remove her wedding band. When it would feel right, instead of wrong.

Now…seemed right.

CHAPTER FIFTEEN

"YOU WANT TO TRY to actually get those bales up here?" Brad said the next morning.

Chance grabbed another sixty-pound bale of straw and tossed it onto the truck, shooting his eldest brother a glare.

"Before I forget, stop by the house before you leave. Gabriella made something for you."

"It's more of that so-called health food *sludge* she tried to get me to drink when I first broke my foot, isn't it?" The concoction smelled like swamp water and tasted worse.

"Vegetarian chocolate chip cookies," Brad said. "They're a little gooey, but you say a word about it and your ass is mine."

Chance kept moving. The sooner the straw was loaded, the sooner he could get out of there. Normally Brad would have been out on the ranch somewhere overseeing things, but this close to the wedding Brad was sticking around because of all the work that had to be done to prepare.

"You know, Gabriella still sets a place for you every Sunday."

Chance grabbed another bale and hefted it high. "Tell her not to do that anymore."

Brad muttered something under his breath Chance decided to ignore. Yeah, he was deliberately missing the point but what did Brad want from him? Being on the ranch wasn't the same without Zane there, and every time he turned around, something else reminded him of the man. Toss old Charlie into the mix and he couldn't stop wondering what had happened to his real father. Was the man even alive?

"Look, I know things are changing around here, but Sunday dinners are tradition. You know you're always welcome. This is your home, too. Zane wanted us to look out for each other."

Chance exhaled and the air blew white, the smell of straw strong in his nose. Sweat prickled his back beneath his clothes but he kept lifting the squares and tossing it to Brad. There was nothing like hard work to ward off the cold of a Montana winter day. "Looks to me like we're all doing just fine."

"Not from where I'm standing. You haven't stopped scowling and growling at people since you got here."

"Mind your own business, brother."

"Can't."

"And why's that?" Chance asked, his muscles finally loosening up.

"Because I've never seen you like this. Not about a woman."

"Yeah, well, you're not seeing it now, either."

Brad took a breather, his gloved hands on his hips.

"If you want her that bad, what's stopping you?"

"Her dead husband." Just saying the words got his dander up and Chance tossed the straw with more zest.

Brad wasn't prepared and grunted on impact.

"Break my ribs and Gabriella will have your hide."

Gabriella was as tall as he was but reed thin and anti-violence. She wouldn't hurt a fly. "Not even married yet and already hiding behind her skirts."

"Don't pick a fight with me, boy. I don't kick a man when he's down. If you want Jenna that bad, figure out a way to change her mind."

Chance couldn't restrain his curse. "Is that supposed to be some kind of reverse psychology? Weren't you and Liam the ones telling me to keep my hands to myself?"

"Did you?"

He swore softly. "No."

"Exactly."

The next square he tossed landed five feet short of Brad, forcing his brother to leave his perch atop the bottom layer and walk to retrieve it. If Brad had so much energy to burn that he could run his mouth, he could get the straw from the *end* of the long bed. "Can't you just stack the damn straw? I have to get back to the store."

"You know, Gabriella and I are different, really different, but we make it work. Maybe you two could, too."

Relationship advice from a guy who wasn't even married yet? "Like I said—dead husband. Jenna and I would argue every damn time the subject of climbing came up."

"So argue. Make up sex is great."

Chance groaned and shook his head. He didn't want to think about sex with Jenna, much less make up sex. If he did, he wouldn't be able to walk. Holding her last night had given him the hottest dreams in history.

"You weren't around much when Gabriella first came here."

"If this is another guilt trip about climbing," Chance growled, "save it."

He turned toward Brad with a bale in his hands, only to see Brad tossing the last one back at him. Hands full, he couldn't avoid it and went down with a curse. "What the hell was that for?"

"Someone has to bring you down a notch and until that foot is healed completely and you can fight fair, that'll have to do. Now shut up and listen. You want Jenna or not?" Brad waited, his gloved hands at his sides like he was ready for a fast-draw. "Well?"

"I don't know," he said honestly, shoving himself up to a sitting position. "That's just it. I've only kissed her once but she drives me crazy. I want to take her to bed, but then what? She's a mom with two kids. I don't want to mess up her life."

"Who says you would?"

He was getting a headache from trying to figure out Brad's thinking. "I do. *She* does. I've never met a girl I haven't been able to walk away from. And even if Jenna slept with me, Jeff's ghost would probably be there in the bed with us. Every time I turn around, she's bringing him up."

"And you don't like that."

He kicked at a pile of straw lying on the floor, realizing Brad was probably his best choice if he hoped to gain some objectivity. "You think I'm too stupid to know I'm jealous of a dead man?" He knew how he sounded. Knew it was crazy. But last night a part of him had been glad Mark had decided to drop his father's name, because it was one less mention of Jeff. And when he'd almost kissed her, he could have sworn Jenna wanted to kiss him just as bad. But she'd pushed him away. And it had taken everything in him to walk out the door. "She still wears his ring."

"Chance, I don't know what to tell you. Schedule her to work with Dooley and steer clear of her, but find a way to take the edge off that *doesn't* include you tak-

ing off and missing my wedding," Brad said. "The rehearsal dinner is Thursday, the bachelor party's Friday
and the wedding Saturday."

"I know the damn schedule," he growled.

"Good. Because with Zane gone...I need you and
Liam to be there."

So he could see the happy couples in action? Not
how he wanted to spend his time.

"You can't compromise seeing as how Jenna's husband died?"

A compromise? As in give up climbing? Fat chance.

And why should he? In telling him about her childhood, Jenna's face had lit up. She'd liked traveling, liked
exploring and going on adventures. They had that in
common. But after what had happened with her mother
and Jeff, Jenna had shut that part of herself down: out
of fear, out of the burden of responsibility she carried,
necessity, because she had to find that so-called security and stability her family needed. But he didn't fit
into that picture. "Climbing is a part of me and I can't
change that." He turned and met Brad's gaze. "I didn't
stop for Zane, and I'm not going to stop for Jenna."

Brad looked disappointed by the news. "Guess that's
your answer then."

"Mom, where are we *going?*" Tori asked for the hun-
dredth time, drawing out the words.

"You'll see. I told you, it's a surprise," she said, smiling at the twins' excitement, even though she was more
nervous than anything.

All week, she'd been trying to come up with a fun
idea of something they could do to celebrate Jeff's birthday, and despite the Christmas special at Bowl-a-Ball,
and the kids-eat-free restaurant ad, her gaze had con-

tinually landed on the ad for Treehouse Rock, the indoor climbing and fun center. The kids would not be participating in the rodeo, but she had allowed Mark to rappel and Tori deserved the same opportunity.

In addition, she'd packed a bag for each of them for a special skip-school day tomorrow—not a big deal since the rodeo participants wouldn't be at school anyway—to spend the weekend with Les and Karen to have a celebration for Jeff and attend the rodeo with their grandparents.

Better still, Jenna had her own reasons to splurge. When Rachel had let herself in the house this afternoon to walk Snickers she'd overheard the end of a message being left on the machine by the school principal informing Jenna that a two-year grant had been approved for the new year. If she wanted her old job, she could begin on January 3 when school resumed. She would have better pay, insurance and no need to hire a babysitter for the kids. She had returned the call to the principal on her lunch break, but still needed to inform Chance, even though it wouldn't be a problem.

"No. Way. *Mom!*" Tori screamed when she saw their destination. "Really?"

"Really?" Mark repeated, his eyes almost as wide as his grin.

"Really," Jenna said, despite her parental trepidation. "But there are rules. Helmets and full gear at all times. And no horsing around. You listen to the instructors and do what they say, got it?" She pulled into an empty parking spot.

"Yes! I don't believe this," Tori said.

"Me, either. Mom, thank you."

Both kids simultaneously unbuckled seat belts and squished Jenna against the door in a mash-up hug Jenna took way too much pleasure in. They were growing up so fast. And even if her budget would be a bit strained over the next few weeks despite the coupon, they'd get by until her pay kicked in from the school. More hamburgers and bean soup for dinner seemed like a good trade-off.

She kissed the tops of their heads with loud smacking sounds. "I love you. I know you guys were disappointed about the rodeo but I thought this would be a fun way of celebrating Dad's birthday without bringing wild animals into the equation. You each get two hours for the price of one, so let's go."

Noise bombarded them the moment they stepped through the door. Along one side of the building was a fun center with arcade and video games, party rooms for rent were in the back and on the left was the faux-rock entrance that led to the climbing section.

The kids hurried ahead of her while she reminded herself that climbing wasn't what had killed Jeff. After making that bitter comment to Chance in the parking lot before the Scout trip, she'd firmly reminded herself that it was Jeff's fault that he was dead. His own reckless nature and rash behavior had no doubt been spurred by his need to impress his buddies; but Jeff was the one who'd jumped.

So Chance was right in a way. She had to teach what she preached, which meant letting the twins do things like this in a controlled environment, so that they saw the difference between fun and sheer stupidity.

Nice way to classify that.

Yeah, well, she'd never claimed to be perfect.

"Mom, hurry up," Tori said, motioning for her to join them at the desk. "Aren't you going to do it, too?"

As if she could afford to pay for three. "Not this time. This is all you. I'll watch you guys and guard the cake."

She dug into her purse and presented the coupon torn from the newspaper, handing over her hard-earned cash with barely any hesitation.

"Oh, is it someone's birthday?" the cashier asked.

"Our dad's," Tori said simply, sliding Jenna an uncomfortable look. "He's dead but he liked to climb. We're celebrating."

The cashier's smile faltered before she regained her composure. "I'm sorry for your loss but I think it's really cool what you're doing. Have fun."

"Thank you," the twins said in unison.

Jenna nodded without comment and led the way to the next section where the gear was distributed and instructors or spotters were assigned. Their two hours didn't begin until the instructor started the stopwatch. But there was a short line, even though it was Thursday evening, and a wait while helmets and harnesses were fitted and exchanged for the correct size.

The twins met their spotter and the man quickly explained the rules, which had Tori sliding a glance over her shoulder toward Jenna as though she'd put the man up to it.

"That's it," the instructor said. "Are you ready to go have some fun?"

"Yeah!"

"Ready, Mom?" Mark asked.

"No, she's not ready yet," Chance said from her right.

Jenna turned and found Chance and another man rapidly closing the distance.

"Chance!" Mark said.

"Hey, buddy. Don't you guys look sharp. Jenna, I'd

like you to meet Caleb Jeeter, the owner of Treehouse," he said, performing the rest of the introductions.

"I'm glad you guys decided to make us part of your celebration," Caleb said, "but I'm going to put my foot down and return your money. I haven't been a Rock God for a while, but I knew your dad and he was a big supporter of this place."

Jenna wanted to refuse—the gesture seemed too big—yet she knew better than to protest. "Thank you."

"Not a problem. In fact, I'd consider it an honor if you came back on a regular basis and used these," he said, handing Jenna not only her cash but three VIP cards.

"What are they?" Tori asked.

"Special passes. Anytime your mom can make the drive and bring you here, you three get in free. I insist," Caleb said. "Let me take Jeff's cake, and I'll have a table ready for you when you're done. No hurry."

Jenna was flabbergasted by the offer. "Thank you, but it's too much."

"Not at all. Make this a special day," he said, holding Jenna's gaze. "Make every time you come here special."

She managed a smile and nodded, very aware that Chance watched her every move. "Thank you again."

"Well, I'm going to leave you in Chance's capable hands and get back to work. Have fun."

"Okay, guys, let's go," the twentysomething spotter said to the twins.

They took off, but when Jenna tried to follow them, she made it as far as a shadowy corner before Chance snagged her arm.

"This is for you," he said, a harness in his hand.

When had he picked that up? Jenna eyed the contraption warily. "I wasn't planning on climbing."

"Now you can. I'll spot you."

"Chance, what are you doing here? Did Dooley tell you what I was doing?"

His expression tightened. "I had physical therapy and needed to talk to Caleb about my Nevada trip."

Of course. She should have known.

Jenna held out her hand. "Let me have it." She glanced over her shoulder to check on the twins and saw them facing the wall, ready to take their first hold. She needed to hurry. When she turned back to Chance, she saw that he held the harness out of reach.

"But had I known you'd be here, I would've come anyway," he said, his gray gaze searching her face. "I'm trying to keep my distance, Jenna, but…"

But when they worked together on a daily basis, it was hard to forget that kiss. "I got a phone call today," she said. "I got my old job back and start January 3. It…this…won't be a problem much longer."

His expression grim, Chance dropped onto one knee, his injured foot extended out to his side. "Step in."

Noise and people surrounded them but everything disappeared when he looked at her the way he was now. For experienced climbers the harnesses were simple but for a novice they were a jumbled mess of straps and buckles, especially the older ones, which this was.

She stepped forward and slid her foot into the opening Chance held, but when she put her other foot in, she noticed his gaze focused on her left hand and her fingers curled in reflex.

He'd noticed her wedding band was gone. And the look on his face…

He lifted his gaze to hers. That flare of heat was back, zipping through her like a lightning bolt.

He slowly straightened and pulled the harness up between her legs as he did. His gentle tug unbalanced her until she took a tiny step forward, his hands on the straps holding her in place close enough to his body that she could see the tiny little lines that bracketed his mouth, and the dark shadow of hair along his chin and jawline.

Standing carefully still, she felt his every touch as he fit the straps into position, smoothing his hands around her from the front instead of walking behind her to adjust the straps along her shoulders. His fingers beneath the straps, between them and her clothes, he stepped back and knelt in front of her again, one hand sliding between her thighs to hold the belt in position while he fastened the buckle on her outer thigh. He did the same to the other and by the time he fastened the last buckle into place directly over her breasts, she struggled to hold herself together so he wouldn't see the way she trembled.

"All set," he said close to her ear, his voice huskier and richer than she'd ever heard it. He stepped back, his gaze smoldering as it lowered to the vicinity of her mouth.

She walked toward the kids, unsteady, aware of Chance behind her every step of the way....

He stayed for cake. And even though he wasn't part of her plan to celebrate Jeff's birthday with the kids, she had to admit, despite the tension between them, Chance helped make the evening more fun. While the twins' instructor checked out the teen girls and let the twins do their own thing, Chance called out encouragement and advice, teased and congratulated them all when they reached the top of the wall.

It wasn't until they were stuffed with sweets and on their way out of the building that the tension between her and Chance rose again because Tori informed him that they were spending the night at Grandma and Grandpa's house and skipping school tomorrow.

"Sounds like fun. You can tell me about it when you're at the store on Monday," he said, opening the passenger door of the truck for them to climb in before walking to where Jenna stood at the rear bumper. "You're letting them skip?"

His teasing tone brought out a smile she couldn't quite hold back. "I'm just a rebel," she said with a forced laugh. "Thanks for, um, helping us out in there," she said, her fingers twisting in the handle of her purse.

"No problem. It was fun."

It was fun. More fun than she'd had in a long time. "You were good with them. Thanks for stressing the need for care and patience." Her fingers were going numb with the grip she had. "I should, um, get going."

"I'll follow you. Make sure you get home okay."

Since he was headed back to North Star like she was, she couldn't exactly protest. "Thanks. 'Night."

She rounded the rear of the truck when Chance called her name. She turned to find him a single step behind her and before she could even blink, he tugged her behind the van next to hers and kissed her. Not a gentle, tender kiss but one that was hard and fast and deep, one that left her clinging to him and dazed.

"This is crazy. You're crazy," she said, the words low and raspy.

He held her close, his lips brushing hers again. "I've been called worse. Jenna, I like you. I want you."

She closed her eyes at his words. "For how long? A night? A week? Until winter's over? Until you grow bored with a mom and two kids?"

"Why can't it be as long as we want it to be?"

"Mom, hurry up, it's cold," Tori called.

"Think about it. Drive safe," he said, giving her one last lingering sex-me-down stare that did nothing to steady the uneven pace of her heart.

Without a word, Chance led the way to the truck and opened the door for her to climb in. The kids called out last goodbyes to Chance, but Jenna couldn't look at him and when Mark asked why her hands were shaking she reminded him of the cold.

The beginning of the forty-five-minute drive was spent with the twins arguing over the best radio station. Finally their long day kicked in and they quieted but Jenna didn't welcome the silence because it gave her too much time to think about what Chance had said and to notice his lights in her rearview mirror.

In North Star, she dropped off the twins at Jeff's parents with little fuss, then continued on her way home. As she approached the store, she slowed, seemingly drawn by some invisible force as Chance's words repeated in her head. Combined with Rachel's hump-guy theory, Jenna's body filled with a combustible urge that had her turning onto the lot and driving around to the back to where Chance usually parked when he was home.

His truck was there. That meant he was there....

Biting her lip and trying to slow the frantic, dizzying pace of her heart, she parked her small S-10 on the other side of the Dumpster, out of sight, just in case.

Then... Then she got out and walked to the door.

CHAPTER SIXTEEN

CHANCE WANTED TO FOLLOW Jenna all the way home, but after kissing her again and saying what he had, he knew the next step had to be hers. Even if keeping his distance was going to be nothing short of torture.

He'd removed his shoe and stripped down to his boxers when a soft knock sounded on the door. His heart slammed against his ribs in response and he nearly tripped himself getting there to answer.

A quick check through the peephole sent blood pulsing faster through his chest and he opened the door with a yank. Jenna stood on the other side, her eyes wide but startlingly frank.

"This isn't happening," she whispered, holding his gaze. "I'm *not* here."

Willing to take her any way he could get her, Chance opened the door wide.

The moment she crossed the threshold of her own free will, he slammed the door shut and flipped the lock before he crowded her against it, one arm braced above her head, the other at her waist.

She lifted her face, parted her lips but he didn't make another move. This was *her* decision.

Finally she released a frustrated sound and palmed his face, tugging his head lower before sliding her arms around his neck. She raised herself on tiptoes, her mouth on his, her nose cold against his cheek.

The kiss was awkward, her aim slightly off, but Jenna's taste filled him with the first nudge of her tongue against his. His hands fisted where they were, because it took all of his control to go at her pace when he wanted her hard and fast and now.

The kisses deepened, lengthened, and when he couldn't take it anymore, he lifted her into his arms and helped her wrap her legs around his waist, carrying her into the warmth of his apartment.

The light over the kitchen was on and bathed the room in a soft glow. He lowered her to her feet and shoved her coat to the floor. Her layered shirts were next and once they were gone, she was clad in her bra, jeans and boots. His knees went weak. "You are beautiful," he whispered, his hands at her waist, his thumbs dipping beneath the band of her jeans to stroke.

She gasped at the touch and he repeated it, watched as her eyes darkened. She was responsive and sensual, and it turned him on seeing the way he got to her.

He lowered himself to sit on the edge of the bed and pulled her to stand between his legs. He kissed her ribs and the softness of her belly, tugged off her boots. Finally he unbuttoned her jeans with a quick twist of his fingers. "Take them off."

She swallowed but didn't balk at the directive. She slid her thumbs beneath the material and did a very seductive, feminine shimmy that left the pants at her ankles. She stepped out and used one narrow, sock-covered foot to kick them away.

He yanked his shirt over his head and pulled her back into his arms. He kissed her stomach and smiled when she sucked in and held her breath, as though to disguise that she was soft and curvy instead of hard.

That's one of the things he liked about her. That she was all woman.

He liked the feel of her hands running over his shoulders and arms, his back. In response he squeezed her behind, the dark scrap of material cupping her a nice surprise. He'd pictured Jenna as a plain white cotton kind of woman but that obviously wasn't the case. He vowed then and there to make use of Gabriella's business. His soon-to-be sister-in-law specialized in romance, which included selling negligees and lingerie, and he wanted to see Jenna wearing some of the things he'd seen hanging around Gabriella's office at the ranch. *Soon,* he promised himself.

Face buried in Jenna's fragrant skin, he slid his hands up her back and unfastened her bra. The straps slid down her arms, baring her to him. He smiled at the pretty sight and ran his knuckle over the puckered tip.

Her fingers tightened on his shoulders and her mouth parted as though to take in more air.

Smiling, he wound his arms around her and fell back against the mattress, rolling so that he was next to her on the king-size bed. He kissed her hard, relishing the little sound of pleasure she made as she wrapped her arms around him and met him skin to skin.

He slid his hand beneath the material left covering her, shoving it off and smoothing his hand up her leg. He wanted her around him, needed her closer, ached to make her a part of him but unwilling to rush it now that she was here.

He kissed her, stroked his hands over her body and learned the shape of her, until she squirmed against him and he couldn't wait any longer to grab protection from the bedside table.

Jenna followed him to the edge of the bed, kissed his

shoulder and ran her fingertips down the length of him with an exploratory touch that was pure seduction.

Protection in place, he pinned her to the bed and she welcomed him with a voracious kiss and a throaty exhalation as he fitted himself to her. She kissed him hard, her fingers gripping his hair and not letting go as he set a pace that left her crying out in pleasure and gasping his name.

With a few final mind-blowing strokes, he followed her into completion, his head buried in her neck, lips open against her salty skin. He held her close, unwilling to release her, to end this connection.

"Chance?"

His heart pounded so loud in his ears he barely heard her. "Mmm?"

"Do you hear— Oh, no. *No.*" She shoved at him.

"What? What's wrong?" he asked, her panic giving him the strength he needed for a fast recovery.

"The door. Someone's here!"

"What?"

That's when he heard it. Pounding. Not the gentle knock Jenna had used earlier but a closed-fist slam that grew angrier every time it made contact.

"Go." She rolled to the opposite side of the bed as soon as he moved. "No one can know I'm here. Chance, *please.*"

Her shame was tangible and it pissed him off but he didn't have time to argue with her now. "Stay here," he ordered, snatching his clothes and yanking on his boxers and T-shirt, while Jenna dove for her clothes. He caught a quick flash of her breast and the line of her back before he shut the door to the apartment and crossed the expanse of the storage room to the door.

"All right, all right," he called when the pounding continued. "Who is it?"

"Liam. Open up."

Swearing, he hesitated before unlocking the steel door. The moment he did, Liam had him by the throat and against the wall, using enough force to drive the air from Chance's lungs.

"Where the hell were you?" Liam demanded.

The rehearsal dinner. He'd missed it. "Something came up."

"Something came up? You missed Brad and Gabriella's wedding rehearsal because *something came up?*"

"Liam, don't hurt him," Carly said from the threshold.

"I told you to stay in the car," Liam said.

"And I told you what you could do with your orders," Carly replied. "I'll go back to the car because Riley is waiting. But if there is one visible bruise on Chance, you'll answer to me, Liam McKenna. Chance, shame on you. Gabriella and Brad were both hurt that you missed tonight. You could have at least called."

"I'm sorry," he said, meaning it. He'd thought about calling while he was at Treehouse Rock with Jenna and the twins but he hadn't wanted to leave—even for the five minutes it would take to use the phone.

"I hope whatever it was was important," Carly said in a scolding tone.

Chance didn't so much as blink as he stared into Liam's face.

"You should've been there," Liam growled. "We are the only people Brad has and you embarrassed him by not showing up. What were you thinking?"

Chance didn't answer, knowing his silence egged

Liam on. But given Jenna's fear that someone know she was here with him, he wasn't in the best mood himself.

Biting out a curse, Liam pulled Chance forward and slammed him against the wall again when he didn't speak.

"Dammit, Chance, listen up and listen good. You are not allowed to break this family apart. Do you hear me? Zane wanted us to stay together, and he damned well would've kicked your ass for missing tonight."

"But you can't kick my ass. Carly said." He wasn't sure what possessed him to make the taunt.

Lightning fast, Liam drew his fist back and nailed Chance in the gut, letting him drop to the floor on his knees, doubled over and unable to breathe. Liam had a hell of a right arm.

"Smart-ass. Carly said *no visible bruise*. Don't think for a second she wouldn't approve. Now, you planning on letting something come up tomorrow night?" he asked, referencing Brad's bachelor party.

"No," Chance wheezed, coughing as he struggled to recover.

"And the wedding?"

He closed his eyes and shook his head.

"Good."

Chance glared at Liam but knew he'd gotten exactly what he deserved. He should have answered his cell phone one of the *twenty-three* times it had vibrated in his pocket while he was there having cake to celebrate Jeff's birthday.

Chance rolled until he propped himself up against the wall. Cold air blasted through the building from the open door, cooling the sweat covering his face.

"In case it hasn't sunk into that thick skull of yours, we love you, brother."

That said, Liam slammed out.

Seconds passed but his senses were on full alert when Jenna quietly opened the door to the apartment and emerged fully dressed. Seeing him on the floor, she rushed to his side.

"Are you all right?"

"Yeah. Fine."

"I can't believe he hit you. He's a deputy."

"It's fine." He deserved more and he knew it.

"Chance, *why* didn't you go to the rehearsal dinner? Why did you stay with us?"

He held out his hand for her to help him to his feet. When she did, he wrapped his arm around her neck and kissed her. "I was where I wanted to be."

He knew he'd said the wrong thing when he felt her stiffen.

"You shouldn't have done that. Your family comes first. That's the point I keep trying to make."

"I was where I wanted to be," he repeated softly. "And if I hadn't stayed, you wouldn't be here now, would you?"

She pushed him away and stared at him, her head moving back and forth in tiny motions. "Nothing has changed, Chance."

Everything had changed. But he'd admit it wasn't necessarily for the better.

"I meant what I said when you opened the door. This never happened."

"Then give me the three weeks you have left working here," he said, surprising himself—and her if the look on her face was any indication. "We'll be discreet. No one will know."

She closed her eyes and leaned into him briefly before pushing herself away.

"I have to go."

"Looky there. Hop-along isn't hopping anymore," Charlie said Friday afternoon when Chance made his way into the barn where the wedding would take place tomorrow evening.

Despite his sour mood, Chance took the teasing in stride, trying to focus on the fact that he'd done so well in his PT session yesterday that the doc had removed the boot for good. He could wear regular shoes again. *And climb.* "Sorry I'm late," he said. "The appointment took longer than I thought it would, but I'm good to go again."

No one said a word, but Chance caught the look Brad shot toward Liam. With a dark curse the likes of which Brad rarely uttered, Brad turned away and stalked off.

"Cold feet?" Chance asked.

"You really are a moron sometimes, you know that?" Liam said before following Brad. "You breathing okay today?" he called over his shoulder.

The reminder of the punch left Chance scowling. To cool his temper, he looked around the inside of the barn, unable to believe the transformation so far. The base of every support beam had been layered with tree limbs that were painted white and lit with miniature lights. At the front a twenty foot, flocked Christmas tree stood lit and ready.

He couldn't imagine going to so much fuss, but at the same time he knew Zane was watching, no doubt grinning from ear to ear. This was exactly what he had wanted when he'd gambled the ranch's future on Gabriella coming to the ranch and falling in love. Although

Chance did wonder if Zane really intended for her to fall for one of his sons.

Spying the bride-to-be, Chance watched as Gabriella wrapped her arms around Brad and raised her face for a kiss. She was happy. They were happy.

And Chance was jealous as hell.

Instead of the horror of being caught with him, he wanted to see Jenna's face light up the way Gabriella's did at the sight of her man. He wanted to *be* that man. But how could he be when Jenna saw him as the antithesis of everything she wanted?

It's not like you have to worry about it. It never happened, remember?

"Chance, give me a hand?" Charlie asked, motioning toward the lone support pillar with no limbs around it.

Chance shoved off his thoughts and the anger he felt at Jenna's quick departure last night and put his feet into motion. She didn't want anyone to know she'd given into the attraction between them and that told him all he needed to know as to where they stood with each other.

"You sure that foot's not bothering you?" Charlie asked as they set to work wrapping the support beam.

"It's fine."

"All this is something, ain't it? Gonna be a pretty day. Glad I'm here to see it. It means a lot to Brad that you're here, you know," the man said gruffly. "To both the boys."

Yeah, Chance could tell.

"After we're done pitching in here, don't take off. Don't know if Liam told you or not, but the bachelor party's been changed to the bunkhouse."

"What happened with having it at the Honey?" Chance asked.

"Too many strangers on the ranch and too much valuable stuff out in the open. Brad doesn't want to risk someone coming in to take off with things thinking they can make some easy money."

Made sense. Brad was always looking out for the ranch, and he certainly wouldn't want his bride's wedding day ruined by mischief. The whole town was talking about the event as though Gabriella and Brad were royalty. But that meant unwanted attention would probably be focused on the ranch, as well, and everyone knowing the couple would be off on their honeymoon soon.

Maybe Chance should sleep here instead of at the store. The building had a security system. If anything happened there, the sheriff's station wasn't far. But if Brad expected him to stay here to look after things, shouldn't his brother have given him a heads-up? The fact that he hadn't was a pretty good indication of Brad's opinion of him. His brother didn't trust him to stick around. And after missing last night, why would he?

Four hours later, the sun had set and the men were beginning to assemble in the bunkhouse. Chance made his way inside and found several of the local ranchers present, as well as the McKenna ranch hands and Liam's father-in-law, the sheriff. It was a small gathering thanks to tonight being rodeo night, but the size of the crowd suited his very private brother.

Seeing Brad alone at a table, Chance approached. Considering he'd spent the entire afternoon working alongside his brothers, this was the first time he had a chance to speak to Brad alone.

He passed Liam along the way and his expression stated loud and clear that Chance had some ass-kissing to do to make up for last night and he'd better not do anything to screw with Brad's head now. Yeah, he'd gotten the message with the slug to the stomach.

"That's quite a production out there," he said, taking a seat. "Guess since Gabriella's business is to plan events like as this, her wedding has to be a big to do."

Brad lifted his head and from three feet away Chance heard Liam swear.

Chance ran a hand over his face and scooted his chair in closer to try again. "That didn't come out right," he said by way of apology. "I just meant— Look, Brad, I'm sorry about last night."

"Where were you?"

"In Helena. I was on my way to the dinner when… something came up."

"Something?" Brad asked.

Chance sidestepped the question by reaching into the bag he'd retrieved from his truck. He pulled out a long velvet case. "I got this for Gabriella, but considering it's jewelry, I thought you might want to give it to her."

Brad reached for the box, flipping the lid back. The case apparently drew attention, because Liam and Charlie immediately joined them.

Charlie whistled long and low. "Now that's pretty."

Removing the second one from the bag, he gave it to Liam. "For Carly. I never did get you two anything for your wedding."

The white-gold charm bracelets sparkled beneath the lights of the bar, the Circle M brand charm specially designed by a jeweler with a small diamond in the center of the M.

Brad closed the velvet case and tucked it into his jacket for safekeeping.

"Don't be late tomorrow."

"He won't be," Liam said, holding Carly's gift. "Thanks."

"You're welcome." Chance sat back, relieved that he'd been forgiven.

Unlike the last time the four of them had sat around a table drinking while mourning Zane's death, this night was one of celebration. Liam was married, Brad twenty-four hours from tying the knot. The sappy expressions on his brothers' faces made Chance recognize that he'd been looking for a ready excuse to skip out on last night after the awkwardness of Thanksgiving. Spying Jenna and the kids on his way out of Treehouse Rock had been the reason he'd needed to avoid acknowledging the fact that his brothers were moving on. They would spend the holidays with their wives and, while they'd be sure to include him, he didn't like feeling like a fifth wheel.

For the first time, Chance looked around him and re-alized how connected his brothers were to the people of North Star. Local ranchers, law enforcement. The lines between friend and family had blurred for them.

But not for him.

Zane had given Chance a new name, but Chance would always feel like the outsider looking in.

CHAPTER SEVENTEEN

"Three weeks."

Jenna nearly screamed when she heard Chance's tempting voice in her head again. She hadn't been able to think about anything *else* since he'd said those words to her. But how could she even consider such an outrageous proposition?

It was too late to undo the craziness she'd committed last night but that didn't mean she had to slide full-tilt into…what? A fling? With Jeff's *friend?*

And your employer.

And a Rock God.

She'd dreaded coming to work today, but when she'd arrived Dooley had announced they were on their own. Chance had an early-morning doctor's appointment and X-rays, then would be at the ranch helping with the wedding prep and Brad's bachelor party. The relief she'd felt was immeasurable even though she'd have to face him again at some point. And be armed with an answer.

But not tonight. By the time she and Rachel got to the ranch to deliver the last of the flowers and swags, Chance would have already left for Wild Honey. *You're off the hook.*

"You're awfully quiet," Rachel said as she handed a swag for Jenna to load in the delivery van. "You okay?"

"Fine. Just tired."

"I thought you'd be home earlier last night. I went to

bed around eleven and you still weren't there. Was the trip to the climbing center fun? I'll bet the kids were worn out after all the excitement."

"They were. And, yeah, it was fun—and free," she said, explaining the passes and the owner returning her money but leaving out any mention of Chance.

"No way, seriously? That was nice of him. That will be a great tradition to celebrate Jeff's birthday, too."

Yeah, it would be. But Jenna knew she would never celebrate Jeff's birthday again and not think of what she'd done *afterward*.

Jenna wanted to confide in Rachel—needed to, truthfully—but at the same time she couldn't bring herself to do it. One, because she knew Rachel's advice would be to accept the three weeks with Chance and screw convention and morals. And two, because the more people who knew about it, the more she risked Jeff's parents—and possibly even the twins—finding out. And that couldn't happen. "Um, is that it?" she asked, waving her hand to indicate the swags.

"Yes. We have the table arrangements left, then we can go."

They finished stashing everything, then climbed into the van.

"Oh, did I tell you the news?" Rachel asked.

"What news?" Jenna asked, knowing when she was expected to play along.

"Brad changed the location of his bachelor party at the last minute. It was supposed to be at the Honey but now they'll all be at the bunkhouse. I can't wait to see who shows up. Maybe we'll both meet some hunky bachelor," Rachel said, sliding Jenna an ornery grin. "Chance might even be there."

"I told you, I'm not interested in Chance."

Liar.

"So you wouldn't mind if I chatted him up?" Rachel said, her tone doubtful.

Jenna stared out at the passing scenery, images from last night flickering through her head with rapid and breath-catching intensity. Of all the men in North Star, Chance was the last one she wanted to be interested in. And the quickest way to ensure nothing else happened? "Why not? I refuse to repeat history."

"THEY JUST KEEP COMING," Charlie said later that same evening. "Don't think I've ever seen that many flowers before. Women really get into weddings, don't they?"

"And look who it is," Liam added.

Pulled from the cards in his hand by Liam's tone, Chance glanced out the window to see Jenna getting out of a white delivery van with flowers painted along the side—Rachel's Garden. Several others appeared to help empty the van, and he fought the urge to go after her when she was out of sight.

The card games continued with Chance growing antsier by the minute. He lost the next three rounds because of his inability to concentrate. Seth and Jake Rowland made their way over to congratulate Brad, and Chance used the men's appearance as an excuse to toss in his hand and claim the need for a break.

He slipped out the door and walked to the barn, his hands in his pockets to combat the cold. Inside, he found Rachel staring up at the rafters and Jenna…on top of a twelve-foot ladder. "Jenna," he said softly so he didn't scare her, "what are you doing up there?"

Rachel flashed him a welcoming smile and he was uncomfortably aware of Jenna's friend checking him out as though he was the ladder she wanted to climb.

"Um, hi," Jenna said, her voice echoing slightly due to the acoustics of the building. "Rachel's afraid of heights."

"You should have asked someone to help you."

"It's fine," she said, turning back to what she was doing. "I'm almost done. I just need to hook this into place, but I can't quite…reach…"

"Stop before you fall. Give me a second."

"There isn't another ladder," Rachel said. "I looked."

Chance ignored the woman's words and took a two-step run at the wall, used it to propel him above the decorated portion of the support pole and grabbed hold, climbing into the rafters and onto the cross beam Jenna was attempting to decorate.

Seconds later, he straddled the beam and fastened the long piece of pine where she wanted it. "Hi."

She didn't smile.

"Already up to your old tricks after a single afternoon without the boot?" she murmured drily.

"Only because I saw a damsel in distress," he said, watching every flicker that crossed her face.

"Since you're both up there," Rachel called, "how about you add this one?"

Giving Jenna a teasing wink, he waited while she took the end of the long section of pine Rachel held up via a hook on the end of a pole, and helped her fasten it into place, as well.

"You okay?" he asked softly, careful to keep his voice low so Rachel wouldn't hear.

"Fine."

"Here's the last one," Rachel called.

"I'm not ready for it," Jenna said.

"Just drape it over the top of the ladder until you are."

She did as instructed and Rachel moved away to rustle through some bags sitting on one of the tables.

"Jenna." He placed his hand over hers and she froze.

"Hey, Chance," Rachel called. "Would you mind driving Jenna home?"

Jenna's panic was visible. "What? *Rach*—"

"The nurse texted me. Mom's sick and I need to go, but those swags have to be finished."

"I'll drive her." Chance squeezed her hand. "We need to talk," he added for her ears only.

"Great. Thank you so much. Jenna, I'll talk to you later," she said with a cheery wave.

Jenna's face burned hot with fiery color. "She really could be a little less obvious."

Chance chuckled, thankful for his opportunity to talk to Jenna alone. "You don't think her mama's really sick?"

"It's possible, but more likely Rachel is scheming," she said. "Shouldn't you be at the bachelor party?"

"It'll be breaking up soon—Brad's hardly a night owl. Besides, I'd rather spend time with a beautiful woman than a dozen guys talking ranching."

"But you missed last night," she said. "Was Brad angry?"

He fastened the pine into position and used his hands to scoot along the beam to attach the next section.

"He got over it. And he can't get angry with me when I'm helping you do this, can he?"

The last portion in place, Jenna gripped the ladder to climb down when Chance clasped her shoulders so that when he kissed her—and he was going to kiss her—she didn't tumble off in surprise.

"Chance…"

Careful of his balance because he supported her, he

brushed his lips over hers and heard her breath hitch in her throat. Pulling her closer, he deepened the kiss, inhaling the scent of her.

"Stop," she said. "I'll fall if you don't."

He smiled at her, sneaking one last taste. "I get to you that much, huh?"

Jenna's lashes lowered over her eyes and Chance felt a surge of longing shoot through him.

"I wasn't expecting to see you tonight. I'm glad you came with Rachel."

Her eyes glittered, warm and soft. Hungry, despite what they'd done the night before. "Is it wrong of me to be glad, too?"

He stroked his knuckles over her soft skin, his thumb just beneath her lower lip. "No." First time he felt some hope that he could bring her around. Persuade her to say yes to their time together.

Will three weeks be enough?

"Let's get this done," he ordered huskily. "So we can get out of here."

JENNA LAUGHED AS CHANCE grabbed her hand and rushed her out of the barn a half hour later. In the time it had taken them to finish decorating the long beam, check the lights and store the ladder, he'd stopped to sneak a dozen kisses and with each one, her body ached for more.

Hurrying along the side of the stable, away from all the other vehicles and trucks, Chance paused and kissed her again, running his hands under her open coat to cup her breasts and squeeze.

By the time they tumbled into the truck and he got it rolling down the road, she wasn't interested in seat belts or safety. Chance had the boot off. He would be leaving soon, climbing, as his sprint into the rafters attested to, and she'd be working at her old job. She'd missed the right of passage called dating and right now… Right now she wanted to know what it was like to make out in a truck parked somewhere private. "Pull over," she whispered, the light of the dash allowing her to see the look he gave her.

"And here I was trying to think of an excuse." He flashed a smile. "I like the direct approach."

He turned onto one of the many ranch roads and rolled to a stop, flipped off the lights but left the engine running.

Jenna's heart soared into overdrive when he reached for her, and she refused to admit that this was more than attraction or that she cared for Chance. This was what it was. Nothing more.

"Now what?" His tone was filled with challenge.

Despite an ongoing mental diatribe about how she should keep him at arm's length, she plastered herself to him. She kissed him full-on, her tongue tangling with his and unearthing a groan that made her want to whimper in kind. Their combined exhalations quickly fogged the glass behind Chance's head.

"Chance…" She fingered the texture of his hair, held him in place where he nibbled at her neck.

"What, sweetheart?"

She urged him back to her mouth and the slide of his tongue was bested only by the slide of his hand down her body, between her knees, inching ever-so-slowly up. *Oh, please.* "Keep the heat on…"

What happened next was fast and hard and every bit as satisfying as that first time.

A half hour later, Chance reluctantly dropped her off

at her house. Fifteen minutes after that, he reappeared at her door having parked at the diner and walked back.

"You have to stop," she said, barely able to get the words out because of the way he kissed her. "You have to *go*."

Making love to him in the truck had been an experience she'd never forget. But this…this crazy insane attraction she felt for him, the way he turned her inside out, wasn't good. She hadn't even felt this way for Jeff and she'd *loved* Jeff.

Chance ran his knuckles up and down her sleep shirt, over her bare breast beneath it, until she pressed herself closer with a moan.

This was sex. Everyone knew that desire was fickle. So why hadn't it flamed out and disappeared now that they had been together? More than once.

Chance kissed her harder, murmuring praises and telling her how beautiful she was. How she was soft and lush and everything a man wanted. Everything he wanted. She knew they were just words, but she welcomed them anyway.

Chance backed her up step by stumbling step until he sat on the couch and pulled her down with him onto the soft, worn cushions. Thank goodness she'd left Snickers upstairs behind the master bedroom door, otherwise the dog probably would have jumped onto the couch with them, thinking it a game.

"Hey. Don't be mad at me for leaving you with Cha— *Oh!* Oh, my— Sorry. I'm so sorry," Rachel said, reversing out the door as quickly as she'd entered.

Jenna shoved Chance away. "Rachel! Rachel, wait."

But Rach was already gone. What must she think?

"Oh, no. No, no, *no*." Jenna scrambled to get off his

lap, but Chance looped his arms around her waist and held her in position.

"It's fine."

"It's not fine. I should go talk to her, explain."

"What were doing was pretty self-explanatory."

"But no one can know. Chance, you shouldn't have come back."

"Jenna, I'm pretty sure she understands."

She closed her eyes and groaned, unable to look at him. *She* didn't understand, so how could Rachel? "We can't do this anymore."

"Why? I happen to like what we're doing."

"You can get sex anywhere."

He had her flat to the cushions in a split second. "I want you."

She wanted him, too. But it was impossible. Karen and Les, the twins—they would never understand. And even if they did, what about the Rock Gods? "We both know this will never work. I don't even know what *this* is."

"Then let's find out."

She couldn't breathe. "What are you saying? You want us to date?"

"Why not?"

"Do you *know* what people will say?"

He shrugged. "I don't really care."

"I do." She scrambled away from him. "Jeff has been gone only a little over a year."

"I'm very well aware of that, but don't you think they could adjust?" Chance sat forward on the couch, his elbows on his knees, hands clasped loosely in front of him. Hair mussed from where she'd plowed her fingers through it.

She stared at the sexy, beautiful man on her couch

and fought the temptation he posed. "No. Chance... You're not just some guy. They would never understand. Not after losing Jeff."

"I want to be with you."

She closed her eyes at his words. "I want to be with you, too," she whispered, unable to deny the truth. "But if we are going to see each other, it has to be in private. I'll swear Rachel to secrecy and—I won't have people talking about me. I won't embarrass Jeff's parents and I won't have the twins hurt by it."

He looked at his hands, his jaw tight and a dark expression on his face.

"Fine," he said, standing. "We'll keep it quiet."

Chance walked toward her. He held her gaze, not letting her look away, and leaned low to kiss her again in a slow, open-mouthed caress that made her head spin.

"But that's going to be hard to do when they see you with me at Brad's wedding."

"What? *No.*"

"Jenna, I need you there. Brad and me, Liam, we don't always get along. I want you there with me."

"Why don't you get along?" she asked, trying to pretend the quiet request hadn't gotten under her defenses.

Chance squirmed, obviously uncomfortable with the question. "They don't like the Rock Gods anymore than you do."

Because the group was *so* very reckless. It was yet another reason for her to cancel their internet access, because of the videos posted on YouTube. Videos taken before Jeff's death that showcased some of the things they did. Some of the stunts Jeff had done in the name of *fun.* Chance, too.

"Jenna, please? It doesn't have to be a date, just two

friends going to a wedding and enjoying really expensive food."

Oh, he had to remind her of that, didn't he? "Rachel told me about Wes French." The famous chef. Gabriella Thompson-soon-to-be-McKenna was *friends* with Wes French and the man's wedding present to her and Brad was an elaborate five-star meal.

Jenna could eat food by a famous chef she adored watching on television, but at what price? The longer this affair or fling or whatever it was continued, the more painful it would be to end. And if something happened to Chance while they were together?

You would be attending another Rock God funeral.

"Interested now?" Chance asked, watching her much too closely.

"No," she whispered. "People would talk."

"Jenna, all of the McKenna employees are invited to the wedding. They'll talk if they think there is a reason you won't come."

"I didn't get an invitation," she said quickly, desperate for an excuse.

"They went out before you started working at the store. Gabriella's been so busy it's an oversight. You're invited, trust me."

She closed her eyes in an attempt to resist him. Why couldn't anything be easy? Why couldn't one night be one night? Why couldn't she have this intense reaction later, with someone more acceptable?

"Please," he said. "Don't make me go alone." He pulled her close, his fingers in her hair, mouth against her temple.

"It can't be a date," she said. "We are *not* dating. I've already dated one of the Rock Gods. Lesson learned."

The very air between them stilled. Chance pierced

her with a quelling gaze that had her heart pumping blood past her ears in a gush and she knew she'd said too much. Hurt him even though the reminder had been for herself, so she'd remember to keep her emotions in check.

Chance released her. "I may be a member of the Rock Gods, but don't compare me to Jeff. Don't compare me to anyone."

She blinked at the anger she saw on his face. "I'm sorry."

"I'll pick you up tomorrow at four."

"No," she said quickly. "I'll—I'll find my own way there. You can bring me home." Fewer people would notice that way. But walking in with someone, arriving with someone, that was different.

"Fine. Be there at six," he said, leaving without a last goodbye kiss, which made Jenna realize how bad she wanted one, and she questioned her decision all the more.

CHAPTER EIGHTEEN

THE NEXT AFTERNOON after her shift at the store ended, Jenna knocked on Rachel's door and let herself inside. "Help. I'm out of coffee and desperate," she called out.

"Well, we can't have that, can we?" Rachel said from the kitchen.

"How's your mom?"

"Taking a nap. Hungry?" she said, offering Jenna a biscuit and some jam.

"Tell me those aren't homemade, so I don't feel like such a slacker for feeding my kids cereal all the time."

"Just whipped them up. Fresh and hot from the oven."

She slid onto a bar stool and groaned. "I hate you."

"You should, but for walking in on you last night, not the biscuits. I didn't see a thing but I noticed he, um, left soon after."

"It's fine. No problem." She and Chance had needed interrupting.

"That's not the answer I would've given. Come on, follow me. Coffee's brewing in the shop. So, did Chance leave because of me?"

"No."

"Are you sure? Because when I walked in on you, he was totally feeling you up and most men don't walk away after things get that…intense."

Jenna tried and failed to control the surge of heat

flooding into her face. "I thought you didn't see anything?"

Rachel waved her hand in the air. "Don't be embarrassed about that. Now, if you'd like to discuss why you claim you're not interested in Chance when it's totally obvious you are, that's a different story. Was last night the first time something like that's happened?"

Rachel drilled her with a look that compelled Jenna to come clean. "No. We, um, slept together—"

"What?"

"I didn't want to tell you because the fewer people who know, the better."

"Since when did I become *people?*" Rachel argued, looking hurt.

"You're not, it's just— Oh, this is insane. I'm not sure what to say anymore. I'm not sure what to *do.*"

"About?" Rachel waited, her expression expectant. "Don't leave me in suspense. I thought we hated him. You know, for being so similar to Jeff? What's changed?"

Jenna paced the narrow walkway of Rachel's flower shop, not stopping until she stood in front of the display of angels. She'd always had a thing for angels. "Nothing. Rach, that's just it. Nothing has changed and I'm so confused."

"Here. Hot coffee, two sugars and our favorite creamer. Have at it."

She turned to see Rachel set a mug on the counter. If only this was one of those days when clarity came with coffee. "Thanks."

"No problem, just keep talking. So it's a love-hate thing now?"

Rachel had such a way with words.

"It's not love. And I never hated him. Hate takes too

much energy," Jenna said, blowing on the surface of the drink.

"So you *like* him now?"

She knew Rachel was trying to get her to focus on her feelings but *like* was way too mild of a word for how she felt, which made her feel that much worse. "Yes, but no. See what I mean?" Jenna slurped the too-hot coffee and burned her tongue in the process. "Chance McKenna is everything I don't like or want in a man— and yet he is everything I do like or want. Worst of all, he's...caring."

"And that's a bad thing?"

"Yes."

"Okay," Rachel said, her confusion evident.

"Please don't be upset with me for not telling you. I wanted to. But I had to figure out what I'm doing with him. As you can see, it's going well."

"Is it serious?"

That question was easy to answer. "It will never be serious with Chance. It can't be, which goes against everything I was raised to believe in. I messed around with Jeff and we got caught. I blamed it all on being young and stupid. But what am I doing with Chance? I keep telling myself no, but I'm...drawn to him."

"Jenna, it takes two to tango. The guy's got to settle down sometime."

Maybe. But that wouldn't happen anytime soon and as hard as he pushed himself... Why did he feel the need to drive himself the way he did? What did she really know about Chance?

Maybe you need to ask.

"Have you told Chance about your old job?"

"Yes."

"What was his response?"

Ah, yes, his response. "He asked me to spend the next three weeks with him."

"Only three weeks?"

She turned to face Rachel. "Only three weeks." Because he didn't want more? Was afraid of more?

"Do you want it to last longer?"

"I don't know."

In the aftermath of the mudslide, she'd mourned her mother and friends and her connections. She'd felt uprooted. By comparison, Jeff's description of North Star had seemed idyllic. He was handsome and fun and talked of family and friends, so she'd convinced herself his wild abandonment and recklessness were for show.

But what about Chance? He'd skipped out on his brother's rehearsal dinner. And while Chance being upset when she'd compared him to Jeff was understandable, there seemed to be a deeper, underlying issue. She needed to know more, but given the temporariness of their relationship, Chance had no reason to open up and share such intimate details of his past.

He'd proven he wasn't the same man as Jeff in little ways, such as when he'd misdirected the climber to a safer location, and the care Chance had taken with the twins after she'd told him to stop filling their heads with wild adventure stories. But the fear remained… "What if I'm repeating the past?" she asked softly. "Falling into the same old trap? How far can Chance and I go, realistically?"

"Jenna, for what it's worth, my honest to goodness take on Chance McKenna is that he could walk into the Honey or the diner or the *grocery store* and go home with any woman if he so chose. But last night when he looked at you, I swear, there was no one else in the room. There's only one way to find out where it might go."

Rachel was right but that didn't make it any easier to accept. "But how can I not be worried? My children *buried* their father. And what about Jeff's parents?"

"What about them? This is your life, Jenna."

"I don't want to be that woman everyone is whispering about. My kids don't deserve that, Jeff's parents don't deserve that and neither do I."

"That's the risk you take. Nothing you do is going to stop the gossips. It's who they are. And we all face getting our hearts broken. The only question you can answer is whether you feel strongly enough about Chance to give the relationship a try instead of running away because of what happened with Jeff. Do you?"

She believed in love, believed in *commitment*. She wanted to be with someone, grow old with him. Have fun with him. *Love* him. Forever.

But how long could forever last with Chance free climbing on sheer rock faces? "I don't want to bury another man I care for. Not again."

"No one does. But it sounds to me that if something happens to Chance, you're going to hurt no matter what."

The weight and reality of Rachel's words swept through Jenna and left her reeling.

She cared for Chance. *Cared* for him. She couldn't deny it. And with her, love and caring went hand in hand.

Along with crazy. But isn't opening yourself up to be hurt crazy? Because love means letting someone in.

"Jenna, hon, people think they can plan the future, but we both know we can't plan the next minute. Instead of focusing on what might happen in a month, focus on now and let things work out as they will."

"Have faith," she said, her eyes drawn to the word written across an angel on the shelf.

"That's right," Rachel said from behind her. "If I gave into all the worry in my life right now, I'd be huddled in the corner of a padded room. Worry is evil and it's bad for you and you *can't* give into it, otherwise it'll take over and you'll never know what it really means to live."

Jenna wanted to laugh but couldn't because Rachel had repeated the essence of the Rock Gods' philosophy. "I know that rationally, but it's not just me I have to worry about. The kids are already entranced with Chance," she said, relating the name change request to Rachel. It was yet another example of how out-of-control things had gotten so fast.

"That is the sweetest thing I've ever heard. How wonderful that Mark bonded so well with Chance."

Wonderful—and frightening. It cemented the fact that her children needed a father figure, someone they could trust and confide in.

"When are you seeing Chance again? Personally, not professionally."

Jenna released her breath in a gusty sigh. "He asked me to go to his brother's wedding."

"The wedding? What are you going to wear?"

She hadn't even thought that far ahead. She'd gotten up, dragged herself into work and thanked God that Chance had spent the morning at the ranch helping with the last-minute preparations. "I don't know. I have my dress from—"

"Don't you dare say from Jeff's funeral."

"I was going to say the dress from last year's school Christmas party, thank you."

Rachel shook her head firmly. "No, it was pretty but

it screamed 'Mom dress.' Brad and Gabriella's wedding is going to be a *to-do*. She has clients flying in from California. *Hollywood.* You need a dressy dress."

Jenna didn't have the money to buy anything new or formal, and even if she did, it was too late. "That decides it. I'm not going."

"Oh, yes, you are. I know exactly what you can wear. Remember that deep crimson dress I wore to the florist convention several years ago? It would be perfect."

She remembered the dress quite well. "Oh, Rach, I'm not sure I can pull that off."

"You can, trust me. Chance won't know what hit him. Oh, stop looking so worried. You can't tell me that after what I walked in on that you wouldn't mind showing off a bit. Just to prove you've still got it—not that that's in question."

She thought of the fifteen extra pounds she carried and sighed. She should have said no last night.

"It's good to keep a man on his toes and all Chance has ever seen you wear is jeans, right?"

She rubbed her temple, because it was starting to throb. "We work at a feed store. It's hardly the place to wear silk and satin."

"That's what I'm saying. For one night have fun. The kids are at Jeff's parents, so let yourself relax and be the twentysomething girl you haven't ever been able to be."

She was so out of her element, but she had to admit the thought appealed. "Faith, huh?"

"Yep. Having the big man on your side is the only way to roll with the punches. Let's go get that dress. You have to get started getting ready."

"Rach, it's barely one o'clock. Dooley and his wife aren't picking me up until five."

Rachel had grabbed hold of Jenna's hand to tug her toward the stairs, but she stopped long enough to stare at Jenna's chipped, uneven nails. "We'll barely make it in time."

THE WEDDING WAS unbelievably beautiful and heartfelt. Jenna wiped away tears as Brad and Gabriella repeated their vows to one another, and tried to ignore the blatant way Chance stared at her from the altar, rather than focusing on the couple getting married. It unnerved her, the way Chance made her feel.

He looked utterly gorgeous in his black tuxedo and dark red vest, and if she were smart, she'd end things now, before she got in any deeper. But it was too late and she knew it. The question was what to do from here. She either threw herself completely into a three-week relationship with him—fully aware it was temporary— or walked away. Given her feelings for him, neither of those options would leave her whole in the end.

Someone began to sing and, to keep from squirming in her seat due to Chance's unwavering attention, Jenna focused on the decorations, unable to believe how breathtakingly beautiful the barn had become. Old-fashioned candle chandeliers had been added for ambience, and the entire space was filled with twinkling lights, the gorgeous swags of deep red roses, pine and poinsettias topped with sparkling ribbons. It was a Christmas setting from a Hollywood movie set.

The song over, Jenna glanced at Chance. The moment they made eye contact he winked at her, and heat filled her face once more. He was such a flirt. But she'd be lying if she said it didn't make her feel good to note that, with the vast array of beautiful women in the room, he seemed only to see her.

More warning signs went off in her head and she reminded herself of the three-week time limit.

"I now pronounce you husband and wife. You may kiss your bride."

Jenna smiled at the whistles and catcalls and applause. Brad's joy in being married to Gabriella was written into every line of his sun-weathered face and she felt a pinch of envy that Jeff had never looked at her that way. Not even in the beginning. While never saying the words aloud, she suspected he must have felt trapped by her pregnancy. By marrying her and having a family when he wanted other things.

The wedding party made their way down the aisle toward the door.

Jenna joined the other guests in going through the receiving line. She gave her well wishes to the happy couple and moved on when Chance tried to pull her into the line with him. With a drink in her hand, she waited patiently, amusing herself by peeking through the barrier of white glittering trees to watch the change from ceremony to dinner seating taking place.

The sea of white-clad soldiers rearranged the chairs, brought in more tables and had them covered and decorated with Rachel's table arrangements in a matter of minutes. The entire room would be ready before everyone made it through the reception line.

"Got you this time," Chance said, snagging her elbow and tugging her gently into place near Brad and his new bride. "Do a guy a favor, and don't leave me, sweetheart. The vultures are already circling with their unmarried daughters." He turned his back to the crowd and quickly snuck a kiss. "Mmm. You taste good with champagne. I'll have to remember that."

"People will see you," she hissed, torn between

throwing caution to the wind, and preventing gossip. "You'll cause talk I can't afford. Let go."

She pulled her arm from his grip and put a respectable distance between them, aware that Chance's expression darkened at her words.

Since Liam and Chance both served as Brad's best men, they took turns making a toast during dinner. Liam was first, ribbing his brother unmercifully and drawing solemn nods of agreement that Zane McKenna's presence could be felt in the room on such a happy day. Despite her worry over appearances, she couldn't remember the last time she had laughed so much or enjoyed herself more. And the food… Oh, it was divine.

"Glad you came now?" Chance asked later, his arm draped over the back of her chair where they sat at a table for the McKenna employees.

"Yes. Thank you for including me." She smiled and then added for everyone listening, "The food was excellent."

Her suspicions that they were being watched proved true when the table erupted in low laughter and coughs.

Chance's gaze narrowed in seductive warning that made her heart thump hard in her chest. And all she could think of was: *Embrace the rush.*

JENNA WAS WRAPPED UP to ward off the cold and sitting on the porch of the house when she saw the last of the caterers get into their large trucks and vans and leave. Earlier, Brad and Gabriella had departed for their honeymoon to a private lodge in Wyoming, and the California guests had flown back to Hollywood on private jets. It was surreal to consider those circumstances while she wore a borrowed dress and shoes. But like every Cinderella, the pumpkin hour fast approached.

"Sorry about that," Chance said, hurrying up to the porch. Snow crunched under his shoes and he cursed softly when he slid because he was walking too fast.

"Don't fall. You don't want to break that foot again."

"Definitely not. Why are you sitting out here in the cold? Why didn't you go inside?"

She shrugged. It didn't seem right to be in the McKenna house without Chance or one of the others there. "It's a beautiful night."

Chance motioned for her to meet him at the door.

"Shouldn't we be going?"

"Not yet. You must be freezing. Come in and warm up. There's a fire in the den."

She walked into the entry of the beautifully decorated house and wondered if she'd ever have a home as nice as this with its wintery Christmas decorations and pine-draped staircase.

"Let me take that."

That was her coat, another item borrowed from Rachel, though this one came from Rachel's mother. The thick wool cape had a fur-trimmed collar she'd been a little leery of wearing but given the cold, no one seemed to pay any attention to.

"The ceremony was beautiful," she said, needing to fill the void of silence.

"Yeah. I wish Zane could've seen it."

"I'm sure he did."

Her comment drew a hint of a smile and a nod from Chance before he palmed her shoulders and began to run his hands up and down her arms. Watching him, she saw his gaze slide to the cleavage she felt gently bouncing with every stroke, and wondered...

Maybe it was the romance in the air. The beautiful ceremony where two people who obviously loved each

other had vowed to stay together forever. Maybe it was
the twinkling white lights in the darkened entry, and the
cozy, crazy, this-could-be-different whispers she heard
in her head. Whatever it was kept her from protesting
when Chance lowered his head for a kiss and had her
parting her lips to let him inside.

His hands slid over her, gripped her behind and
arched her into the heat of him. "Jenna…"

Her body hummed as he nipped and kissed and she
went on sensory overload. Her hands pushed at his tuxedo jacket, wanting to be closer. She vaguely heard
it drop to the floor and went to work on his vest. Finally she made it to his shirt but it took her forever to
undo the first few tiny buttons and there were *so* many.
"Chance?"

His face was buried in her neck, the whiskery brush
of his chin bringing out shivers of delight. Was she the
only woman who found that sensation a total turn-on?

"What, sweetheart?"

It was so hard to think with him doing that. Obviously he'd caught on to the fact her neck was one of her
erogenous zones and he was taking full advantage. "Do
you own this shirt?"

"Yeah, why?"

Giving into every luscious, do-or-die push in her
head, she firmed her grip on the two sides and yanked
as hard as she could. Buttons flew, Chance growled out
his approval and she whimpered when her hands en-
countered yet another layer of clothes—the undershirt
he wore beneath.

"Now you know how I feel every time you have on
twenty layers." He nipped her just a wee bit harder.

She left the shirts and tackled his belt next, her fingers fumbling, her need taking on a hard edge because she wanted him so bad.

She'd been good. A good daughter, a good wife, a good mother. All her life she'd been *good*. But she needed this. Needed him. No matter the consequences to her heart.

"Sweetheart, let me."

Chance removed the vest and yanked the damaged shirt off his arms. She shoved up the cotton undershirt and he pulled it over his head. The first time they'd made love had been rushed due to the intensity. The second time had been in the dark of the truck. But here, now, it was all about the moment as they touched and stroked. The beauty of his body stole her breath. He was corded muscle and lean strength, just the right amount of chest hair, lickable, mouthwatering abs that drew her hands.

"No way. Not tonight, sweetheart. Tonight is all you." He brushed her fingers away and gathered the material of her dress, tugging it over her head.

She sucked in her belly but Chance's low groan and the thrill it sent barreling through her made it clear he liked her the way she was, and that made her heart soar.

He speared his fingers into her hair, angled her head just so and kissed her, not letting her up for air until she clung to him. Finally he fished a condom from his wallet and the moment it was on, he removed the last of her clothes.

Dazed and breathless, she found herself lifted high and held secure. Her legs automatically slid around his hips as they stumbled into the wall with a bang neither one of them felt because they were too busy trying to get closer.

THREE HOURS LATER, Chance stood in the dark in his old bedroom and stared at the letter from Zane. He had left all of his children—biological and adopted—a letter to be read after his passing.

Jenna snuggled up downstairs looking so beautiful and sex-tossed, Chance had needed some breathing room because making love with her had rocked his world. So much so he thought of the barn outside, still decorated with its wedding finery, and wanted to call the preacher back to the house.

Instead he found himself here, Zane's last words in his hand.

Swallowing hard, Chance read through the letter, his third time tonight, the last paragraphs jumping out at him.

> I'm proud of you, Chance. You've grown into a fine man. But you need to stop running and start believing you're worthy of being a part of things. You're holding back, son, and I know it's because you're afraid to get too attached in case something goes wrong. Family's family, though. And when things go wrong, it's your family who's going to be by your side, even if I'm not.
>
> You deserve to be happy, son. You weren't to blame for what your father did. Stop carrying his punishment on your shoulders and live your life as you were meant to. Some things are worth sticking around for, but you won't find them on mountaintops.

Chance sat on the edge of the bed, staring at Zane's scrawl across the page. There was more to the letter, but those words stood out.

When he thought of settling down, thought of family, his head filled with images of Jenna and the twins.

Some things are worth sticking around for but you won't find them on mountaintops.

Mind churning, he put the letter back in the drawer and made his way downstairs. He grabbed every pillow and throw he could find—they owned an abundance thanks to Gabriella—and tossed them onto the floor before he plucked Jenna from the couch. She woke up when he swung her around to lower her to the makeshift bed in front of the fire.

"Hey," she said, smiling.

"Hey, yourself."

"Something wrong?"

Lowering his head, he kissed her. "Not now…"

CHANCE OPENED HIS EYES several hours later. A muffled noise from the kitchen reminded him he wasn't alone, although a glance at the window said it was barely dawn. Did Jenna always get up this early?

He got to his feet and snagged one of the throws to wrap around his waist until he could find his clothes. "Good morning," he said, entering the kitchen, only to stop in his tracks. "Ah, shit."

Liam raised an eyebrow. "I take it you thought I was someone else? Never mind. I can see that for myself."

Chance tried to act casually. "You're doing the feeding today?"

"It's Charlie's day off. Had I known you spent the night, I would've let you do it."

"How could you not know I was here? My truck's outside," he grumbled, wondering where Jenna had gotten to. He looked down the hall to the entry and while his clothes were still scattered on the floor, hers were gone. Had she heard Liam and scrambled to hide? He didn't like it that she was so worried about what people thought of her dating him. Of course, he would admit the need for delicacy with the twins' feelings at stake.

Liam grabbed a cup from the cabinet and headed toward the coffeemaker, apparently not in any hurry to leave.

"Don't you have coffee at your house?"

"Don't you have a bed at yours?"

"I thought this was my house, too." Chance stomped down the hall, a bad feeling in his gut. He grabbed his shorts and pants, mooning Liam when he turned his back to the kitchen to pull them on. Standing there while Liam lectured him reminded him way too much of the time Zane had caught him with his first girl.

"It is. When you want it to be. But what about the rest of the time?"

Chance ignored the slam and looked around for anything of Jenna's but nothing remained, as if the night had never happened. *Again.*

He hoped Brad and Gabriella's photographer had snagged a picture of Jenna wearing the mind-blowing outfit. He wanted a copy to keep.

As to Liam's comment... It made Chance feel guilty and reinforced Zane's words. For all intents and purposes, Brad and Liam had shown they cared for him as much as any blood brother could. Despite the years they'd spent living under the same roof, however, Chance still had that foster-kid mentality. Don't share too much, don't show weakness, don't get attached.

Time and again he'd learned the hard way to follow the rules. "I guess that means I'm going to have to hang around more. That way, you and Brad won't treat me like a freak when I do."

Liam carried a steaming cup with him into the hall and leaned against the arch separating the rooms. "What about this big trip to Nevada I keep hearing about?"

Word sure spread fast. And even though he hadn't exactly been keeping the news quiet, what did Jenna think about the trip? "I don't know." Dammit, where had she gone? Was she hiding upstairs?

"Would be nice if you were here for Christmas. Brad and Gabriella will be back and the girls are planning to host Christmas dinner. It'll be Riley's first dinner as a McKenna."

The picture Liam painted was a nice one. Chance simply had to figure out where he fit into it, considering Jenna seemed hellbent on keeping their relationship a secret. "We'll see how things go."

Liam lifted the mug in his hand. "I'm going to finish up. Let me know when you're ready to leave."

"Why?" Chance followed Liam to the kitchen.

"Because unless you're in the mood for a long walk, I'm your ride to town."

Liam's words sank in and Chance stalked to the window over the sink, only then realizing his truck wasn't parked outside where he'd left it. No wonder Liam hadn't known the house was occupied. *"She took my truck?"*

"Looks like Jenna Darlington isn't the mouse Brad and I thought she was. I like her more now than ever."

Yeah...so did he.

CHAPTER NINETEEN

Aren't you the sneaky one?

Jenna's hands gripped the steering wheel of her truck as she drove down her street and ignored the taunting voice in her head Sunday morning.

Sneaky? Not hardly. And her adventure-girl, throw-caution-to-the-wind side was *not* back. It had merely…

Had a really fine time last night, thank you.

Jenna groaned aloud and pressed harder on the gas pedal. Somehow she'd managed to drive Chance's massive truck back to North Star and change out of her eye-catching red dress and heels before the sun had shown itself on the horizon.

Now on her way to Jeff's parents to pick up the kids, she wondered if she had a sign on her forehead that read *I had mind-blowing sex last night.* It sure felt like it.

What would Chance do when he woke up and found out she'd taken his truck?

He'd be angry, probably more than a little embarrassed. But that whole morning-after thing? She *so* couldn't do it. What do you say?

The first time she'd slept with Chance could be passed off as one of those things. And in the truck? She had to be the only woman her age who had never had that experience. But last night?

Last night she'd gone in with her eyes wide open. But even if she was ready to admit to others she and

Chance were involved, she had to figure out a way of telling the twins and Jeff's parents first. She owed them that.

Her bid for simply keeping her family's heads above water financially had turned into a complicated mess spiraling out of her control. Her guilt was compounding hourly, and she had to think of a way of bringing up the subject of Chance but how?

Her mind too jumbled for answers, Jenna turned up the radio and then immediately turned it off. She wasn't in the mood for Christmas carols. Pulling into Les and Karen's driveway, she fought her trepidation. They would *not* be able to tell.

Mark had the door open and was waiting on her when she topped the steps. "Hey, Mom. What are you doing here so early?"

Hiding. Managing a smile, she dug her thumbs into her back jean pockets and shrugged. "You guys have been gone so much lately I wanted to spend some time with you. That okay?"

"Sure. But Grandma changed her mind about baking. She's taking us to Helena today to go Christmas shopping. You wanna come?" Mark lowered his voice. "She wants us to pick *clothes* and if we have to get clothes me and Tori want your help." He gave her a pointed stare.

Jenna winced in sympathy. Karen still wanted to dress the kids in matching sets despite their preference for the trendier—and more unique—outfits. Relief poured through her at the excuse to join them, which brought more guilt given her morning so far. "Understood. I'd be happy to go with you. When do we leave?"

An hour later, Jenna felt Karen's gaze on her as they drove to Helena. The kids were in the backseat. Mark with his nose buried in a book about rockets and Tori staring out the window.

"I hope you don't mind that I joined you," she said to Jeff's mother. "But with them in school and staying with you on break, I've missed them."

"Not at all. I will say I'm surprised to see you out and about so early. I saw that last night was quite a to-do."

Jenna stared at Karen, confused. "What?"

"The wedding," Karen said. "You haven't seen today's paper? There is a huge write-up and lots of photos, even one of you."

Jenna faltered, unsure of what to say. Her picture was in the paper?

Karen glanced into the rearview mirror as though checking on the twins, and then back at Jenna.

"Jenna, I realize it was a wedding and allowances are given, but I feel I should warn you."

"Oh?" she said, pretending interest in a billboard along the highway.

"The photo was of you dancing with Chance McKenna," she said, her tone taking on a note of disapproval. "And while I'm quite sure it was perfectly innocent, since he is your employer, for the twins' sake you need to be careful. You don't want your children hearing any unsavory gossip about you so soon after their father's death. It would hurt them."

Karen's words hit hard, and, despite the awareness that this was a great time to admit her relationship with Chance, Jenna couldn't bring herself to do it. Not yet. "I'm very aware of that," she said, reaching out to twist the temperature knob on her side of the car.

Karen gasped.

"What? Is something wrong?" she said, alarmed because the woman was driving at seventy miles an hour.

"Jenna, where's your wedding ring?"

The gasp and questions had drawn the twins' attention. Jenna pinned a smile on her lips and tried to slow the surge of unease sliding through her. "Oh. I, uh, I put it away, for safekeeping."

Karen looked upset by the news. And Jenna knew the topic was far from closed.

"HEY, CHANCE! GOOD TO SEE you again, man," the owner of Treehouse Rock greeted later that afternoon. Caleb held out his hand for Chance to shake. "Looking different, too. How's the foot?"

"That's what I want to find out. The boot is finally off so I'm ready to hit the wall. My PT gave me a thumbs-up."

"I love it. Gotta feed the addiction, right? Let's get you set up."

"Thanks." He'd spent the ride into town this morning listening to Liam rib him about Jenna making off with his truck. Finding it parked at the sheriff's station set off another round of jokes Chance knew he'd never live down.

Never in a million years would he have expected Jenna to take his truck like that but that only proved how desperate she was to keep people from finding out about them. *Him.* On the one hand he understood, but on the other?

He already felt enough shame for an army of people. He didn't need to feel more.

Chance paid the fee and changed out of his jeans and shoes into loose pants and climbing shoes. He skipped the easier, straight-up walls designed for beginners and went to the back where Caleb, the other members of the Rock Gods and more skilled climbers practiced.

This wall was different with all its curves and pitches. At around fourteen feet, the wall jutted out and banked up, the various pits and sharp edges challenging even to the experienced. The climber had to start at the bottom and go up, belly to the rock and back to the floor, around the tip of the faux-cliff, then up the wall that shot all the way up to the building's metal roof three stories above his head.

Thankfully no one was in this section right now, so the area and his thoughts were his own to muddle through.

Jenna's face appeared in his mind as he stretched, and, like it or not, his blood began a low boil. He'd phoned her repeatedly throughout the morning, only to hang up in frustration when she didn't answer.

He'd even gone as far as to drive by her house like a love-sick teenager hoping to see her truck in the driveway. Nothing. Wherever she'd gone, she didn't want to be found and for a split second it reminded him way too much of himself.

Chance chalked up his hands, then jumped up, gripping the wall with his fingertips. He hung there a moment, feeling every muscle in his body respond to the effort it took to hold that position, then lifted his feet to the wall. His ankle ached a bit from the strain but he kept going. When the time came, he chose the most difficult path that ran over the very tip of the outcropping. He hung there for a second to chalk up again.

Climbing was all about strategy and skill, the drive to conquer the wall or the mountain—or the woman— without damaging them or leaving a path of destruction behind. To him, climbing was a love affair with something bigger. It was taking on the challenge, being stronger, knowing one tiny mistake would be humbling. It had to be done—literally—one fingerhold move at a time.

On this cold Sunday, this was his church. Every shift of his hands and feet, every thought in his head was a prayer for the future, and thanks for the life he'd been given. Nothing reminded a man that he was only a man like hanging from his fingertips and staring up at the sky, even if it was through skylights in the roof.

You're holding back, son, and I know it's because you're afraid to get too attached in case something goes wrong.

His eyes burned from the chalk dust floating down from the hand stretched above his head. Zane's words echoing, repeating, drilling the awareness home. Maybe… Maybe Zane was right about thinking himself worthy. Believing it.

Chance didn't want a few winter nights with Jenna. But with his past and her issues with the Rock Gods, he felt like he was climbing a mountain that had no top.

All he could do was fall.

"You look different."

Jenna was deep in dishwater when Mark made the announcement that evening after a long day spent shopping along the pedestrian mall in Helena. She'd helped the twins pick out tolerable clothes to be wrapped up and placed beneath Karen and Les's tree, and they had even managed to find quite an expensive bird feeder on clearance for Les's collection in the backyard. But after the conversation with Karen on the drive things between them had grown uncomfortable, making for a strained afternoon. By the time they'd arrived home, Jenna was exhausted—and unsure of whether she was happy or disappointed that Chance wasn't there. "Oh?"

Thanks to her brother's comment, Tori studied Jenna with blatant curiosity. "You *do* look different."

"How so?" Jenna asked, even though she knew she ought to change the subject.

"Not as old."

Tori started giggling and Jenna turned to stare at Mark, giving him her best mother look with eyebrows raised. "Less *old?*"

"Good one, moron."

"Sorry, Mom."

"Well, I'll take it as a compliment since I think you meant it as one. Tori, no names. What do you say?"

Tori rolled her eyes. "Sorry, Mark."

"Here," Jenna said, handing off the roasting pan for Tori to rinse and dry.

"You looked pretty today," Mark said, like he was trying to backpedal the way every red-blooded male did when they believed they had insulted a woman. "Didn't she, Tori?"

Jenna smiled until she noticed Tori watching her with a frown. "Last one," she said, handing Tori a metal spatula. "Finish those and I'll—"

The doorbell ended her words.

"I'll get it." Mark took off like a shot.

"Don't open the door until you know who it is," she called, reaching for a towel to dry her hands.

"I know," he replied. "It's Chance!"

"Why's he here?" Tori asked, suspicion all over her face.

Dread filled Jenna. Surely Chance wouldn't say anything in front of the kids. The moment they had arrived home, Tori had ran to the mailbox to grab the newspaper and read the wedding article for herself. But other than a suspicious glance at the photo, her daughter hadn't commented. "I don't know. Let's go find out."

"Yeah, yeah, you got it," Mark said. "A little lower. You're in."

Jenna felt her heart squeeze when she saw a Blue Spruce being shoved through her front door. She'd commented on how pretty the Christmas tree was at Gabriella and Brad's wedding. Now here was a smaller version of it.

"Mom, isn't it cool? Chance brought us a tree."

"Yeah. It is." But it was an expensive tree. One she couldn't afford. "Chance, you shouldn't have done this."

Chance gave her a look no adult could misinterpret, especially not two consenting adults who had spent the night doing what they had done.

"It's no big deal. I noticed you didn't have one and no house should be without a tree two weeks before the big day."

"Will you stay and help us decorate it?" Mark asked.

"I'd love to, if your mom says it's okay." Chance's gaze met hers and despite the urge to send him on his way, how could she with the way he'd worded his acceptance?

With a reluctant nod and a quelling glare indicating that he'd better not push too far, she agreed.

"Where do you want the tree?" Chance asked.

She pointed to the window in the living room. "There. I need to move the couch first, though."

"You go back to doing what you were doing. Mark and I will get it moved."

"Oh, but it's heavy. I'll—"

"Mom, I can *do* it," Mark said with a put-out sigh and

a shove to his glasses. "You've got to stop babying me. Right, Chance?"

"Hey, me, too," Tori quickly interjected.

Raising her hands in surrender, Jenna nodded. "Fine, fine, you guys move the couch."

"So what do I get to do?" Tori asked.

"Dishes," Mark said. "It's what girls d—"

Mark's words cut off when he caught sight of his mother watching, waiting to see if he dared finish that statement.

"I'll handle the last of the dishes. Tori, scoot the chair over while they get the couch, please."

Jenna finished drying the dishes, stopping every little bit to watch the trio move the couch, chair and coffee table. With every push and shove and laugh, still more of her protective walls crumbled, leaving her feeling dangerously exposed.

Chance made both kids feel as though they were doing their share and were involved with the process. The sight was sweet and touching and more appealing than Jenna wanted it to be, too, but she couldn't shake the anxiety she felt with Chance here in her home. After seeing their photo in the newspaper, her neighbors were sure to make note of his presence.

Why was he here? He certainly didn't act like a man angry about the disappearance of his truck. And what did it mean, him bringing them a tree? Spending the evening with them?

Someone turned on Christmas carols and Chance and the kids began to sing along. Suddenly *boughs of green* became *balls are green* and she barely managed to stifle a laugh. Then she thought, why should she? They were having fun.

And wasn't that the point?

CHANCE TOOK A STEP BACK to survey the tree. Not bad for his first time, but he wished he'd done a little better job on the lights.

Jenna and the kids seemed to have tree trimming down pat, complete with a plan as to how things *had* to be done—lights, then garland, then decorations—so he hadn't had a lot of time to get particular and changing anything now would require a total overhaul.

"Here, you do it," Mark said, holding out the plastic star made to resemble stained glass. It had little white lights inside it and the star gleamed with color once it was plugged in.

"You sure?"

"Yeah. Grandpa says the man of the house puts on the star."

Uncomfortable, Chance glanced around and saw Jenna and Tori looking through another box for ornaments. They hadn't heard what Mark had said. "Mark, that's quite a compliment you're giving me, but I'm not sure I fit that description." Or if he ever could.

"No. It should be you. I'm okay with it."

As though sensing something going on, Jenna straightened and looked at Chance. Her gaze lowered to the star he held and he saw the moment the significance registered with her. Jenna blinked and swallowed, her gaze softening with worry when she looked at her son.

Jenna didn't want him messing with her kids' heads. And he couldn't blame her. He knew firsthand how screwed up kids could get with the wrong person in their lives.

Chance ignored his unease and snagged the step stool used to decorate the top of the tree. He balanced on the top step, aware that every move he made was being watched by the little family. Getting the star just right required some wrangling and angling but finally it was in place. "There. How's that look?"

"It looks straight," Mark said. "Good job, Chance."

"Couldn't have done it without your help, bud."

"Or mine," Tori added.

"That goes without saying," Chance agreed. He glanced down to find Jenna staring at her kids and smiling, and his gut tightened because it was such a motherly, *family* thing to do and the sight of it made him wonder what the hell he was doing there. Why was he pushing so hard when he knew the end result?

Jenna turned away and began to gather up all the tissue paper tossed aside as ornaments were unwrapped and placed on the tree. "Guys, it's late. Way past bedtime. Chance needs to go home."

"Mom, we're not little kids," Tori complained.

And he wasn't going anywhere.

"No arguments. You have school tomorrow. Go wash your hands, brush your teeth and get settled. I'll be up in a few minutes to tuck you in."

"Can Chance do it? Not that I need tucking in, just... can he?" Mark asked, trying to sound older.

Jenna looked stunned by the request and wary of his response.

"You got it, Mark," he said, folding up the stepladder.

Tori regarded him with blatant suspicion. "'Night, Chance."

"Good night, sweetheart."

Jenna turned off the Christmas carols with a quick press of a button. The kids tromped upstairs and Snickers lifted her head from the floor where she had been snoozing, then bounded up after them.

"You don't have to stay. I'll tuck them in. Thank you for the tree. I'll add the cost to my bill and pay you back."

"I want to stay, and no, you won't." He moved close to give her a slow kiss despite her board-stiff stance.

"Chance—"

"Don't take the fun of decorating my first tree away from me."

"Your first?" Her expression made it clear the lack of a tree was yet another example of his screwed-up life.

"Yeah. Until tonight I was a Christmas tree decorating virgin." He gave her a salacious wink. "Thanks for making it gentle for me."

A blush warmed her cheeks and she shook her head. "You're incorrigible. You've *never* decorated a tree?"

"Nope."

"After you tuck Mark in, will you tell me why?"

A multitude of expressions flickered across her face as she stared up at him. "Maybe."

Smiling, she grasped his hand and led the way upstairs but once she reached the top she let go—and he wondered once again why he was there.

UPSTAIRS, JENNA EXCUSED herself from Mark's room and hurried into the master bath to grab the makeup bag stashed beneath the sink. Finding it, she lifted her lashes and caught sight of herself in the mirror. Little lines were beginning to form at the edges of her eyes from squinting and the line around her mouth was getting deeper. But Mark was right. She looked different.

There was a sparkle in her eyes that hadn't been there for quite some time. Her mouth looked fuller, softer. Her cheeks rosier. And it was enough of a difference that, even though she hadn't taken more than a passing glance at herself in months, she noticed. *They* had noticed.

She had to get a grip on herself. Had to gain control of this situation with Chance.

Through the thin walls of her house, she heard the unmistakable sound of Chance talking to Mark. More heart-rending and rare was her son's low, boyish laughter. Oh, how she loved that sound.

There was no denying that her children had soaked up Chance's company tonight and gotten along in a way they hadn't in a long time. But they were fragile, only now recovering from the haze that had enveloped them after the loss of their father.

Could she allow Chance to become even a small part of their lives? Could she risk their happiness?

Drawn to the sound of their voices, Jenna left the bathroom and tiptoed down the hall. Mark's door was open, his nightlight on. And despite having been tucked into bed moments ago, Tori sat in the miniature recliner in the corner of Mark's room, her knees drawn up to her chest, zebra-striped slippers in place.

"What happened then?" Mark asked.

Chance shook his head slowly back and forth. Jenna couldn't see his expression, only part of his face.

"Well, needless to say Zane wasn't happy. He loaded us up and took us back to the home for boys, marched us in—"

"He didn't take you to *jail?*" Tori asked, eyes wide.

"No. He could have. We'd done that much damage to the ranch. It was really bad on our parts, wrong of us. But instead of having us arrested, Zane told the person in charge at the home that he wanted us—all three of us. He said he didn't want us getting off *easy,* and that we had to work off the money we owed him."

"He kept you *hostage?*" Mark asked, his eyes wide behind his glasses.

Chance's chuckle and the expressions on the twins' faces brought out a smile until Jenna squelched it and schooled her features into something more somber.

"Not quite. But we worked, hard, and by the time we'd paid off what we owed Zane, none of us wanted to leave. We thought we were so tough. Brad and Liam and I wouldn't say anything about wanting to stay, not even when Zane asked us if we wanted to."

"So how did you get to?" Tori asked.

"Zane finally changed how he worded things. One day he looked at us and said flat-out that he was adopting us—unless we spoke up and said no. Folks around here thought he was crazy but that was the last time we ever had to stay at the boys' home. From then on…we were McKennas." Chance's last words rang with a quiet pride Jenna couldn't help but find endearing.

Mark asked a couple more questions and somewhere along the way, Tori leaned her head back against the seat and closed her eyes.

"That's enough for tonight. Lights out before your mama gets mad at me," Chance told Mark. "Sleep tight, buddy."

"Chance?"

"Yeah."

"Thanks for telling my mom about the name thing. You were right. She wasn't mad."

Knowing her son didn't want a big deal made over the situation Jenna had simply began calling him Mark and commented casually that if he ever needed to talk about anything, he could. Before long, Tori had begun calling him Mark, as well. Jenna hadn't mentioned the name change request to Karen or Les, knowing if she did it would probably become an issue. Maybe after a while they would also catch on to the name choice. Either way, it was best left for after the Christmas holiday.

"Good to hear it."

Chance stood and hesitated when he realized Tori was asleep.

"Her room's this way," Jenna said softly.

Chance picked up Tori, awkwardly cradling her against his chest. And the sight of her daughter held so tenderly in his arms, the look on his face, gave Jenna the courage she needed to forge ahead. She could face the future so long as she had faith.

She opened the door wider when he approached and smiled at his somewhat awestruck expression. Sound asleep, Tori looked like an angel and the fact had obviously caught him off guard.

Inside Tori's messy room, Jenna pulled the covers back and waited while he lowered Tori to the mattress.

"Not even a flicker," Chance murmured. "She sleeps like you."

She wanted to add *and you* because she'd managed to sneak out while he slept but that would remind Chance of her departure.

After a final kiss on Mark's cheek, she shut his door and continued downstairs. She bent to pick up more tissue paper when Chance wrapped his arms around her from behind.

"Leave it."

"Snickers will get into it. I'd rather pick up ten pieces of paper instead of a hundred."

He exhaled roughly, the sound revealing every ounce of frustration he hadn't expressed the entire night spent with the kids, and began to quickly grab the tissue paper. "You stole my truck, woman. That's as bad as stealing a man's horse."

The statement caught her by surprise and she laughed. "Bruised ego?"

"What do you think? Liam found me naked in the den and informed me my truck was gone," he muttered.

She winced. "I'm sorry. I just didn't know what else to do."

Chance caught her arm and turned her to face him. "You could've stayed. I would've driven you home."

She pictured that and grimaced. "Not a good idea," she said, watching as his expression tightened, "but maybe next time?"

CHANCE STARED INTO Jenna's face and fought a lifetime of insecurities. With her promise of next time he knew he was making progress with her, so why did he suddenly feel as though he was on a ledge with nowhere to go?

She fingered the material of his shirt, her teeth worrying her lower lip until he wanted to kiss her and make her stop.

"I've been doing a lot of thinking today. I still want to take things slow and keep things quiet—for now. But I want to know more about you. Your story about Zane… How did you wind up in Children's Services?"

He looked away from her and glanced around her home. At the plants and dog, pictures of the kids upstairs. The stack of bills in a basket on a shelf. Once he told her there was no going back. But maybe this would be what kept him from wanting too much.

Chance wrapped her in his arms and kissed her until Jenna moaned. But knowing the kids were upstairs and could interrupt at any moment, he pulled away and shifted so that her back was to his front, his lips against her temple. So he couldn't see her eyes, her face, when he told her. "You asked me once if my father was dead," he said softly. "He's not. He's in prison, and has served twenty-four years of a life sentence with no parole."

He felt her stiffen against him.

"Oh, Chance, I'm sorry. That's why you were put up for adoption?"

Staring into the multicolored lights glowing from within the recesses of the tree, he inhaled. "No. Long story short—when Zane decided he wanted to adopt us, he went to the prison and my father signed over his rights. Until then I was shipped from house to house in foster care, or else in the boys' home near here."

"Do you see him?"

Every damn day.

He saw his father's face every time he closed his eyes to go to sleep. Especially recently. Shortly after Zane's death he and his brothers had gotten into a fight at the Honey and it had resurrected nightmares he'd thought long buried. All because he'd looked at his hands when the brawl was over and his knuckles were covered in blood.

Just like his old man's had been when the police had cuffed him.

That's why Chance had pushed himself so hard in PT. Zane's death, the fight. Even the story of the foster kid Liam was adopting had kept the nightmares alive and well. Not that they'd ever completely stopped.

How many times had his foster parents or the boys' home officials warned him that if he kept acting out, he would follow in his father's footsteps? How many times had he wondered if he already was? "I haven't seen him since the police took him away. Zane was the only man I'll ever claim as a father."

"That's understandable. I've only ever heard good things about Zane. I wish I could've met him."

He squeezed her tight, relishing the feel of her in his arms, the comfort her softness and scent gave to him.

"Why was it your first tree?"

"Just happened that way. Seems like in all the homes I was in, it either wasn't Christmas or the tree was already up when I got there. After Zane adopted us, Sally—the housekeeper—usually put up the tree."

"Zane didn't?"

"No. I think it reminded him too much of his wife, Noelle, and Gabriella. Sometimes the others would help Sally but...I never did."

Jenna leaned her head on his shoulder and snuggled against him. "Why?"

He was torn between staring at the mesmerizing lights on the tree, and staring at Jenna. "I guess because I learned not to count on it much."

"Christmas?"

"Yeah. Jenna, I was five. I'd say my prayers at night and ask for my mom to come back."

"Oh, Chance..."

"And then I watched my father turn into a monster. It all seemed like a bad dream but I couldn't wake up. I made a lot of wishes." He'd wished to go home, for it all to be over. For none of the things being said about his dad to be true. Wished for so many things. "I said my prayers like I was supposed to, and I stayed out of trouble but I didn't get what I asked for. It wasn't too long after that when I stopped."

"You lost faith."

Yeah, he had lost faith. His whole world had collapsed in a matter of months and no one seemed to care.

He tightened his arms around her and slid his hand into her hair. He loved her hair. Shoulder-length, it was mostly straight but curled on the ends, wrapping around his wrists whenever he held her.

"Tell me what you wished for."

Staring into her eyes, he drew her face to his. "It doesn't matter now."

"It does to me."

He brushed his lips over hers and watched as her eyes glazed a bit. Talk about a powerful feeling, being able to do that to a woman. And to be able to do that to Jenna?

He stroked her tongue with his, careful to keep things light. But light though it was, one kiss turned into several and his hand found her breast, squeezing lightly. She felt so good. "I should probably go."

Jenna's lashes hung low over her eyes and her lips were wet from their kisses. He pressed another to her mouth, wondering if anything could smell as good as she did—like pine and fruit and cookies. That mysterious fragrance that was just her.

He ended the long embrace with reluctance, and tugged her behind him as he walked to the door. Another kiss, this one to her forehead and he grabbed his coat and stepped out into the cold.

"Thank you again. For the tree."

"My pleasure. Wait, I have something else for you. Here." He handed her the photo and waited for her reaction.

"The kids looked so happy when they finally reached the top of that wall."

Yeah, they had. But then—so had she. "You like it?"

Jenna held the photo to her chest as though she cherished it and it made him feel good that he'd given it to her. "I love it."

Hearing that particular word pass her lips upped his blood pressure and did things to his insides he didn't want to ponder too closely. Not on the heels of the discussion about his father. Once she had time to think about all he'd told her, she'd probably continue to make excuses for not wanting to be seen together until she went to work at the school and things ended anyway. He had to be okay with that. "Good night, sweetheart."

"'Night."

Chance stepped off the porch, pausing in the darkness of her sidewalk to listen for the click of the latch before continuing to his truck. He started the engine, then made a point of sitting there with his lights on so her neighbors would note he wasn't spending the night.

He reversed out of her driveway but one last glance at the house had him hesitating. Jenna had stepped in front of the window by the tree and he could see her as she stared at the photo. She looked so pretty there in the glow of the lights.

And he knew this year he'd be making another wish.

CHAPTER TWENTY

JENNA WAS IN THE BREAK room getting her cooler from the locker for the kids' after-school snack when Chance pushed through the swing door and gave her a grin.

"Come here."

"Chance, they'll be here any second."

"Better hurry then."

"Dooley's out front," she said, holding up her hand to ward him off, as though that would help. Chance McKenna on a mission was unstoppable.

"That means he's not back here." Grinning, he pinned her against her locker and lowered his head for a voracious kiss that left her gasping.

After their discussion last night, every time she began to lecture herself about what could and could not be, the words stalled out, followed by, what if? What if Chance *was* different? What if with time and patience they could make it work? Chance seemed to be struggling with his emotions as much as she was.

"Mmm, remind me to feed you Mrs. Morton's peanut butter balls more often. You taste good."

"So do you." She laughed, unable to hold in her happiness. Maybe she should feel guilty for feeling this way but… "Chance—"

He put his finger over her mouth to silence her. "I know that tone. One day at a time, Jenna." Chance smoothed his palms over her hair, his thumbs gently following the arch of her cheekbones. He lowered his head and kissed her again, this one soft and slow and tender, lingering.

She closed her eyes and leaned into him. If only—

"Mom?"

Mark. Jenna pulled away just in time. Mark walked through the door followed closely by Tori. But unlike her son's oblivious gaze, Tori's held way too much maturity and knowing speculation.

"Um, hi, guys. How was school? You hungry?"

"I am," Mark said.

"You're always hungry," Jenna teased.

"A growing boy," Chance added.

"Can we watch TV after we get our homework done?" Mark asked.

"Oh, I don't know. I don't know if Chance—"

"I don't mind. After your homework is done." Chance smiled at Tori. "Tori, you, too."

"He watches stupid science stuff."

"Better than stupid girl shows."

"But no TV unless you get along," Chance corrected. "You two can take turns picking the show but while the other show is on, you have to promise not to do anything disruptive to ruin it."

"Whatever," Tori said, rolling her eyes.

"Tori." Jenna gave her daughter a quelling stare.

"What? He's giving us orders and he's not our dad. Why do we have to do anything he says?"

"Apologize, right now," Jenna said.

"Why should I?"

"Because you are being very rude to my boss and that is not acceptable."

"But it's okay to *kiss* your boss? He's wearing your lip gloss."

The air rushed from Jenna's lungs. She faltered, her attention divided between her children. Tori's all-knowing displeasure and Mark's— Jenna couldn't believe the hope she saw shining on Mark's face. "I— I—"

Chance drew her attention when he wiped his thumb over his mouth. "Tori, your mom deserves your respect, not that tone of voice. Yes, we were kissing but that's between us adults and not up for discussion by you."

Jenna turned her head to glare at Chance so fast her neck popped. *"Chance."*

He gave her an apologetic glance. "Better to be honest with them than lie, Jenna. And we were caught red-handed," he added for her ears only.

"Yeah, Mom, you always tell us to tell the truth," Tori challenged.

"Tori, that is enough," Chance said. His order managed to close Tori's mouth, whereas Jenna's warning had gone unheeded.

"So, here's the deal. I kissed your mom," Chance said, staring directly at Mark. "Because I— I really like your mom a lot and I want to get to know her better."

"Cool," Mark said.

"Thanks, buddy. You're pretty cool yourself."

Jenna waited for Tori's response, wondering if she dared to hope for something positive.

"You're not ever going to be our dad."

"Tori, be nice," Mark said. "It's okay, Chance. We know why Mom likes you."

Jenna's nails bit into her palms and she struggled to breathe.

"If she likes you, it's only because you're so much like our *dad*," Tori argued.

"Victoria, that is not true," Jenna said, knowing

now wasn't the time or the place to have a discussion about her feelings for Chance when she wasn't sure of Chance's feelings for her, other than that he desired her.

But the fact remained that Chance and Jeff were different in so many ways, and she felt bad for comparing them.

Chance removed his hand from Jenna's shoulder, avoiding her gaze.

"Wait," she said. "I'm only going to say this once, Tori, and I want you to listen up. Chance and your father shared some of the same hobbies but they aren't the same man. There's no need for you to be disrespectful."

"Whatever," Tori said, turning on her heel to leave. "I have to do my homework."

Jenna stared at the swinging door. The fact that Tori *wanted* to do her homework to escape spoke volumes. But the store wasn't the place to have this discussion. She needed to talk to Tori and Mark about what had taken place, but what would she say? It *was* happening fast.

Too soon?

Guilt stirred as it always did but this time it surfaced because it didn't *feel* too soon. This thing with Chance actually felt right. Maybe if she asked Chance to spend some time over Christmas with them Tori would let down her guard enough to... What?

Let Chance in?

"I have some things to do in the office," Chance said, heading in that direction without so much as a glance at her.

"You okay, Mom?"

She stared into Mark's eyes and smiled, ignoring the confusing mix of doubts and fears and worries over what had taken place. No matter what unfolded between her and Chance, she was a mother first, the twins' only surviving parent, and she couldn't forget it. "I'm fine. Let's get you something to eat."

LATER THAT NIGHT, Jenna knocked on Tori's bedroom door and let herself in, careful not to notice the way Tori shoved her much-loved stuffed animal under the covers. Tori had stopped carrying Mrs. Wiggles not long after Jeff's death but tonight she was tucked into bed beside her. "Hey. Teeth brushed?"

"Yeah. 'Night, Mom."

Jenna chose not to take the hint and stepped deeper into the room. Beneath the covers, Tori's hand shoved something a little farther down. "I wanted to talk to you, about what you said to Chance."

A mulish frown pulled Tori's lower lip to full pout mode.

"Why were you so rude to him today?" she asked her daughter. A shrug was her answer. "Come on, I know you can do better than that. Does Chance remind you that much of Dad?"

"No. Not really."

Surprised by Tori's answer, Jenna was at a loss as to what to say next.

"I saw the picture," Tori said, "the one of us on Dad's birthday, climbing."

Jenna sat on the side of Tori's bed. "I put that in my room. What were you doing in there?" After too many incidences with water balloons, gum, paint spills and food stains, she'd established a rule about the twins sticking to the other areas of the house and staying out of her bedroom unless she was in there with them.

Tori's face grew splotchy with a torrid blush. "I had to get something."

"Oh?"

"From the cabinet."

The cabinet? The *cabinet?* "A pad?" Tori would turn eleven next month, and the mood swings, the temper and the tears... Jenna had known it was coming but— "Are you okay? You took care of things?"

Tori nodded and drew her knees up and Jenna straightened on the bed to give Tori room, but a glance gave Jenna a better idea of how upsetting the day been for her little girl. Mrs. Wiggle's ruffled bloomers peaked out from beneath Tori's purple sheet but the *thing* Tori had been hiding when Jenna had walked in the room— "Your body book," she whispered, referencing the book purchased to help answer the questions Tori was too embarrassed to ask. "Oh, Tori, if you'd only told me. Were you scared?"

Tori launched herself against Jenna's chest, her thin arms nearly strangling her.

"I *hate* it. I hate it and I don't wanna be a *girl.*"

"Shh, it's okay," she said, beginning that gentle rocking motion every mother knew to do from the moment she held a child in her arms. "It'll be okay."

"No, it won't. It's *horrible.* I forgot what you said and when I saw it at school I thought I was *dying.*"

Jenna squeezed her eyes shut at the word, the image so painful she couldn't breathe for several seconds. She couldn't bear the thought of ever losing either of her children. Over a year after Jeff's death Karen still struggled and no wonder.

Jenna needed to be more empathetic, but she had to stand firm about her desire to move forward. However that happened. "Were you upset at school today, too?"

"Yeah. Kenzie's mad at me now but I don't care. I told her in secret and she told *every*one."

No. "Everyone?"

A sob rocked Tori's chest. "All the g-girls. I'm the first one and all the girls were whispering about me."

"Oh, baby, I'm so sorry." She focused on the feel of her daughter in her arms, the smell of her hair and the way she held on. "Just remember what I told you, okay? Every healthy girl gets a period and no one likes it but once you get used to how things work, you learn to deal with it. Do you remember what it means?"

"Yeah. But I don't ever want to have a baby."

Fighting her emotions, Jenna hugged Tori tighter. "Babies are precious. I can't imagine my life without you and Mark. It'll be okay. I promise. Do you have any questions?"

Like thousands of times before, Tori wiped her tears on Jenna's shirt. "Does it really happen *every* month?"

"'Fraid so."

"This *sucks*."

Tori seemed to be okay talking about it so long as she kept her face buried. "I know. But one day you'll understand how wonderful it can be. We can do things no boy can do," she said, trying to appeal to Tori's competitive side.

"So do you like Chance? Enough to kiss him?"

The abrupt change of topic threw her momentarily. And answering the tough questions never got any easier. "Yeah, I do," she said, forcing herself to be honest. "Do you?"

"I don't know. I miss Dad."

"I know you do. That's why I haven't said much about Chance."

"But you *kissed* him," Tori said.

"Yes, but friendship is different for adults, Tori. What you need to remember is that no matter what happens, I love you, and I'll always do what is best for you." Jenna kissed the top of Tori's head and lowered her daughter onto the mattress, smiling at the drowsy innocence that disappeared beneath the attitude when Tori was fully awake.

"Will Dad be mad if we like Chance?"

"No. I think your dad would completely understand. He liked Chance enough to consider him a friend."

"But what if Chance falls when he's climbing? Like Dad? What if he dies? Aren't you scared? That'll make you sad again."

Jenna smoothed her hand over Tori's soft hair. "It would make me very sad. And, yes, I'm a little scared, too. But I think knowing what we've been through will make Chance very careful when he climbs." She smiled at her daughter. "So are we good?"

Tori nodded and cuddled beneath the blanket.

"Good night, Tori." Jenna shut Tori's bedroom door with a soft click but leaned against the wall outside, their conversation slowly sinking in.

Was she scared?

No.

She was terrified.

"DUDE, LONG TIME NO SEE."

Chance turned from where he salted the sidewalk outside the store on Friday to see Vic and Dillon Sayer grinning at him from within Vic's Jeep. "Hey. What are you two doing here?" he asked, approaching the vehicle.

"We heard you're back in the game, so we thought we'd swing by. Came up to visit the grandparents but wanted to let you know we're scrapin' some ice over Christmas if you want to join up," Vic said.

The mere mention of an ice climb sent Chance's blood gushing through his veins a little faster. But as quickly came the awareness of the timing. Jenna had yet to say a word about her plans for Christmas, but he was really going to turn down a chance to climb *in case* Jenna asked him to spend Christmas with them? "Where you headed?"

He battled the urge to say yes. He'd put his trip to Nevada on hold until after the holidays, but maybe a trip closer to home wasn't out of the question. Especially since this would be his first opportunity for a real climb in months.

"Bozeman," Dillon said from the passenger seat.

"Whoa, dude, check it out," Vic said, pointing to something, then giving Chance a surprised look. "You mean, it's true?"

"What?" he asked, turning to see Jenna bent over as she retrieved a wreath from the ground where the wind gusts had knocked it off the display.

"You and Jeff's wife?" Vic said. "Remind me not to leave you alone with my girlfriend."

Chance braced his hands on Vic's lowered window and leaned closer so his words wouldn't carry to where Jenna worked. "Watch your mouth. Jenna *works* here. She's one of my employees."

"Hey, Chance, no offense. Just making an observation. So, you coming to climb with us or not?"

"I'll have to let you know." It was a lackluster response, but Vic had ticked him off.

His comment was proof that people were talking. Proof that Jenna was smart to be wary. And even though Chance was long overdue to try his skills on a mountain face, something held him back.

"That's cool. Just give me or Dillon a call. Catch you later."

"Yeah." Chance lifted his chin in goodbye as the brothers sped off the lot, noting the way Vic's head turned as he passed Jenna.

Chance spread the salt with a little more force, aware of Jenna's approach.

"What was the dynamic duo up to?"

Jenna was bundled against the cold and wearing one of his hats because she'd forgotten her own, but even layered and mismatched she looked beautiful.

"They heard my cast was off and invited me to go on a climb over Christmas," he said. "I'm thinking of taking them up on it."

"I see."

"You don't want me to go?" He hoped she'd give him a straight answer. If she had issues with him climbing, they had to be settled.

"Not with that group. You'll wind up hurt again."

"You don't think I have enough common sense to go anywhere unless you're there to keep me in line?" He resented that her opinion made him seem too much like his father, unable to control himself or his actions.

Unease tightened his gut into a hard knot.

"No. I just want you to be safe," she said, not looking at him. "You don't need my permission or consent. Go. Have fun."

"Don't be a wise-ass," he said, losing his patience.

"Me? Wise? How *wise* is it to go climbing when you just got your cast off?"

"My foot is fine."

"Fine," she repeated, her nostrils flaring with her inhalations.

The school bus appeared at the stoplight and turned

with a loud squeak of the brakes. The kids were there and Chance knew Jenna wouldn't want the twins getting off the bus to find them arguing. He didn't want it, either. "You know who I am, Jenna. What I do. That's not going to change. We can't argue about climbing every time it comes up."

"I know."

"You can't expect me to give it up," he added.

"I don't," she whispered, swallowing. "I know it's a part of you and so long as we are...together...I have to accept that."

Did she mean that? Could she truly accept that? "Vic said something that makes me think people are talking."

Jenna winced and tucked her blowing hair behind her ear, under the cap. "It'll blow over." She paused. "Chance, I can't tell you what to do but I hope you won't go on that trip."

Every muscle in his body tensed. He'd known it was coming. "Why not?"

She gazed into his face, her expression intense. "Because it's Christmas, and I heard about your family's plans at the wedding. Gabriella and Carly are making a big dinner for you and your brothers. They want you there. *Home.*"

Unwanted disappointment barreled through him as she walked away. Jenna didn't want him to go—but not so he could spend Christmas with her and the kids. Come to think of it, she'd probably spend Christmas with the Darlingtons. Everybody and their big, old happy families.

He tossed another handful of salt. Nevada was looking better and better.

CHAPTER TWENTY-ONE

DESPITE ZANE'S DEATH, the McKenna Christmas party went ahead on Saturday as planned. Apparently in years past he had held the gathering for his ranch hands, as well as the employees at the store, and according to Dooley, Gabriella and Brad wanted the tradition continued.

The party was surprisingly fun and well attended. Most of the employees and their families were gathered in the living room around the piano. Guitars had been carried in along with the covered dishes, and the chatter that filled the house was highlighted by the light strains of old trail songs and Christmas melodies.

After her words with Chance over climbing, Jenna wasn't in a particularly festive mood but she couldn't cancel because she refused to let Chance think she was upset about his decision. She knew who he was. She just didn't know why he felt so compelled to test his body that way.

She leaned against a wall in the living room near the door, her gaze drawn to Chance. He stood across the room with his brothers and talked with Sally, the longtime housekeeper, and her fiancé. They were an odd pairing—Sally, a bulky woman about six feet tall and him, maybe five-feet-six and as thin as a rail. But anyone with eyes could see the love the couple shared. All dressed up in her Christmas finery, Sally was on the receiving end of quite a few heated glances from her man.

"Would you like one? They're absolutely delicious," Gabriella asked, holding out a platter.

Jenna patted her already stuffed stomach and declined. "If I eat anything else, you might have to roll me out of here."

Gabriella's eyes twinkled. "Okay, but I'll be back with more goodies in a bit. Just warning you."

Jenna smiled and groaned, playing along. When Gabriella was gone, Jenna took a sip of her eggnog and felt someone watching her. She searched the room until her gaze locked with Chance's and her entire body went on full alert. Oh, how the man unnerved her.

Chance said something to his companions and looked as though he was about to excuse himself. To come talk to her?

Jenna quickly retreated into the hallway and made a beeline for the kitchen. Thankfully it was empty.

"Can I help you find something?"

"A spot of courage, maybe?" She turned to face Chance, catching him in the act of giving her body a complete and thorough once-over.

Always cold, she'd worn her typical layers. A lace-edged cami, a long-sleeved black sweater T-shirt that trimmed her waist and never went out of style, along with comfortable jeans and her favorite black suede boots. As a whole outfit, *enticing* wasn't the word she'd use to describe it but the expression Chance wore made her feel as though she was about to hit a runway dressed in nothing but lingerie.

"You want something stronger than the eggnog?" he asked, obviously not following.

"Yeah," she said, nodding a little too vigorously in her giddiness to get it all out there. "I want you."

Uncaring if anyone was behind him in the hall, she rose onto her tiptoes and brushed her lips over his. She kept the kiss light, casual, but in an instant Chance pinned her to the counter and deepened the caress, drawing the kiss out so long her head began to spin.

He kissed her again. And again. Until their breathing grew labored and Chance's hand slid beneath her sweater and slid beneath her tank. The burning swipe of his thumb against her skin had her lifting herself onto her toes to be closer to him. Chance pressed her against the cabinets, one hand moving to her leg to lift it so that she felt all of him.

"Daddy."

The child's terrified shout and the sound of utter chaos in the house brought them back to awareness like a dunk in an icy lake.

Chance let her leg lower but before he could even move, the party seemed to stampede into the kitchen.

"Riley, what's wrong?"

Ducking behind Chance's chest to regain control of her senses, she recognized Liam McKenna's voice.

"She's hurt!"

"Who's hurt?" Carly asked.

"The girl—Tori. Mark's tryin' to save her!"

"ANY WORD?" CHANCE asked, surging to his feet the moment he saw Liam striding down the hospital hallway toward him.

"You nailed it at the scene. Her shoulder was dislocated, broken collarbone and her wrist is badly sprained. Jarring and painful, but nothing time won't heal. The doctor said they're going to keep Tori overnight for observation, but she'll be released first thing in the morning."

"Thank God." He ran his hands over his head and face, resisting the urge to sit because his legs felt weak. He still couldn't get Tori's screams out of his head. Once she'd managed to get her breath back, the girl had screamed like nothing Chance had ever heard before or wanted to again.

Thanks to you and your stupid stories glorifying the rodeo.

"I should get out of here."

"Why?" Liam demanded.

"I saw Jeff's parents arrive," he said. The last thing he wanted was to cause Jenna more pain. "Tell Jenna to...call me if she needs me."

"You're leaving?"

He'd been so focused on his adoptive brother's list of Tori's injuries that he'd missed Jenna joining them in the hall by the waiting area.

Liam patted Chance on the shoulder and gave him a stern yet pitying look. "Remember it's her kid in there and she needs you," Liam said before walking away.

"How are you?" he asked.

Jenna looked like hell. Her eye makeup had smudged, and she was pale as a ghost from worry. "Better now that I know she'll be okay."

His guilt thickened, burying him even deeper. "What can I do?"

"Hold me?"

Jenna stepped close but Chance made no move to take her into his arms. Some things a hug couldn't fix.

"Chance, please, it's okay. I told Jeff's parents about us."

"You shouldn't have done that."

She blinked up at him. "They asked where I was when it happened and I didn't want to lie." She gave him a weak smile, shrugging. "It's not like all those people didn't see us. It's fine. Karen is very upset, but she'll get over it."

That was unlikely. "Jenna, do you *know* what Tori was trying to do?"

She swallowed audibly. "You know I do. We were both there when the boys told us."

They were but with everyone crowded around and Tori screaming, he'd wondered if Jenna had heard why Tori had tried to ride that horse. *She'd intended to stand up on it.* "Then it's obvious why I shouldn't be here. I wanted to make sure she's okay but—"

"But what? You don't have to deal with the fallout? Chance, you didn't put Tori on that horse. My daughter has a mind of her own."

"And right now she needs you."

"Well, I need you."

"I think tonight proves I'm the last thing you or your kids need," he said.

"What are you saying?"

The color drained from her face and he felt like more of a monster. "We said it would last as long as we wanted it to last, Jenna. Your new job starts in two weeks when the kids go back to school. Take the time off to care for Tori and consider it paid vacation."

"Chance..." A breath huffed out of her lungs. "You're serious."

He forced himself to nod. "I am. Two weeks vacation. I'll send your check to the house," he said, ignoring the way she looked at him, because he knew he was hurting her and his guilt was eating him alive. But it was better to do this now. Before anyone else got hurt.

Before either of twins pulled another stunt to be like him. "I've already talked to the hospital. The expenses are covered so if you get a bill, refer them to me."

"What are you doing?" she asked softly. "You're leaving? Now? *Look at me.*"

Chance ran his hand through his hair and pulled hard. "You told me you didn't want the kids acting like Jeff, to have his impulsiveness. *I* am responsible for tonight, Jenna. You had it right all along. I should've stayed away from you and the kids." He turned to walk toward the elevator.

"But you didn't," she said as she followed him. "And what about all that stuff you said to me? About *wanting* me? Wanting to be with me? Was that a lie?"

"No."

"What about how you're not like Jeff?" she continued. "Because this is something he would do. All I ever had to do was say the kids had the sniffles and he made an excuse to leave the house because he didn't want to deal with it, couldn't handle it. He loved them, I know that, but it terrified him when they were sick because he felt helpless. So he left it all to me."

"I'm sorry," he said, punching the elevator button. "You have no idea how much."

"Chance, you *are* different than Jeff, and you're nothing like your father. Yet you're running away from your fears and problems anyway. You're acting like them."

"Don't compare me," he said, the walls closing in on him. He'd had this conversation before with Zane. About how he had to stop running when the pressure got bad. But he was suffocating, and only one thing would take that feeling away.

"Why not?" she demanded, growing loud enough to draw the attention of a nearby orderly. "Isn't that what you're doing? Chance, I'm scared, too, but real men don't leave. For years I was upset with my father because he wouldn't bring me home to the States after my mother's death. But I realize he was following through on the mission he and my mother started together. He knew I would go to college if I didn't wind up with Jeff so he stuck by my mother the only way he could. And by adopting you Zane *stuck it out* and fulfilled the responsibility he had to the family he'd made when he took you in."

"And what about my father? That's the example I know, Jenna. Stop romanticizing things. Happily-ever-afters only exist in books. Tori could've *died* tonight. You could be planning your daughter's funeral right now and if that were the case, *you'd be blaming me.*"

He barely kept from swearing at the elevator when it dinged but the door took too long to open. Finally it did and he stepped on but then had to turn and face Jenna one last time.

"Did you put them on a sled out in the street that first day? Chance, my children need someone able to teach them how to balance fun and safety, and for the record, I don't *want* a fantasy with a prince or some flipping tiara. You know what I want? I want someone brave enough to help me pick up the pieces when things go wrong because I'm *tired* of always having to do it myself." She shook her head, disgust on her face. "If you can't handle that, then you're right. You should go. I need the man I see, not the one you think you are."

She turned away with one last look over her shoulder as the elevator doors closed.

Liam was waiting for him when Chance exited the elevator amid the ground-level waiting room.

"You okay?"

He didn't slow his stride but kept going, out the hospital doors, and welcomed the bitter cold wind on his face. He wanted to punch something, climb something. "Yeah."

"Whatever she said, ignore it. Give her time to calm down, and go talk to her again. Her kid is lying in a hospital bed. Cut her some slack."

If Liam knew what had gone down, Chance was sure another punch would be headed his way. So he kept his mouth shut and hoped his brother would get the hint and back off.

"Where you headed?" Liam asked.

"I don't know." Chance climbed into his truck and jabbed the keys into the ignition. He gunned the engine, the itch to be anywhere but there stronger than it had been.

CHANCE PACKED UP HIS GEAR and got out of town as quickly as possible, seeking solace from the only thing to give him peace and calm.

But this time that peace, the sheer joy he felt when he climbed wasn't to be found. And after two sleepless nights dreaming of Jenna and hearing her accusation that he was running away, he swung listlessly from a rope, lacking the energy to reach the top because he was so bitterly aware that Jenna was right. He was running. From the past, from what he felt about it and what had happened. From the monster he feared lurked inside him. But the only way to end the fear was to face it.

And that meant sitting face-to-face with the man locked behind prison walls.

Chance had left the eight Rock Gods gathered to climb behind and hiked out of the canyon alone, driven all night to Deer Lodge, only to discover a background check and three days' notice were required for all visitors.

After checking into a nearby motel, he'd spent three days pacing the floor trying to figure out if seeing his father was really the answer. Chance still wasn't sure. But a phone call to Liam had pulled some strings and rushed the background check, while the sheriff had called the warden—a buddy from way back—and finished the job until all that was left was to wait for visiting hours to begin. Still, Chance had sat outside the prison gates unable to find the courage to go in. Finally it dawned on him that he couldn't return to North Star or be with Jenna unless he followed through on what he had come to do.

That was how Chance came to be one of three people sitting in the hard plastic chairs opposite the glass window in the visitor's room on Christmas Eve.

For most of his life, his father's actions had held him captive. He'd had nightmares for years—still did—and every time he got angry or felt closed in, he thought about that night and wondered if his old man's DNA was surfacing.

Chance had closed himself off, kept his distance. Afraid to get too close to anyone because... Because he might hurt them.

On the other side of the glass, a door opened inside a gray room. A guard entered first, followed by three men dressed in orange jumpsuits, hands shackled in front of them. Another guard brought up the rear.

The men lined up and the guards said something to the offenders, no doubt instructions. Chance searched what he could see of their faces, looking for something that would identify his father. One of the men was obviously younger than Chance by a good five years or more. But the other two… Both appeared to be in their fifties, both gray, both lined and aged.

Then Chance locked gazes with one of the men and any question of identity fled his mind because of the way the inmate stared at him. He wasn't sure what kind of reaction to expect, considering it had been twenty-four years since they had last seen each other, but the steady gaze and grim expression wasn't it.

Keith Stark was slower than the other inmates to take the seat opposite, his gaze searching Chance's face.

With some amazement, Chance realized Stark wasn't the monster he remembered from that night so long ago. In fact, Stark didn't even look like a killer. He was average height, average weight, average looks.

His father slowly reached both hands out and picked up the phone on his side of the glass. Chance did the same, even though he had no idea what to say. He'd simply wanted to see Keith Stark and put an end to the questions in his mind. To *stop running* as Jenna said.

"You resemble her," Stark said into the phone. "You look like your mother."

That was a welcome statement. "I wouldn't know. I don't remember what she looks like."

When he'd been taken into custody by Children's Services, he'd had nothing but the clothes on his back. No pictures, no stuffed animals. His father had hustled him out of the house that night, desperate for a drink and when Chance had dropped his favorite stuffed dog by the door, Stark hadn't allowed him to pick it up.

An awkward silence extended, broken only by the bits of conversation taking place with the other two visitors.

"You grew up big for such a little guy. You look good. Healthy and strong."

Chance sat there, unable to carry on a conversation.

His father inhaled and when he released his breath the phone crackled with static. "Zane doing okay? He hasn't been in to see me for a while."

"Zane visited you?" Chance asked, unable to hide his surprise.

"Came every few months. Ever since I signed those papers." The man's gaze sharpened. "He was good to you?"

The plastic handset grew hot and sweaty beneath Chance's palm. "Yeah, he was. You did the right thing. That time," he couldn't help but add.

His father's stare never faltered. "Why are you here? Twenty-four years is a long time to suddenly decide to visit."

"I need to know why you did it."

Stark blinked a few times before shaking his head. "You don't need to hear excuses."

"Tell me anyway," he said.

"I was stupid. I let my anger get the best of me. I always had a hot temper that was quick to flash but after your mother passed... You probably remember how bad things got there right before."

Yeah, he did. That's just it. He remembered the bad, not the good. And crystal clear in the mix was his father's defining moment.

"It wasn't intentional. What I did. I'd come out to check on you and I saw him hit her and all hell broke loose. Then I couldn't undo it."

"You killed a man with your bare hands."

"Yeah. I did."

One glance said Stark wasn't sorry for it, either.

"I did wrong, and I know I deserve to be here, but you deserved better. When McKenna showed up and said he wanted to adopt you, I knew what I had to do. I wanted to give you better than you'd gotten from me."

"Zane's dead," Chance said, the words spilling from his mouth and bringing a slew of emotions with them. Things he hadn't let himself feel.

"I'm sorry to hear that. He seemed like a good man."

"He was," Chance said, a lump growing thick in his throat until he cleared it.

"Zane said you liked the ladies. You got a girl?"

An image of Jenna immediately filled his head. "Not anymore."

"You tell her about me?"

He nodded once.

"Why?"

Because he thought it would keep Jenna away? "I wanted to be honest," he said simply.

"So is that what this visit is about?"

"Some. But it is more about me." He'd needed to exorcise his demons, to know he wasn't his father's son. "Would you do it again?"

Stark's lips pulled back over his teeth as he made a face. "Yeah, I probably would. Seeing that idiot abuse his woman when mine had been taken from me… The man deserved to die. I wasn't ever a saint. I just hated that you got caught in the middle."

"Five minutes," the guard on Chance's side of the enclosure called out.

"Go back to your girl and tell her you love her. Buy her something pretty for Christmas. She'll forgive you."

It was what he wanted to do but after walking out on her, how could he expect Jenna to let him back into her life? "I don't believe in Christmas miracles."

Stark didn't move. "I do."

CHAPTER TWENTY-TWO

AFTER TORI'S RELEASE from the hospital Sunday afternoon, Jenna spent the next four days dispensing pain medication, snuggling and trying to disguise her broken heart. Tori's room was filled with flowers, balloons and stuffed animals sent by friends and family. The McKennas had even sent a basket of candy Tori grudgingly shared with Mark.

It was when Rachel came over every night for a few minutes that Jenna was able to vent about getting involved with Chance.

By Christmas Eve, Jenna was exhausted and even more heartbroken because she'd honestly thought she would have heard *something* from Chance. Worse still was the fact that Tori and Mark asked about Chance every day, and Jenna was tired of changing the subject or making excuses, hoping Chance might show up.

Jenna tucked her daughter into bed and turned off the bedside lamp, aware of Mark's shadow in the hallway outside the door.

"Is Chance coming over tomorrow?" Mark asked, much too hopeful. Even in the dark illuminated by the hall light, she could make out Mark shoving his glasses up his nose.

"No, Chance isn't coming over. You'll see him around town sometime, I'm sure."

"What if we want to go see him?" Mark asked. "Can we?"

How did you explain life and relationships and break-ups to children? "Do you remember the night Dad died? How we got the phone call, and we went to the hospital?"

"I was scared," Mark said.

"We were all scared," she whispered. "You guys are growing up so fast. You're not little kids anymore, so I'm going to be very honest with you right now, okay? Chance and I were seeing each other—dating—but we're not anymore."

"Because he climbs? Because I don't want to get another one of those phone calls," Tori said.

"Me, either," Jenna whispered, "but that's not why. Not entirely."

"I like Chance, but I don't want you to be sad," Tori said in a very adult voice.

"I don't, either. But you *did* like him," Mark said. "Right?"

"Yes. I did."

"Were you falling in love?" Tori asked.

Images flooded Jenna's mind. Chance dressed up as Santa. Chance kissing her on the ladder. Chance making love to her. But talking in the past tense hammered the proverbial nail. "Yes, but one person can't love enough for two people, and Chance… He needs to figure out some things. Now, it's bedtime. Santa won't be coming if you're not asleep."

"*Mom,* we know Santa's not real."

"You sure about that? Really?" There was just enough doubt in the silence that followed her statement to bring a smile. "That's what I thought. Kisses," she said, smooching both of them, "hugs, tickles."

"That is so lame."

"Hey, it's Christmas. Give me a break here."

"Do Christmas wishes come true?" Mark asked.

Jenna immediately thought of Chance's story about his childhood Christmases and frowned. "Not always, sweetheart."

"But maybe?"

"Maybe," she whispered, praying the twins received their wishes for—

Oh, no. No, no, no.

She'd stored Mark's Big Green Fishing Machine in Chance's apartment at work for safekeeping and with the events of the past week, she'd forgotten to get it. How could she have let that happen?

"Can I sleep in Tori's spare bed? Like we used to?"

"Tori?" she asked, her mind scrambling to figure out how to get into the store with Chance gone. Dooley lived too far away, Brad was out at the ranch. Maybe Liam.

"I don't care. It *is* Christmas. Can Snickers stay, too?"

Jenna nodded, distracted. "Sure. But on Mark's bed so she doesn't jostle your collarbone."

"Come on, Snickers," Mark said, patting the bed. "Come on!"

Snickers leaped onto the bed with so much doggy delight Jenna laughed and stood, trying not to rush too much as she moved toward the door. "'Night, guys. I love you."

Closing it behind her, she leaned against the wood. What was she going to do now? She'd managed to ruin Christmas after all.

Five minutes later, Jenna still couldn't believe she'd made such a mistake as she stared at the phone and debated on whether or not to call Chance. Maybe he had come back to town to spend Christmas with his family.

What could she say? *I miss you. I like you. And oh, can you bring Mark's gift to me, because I forgot it and it's Christmas?*

Jenna moaned and rubbed her hands over her face.

Figure it out fast because you're calling. She snagged the phone off the base and dialed Chance's cell number but got his voicemail.

Perfect.

"Chance, it's me—Jenna. I'm sorry to call so late but Mark's present is at your place and— Please give me a call as soon as you get this message and tell me the best way of going about getting it before…tomorrow. I'm sorry, I— Bye."

She pressed End and tossed the phone aside to get the phone book when she heard a noise and saw a shadow lurking outside Rachel's house. What the—

Jenna rushed to the window to get a better look. The person across the street looked like Scrooge dressed in a nightdress. "Rachel, what on *earth?*"

She shoved her feet into snow boots, grabbed her coat and the closest throw and headed out into the cold. "Rachel, what are you doing?" she called, careful to keep her voice low in an effort not to wake the neighbors.

Rachel was indeed dressed in her nightgown and snow boots. Tears streamed down her cheeks but she'd positioned the ladder in front of her house.

"I figured it out."

Jenna wrapped the throw around Rachel's shoulders. "You're going to freeze out here. Let's go inside."

"No, I have to put them up. Jenna, stop."

For the first time, Jenna noticed Rachel had a long

strand of Christmas lights draped over her shoulder. "What? Rach, you're scaring me here. What is going on?"

"I was looking through old photos from when I was a kid. I found one of the house, all decked out. That's what Mom was trying to tell me that day, when she got so upset. She was trying to tell me that I hadn't done it right. Dad always put lights around the upstairs window."

"Oh, *Rach*."

The note of sympathy in her voice must have triggered another flow of tears. Rachel's shoulders shook as she sobbed. "I'm going to have to put my mom in a home, Jenna. A *home*. I have to make this Christmas perfect."

All week, Jenna had been so wrapped up in herself and her problems with Chance and Tori and her in-laws she'd forgotten all about the ticking clock Rachel faced. "Rach, I understand, but it's ten degrees out here."

"It's going to be her last Christmas." The lights clinked together. "I have to go up there. I have to put these on so she can see them."

"Hon, what are the odds that she'll understand?"

"She will. I know she will."

"Fine. But you're not going anywhere. I'll do it. Give me the lights. I'm serious," she said when Rachel just stood there and looked at her. "You're too upset to be on the ladder, and you don't like heights anyway. I'll do it. Even though we said no gifts and I know you bought me something so consider this is my gift to you, okay? Give me the lights and show me the picture of what it's supposed to look like. I'll put them up for you."

Oh, poor Rach. Still more tears flowed down her cheeks. "I'm sorry I'm such a mess."

Remembering her reaction when her mother remained missing after the mudslide, Jenna thought Rachel was handling her mother's slow descent into Alzheimer's very well. "It's what happens when we love."

Sniffling and wiping at her tears, Rachel shakily reached into her pocket and pulled out the picture.

"This is it."

Jenna's heart sank. She'd hoped the photo would show the lights tacked up inside the window. Instead they lined the outer dormer from the base of the slanting roof to the peak of the dormer and down the other side. And the only way to put them up was by climbing that ladder.

That really, *really* high ladder.

"Okay, then," she murmured, "here we go."

She made sure the ladder was secure before she began the climb, each step on the rungs carefully placed. She made it all the way to the porch roof before she made the mistake of glancing down.

Suddenly in her head the only thing that existed was the word, the feeling, the total being, of faith. If she could keep her faith despite the tests, things changed.

Using the staple gun Rachel had handed to her, Jenna looped her arms through the ladder and began on the right side and inched her way higher up the dormer, one staple and a few clear lights at a time. It was so cold her teeth chattered but she kept going, kept praying.

You can do this. A few more lights and then you're on your way down again. That's it, a few more.

She topped the dormer, began the descent, the staple gun echoing against the house with every pull of the trigger. Hold the lights into place, staple. Lights in place, staple.

Finally she was done and she plugged the lights into the extension cord Rachel had already shoved out the dormer window.

"Oh, Jenna, they're beautiful!"

The joy in Rachel's voice warmed Jenna from the inside out. This was the meaning of Christmas. Not the lights or the presents but the joy, the happiness of love and friendship.

"Oh, thank you! Jenna, *thank you*."

Mighty happy now that she wasn't stretched toe to fingertip from the ladder to the dormer, she began her downward climb. Once she made it to the roof, she turned to face her friend, doing a little jig of success. "They are pretty, aren't they?"

"They're perfect!"

Smiling because Rachel was no longer crying, Jenna swung her upper body back toward the ladder. But her momentum carried her too far and she fell against the rungs. The staple gun caught on something, pulled at her coat and, because she was so prepared to step down another step, her balance was compromised and her foot slipped off entirely, her chin banging against a rung and rattling her brain.

"Jenna!"

Down she went in a rush of air and cold and adrenaline. It took only seconds but she had the presence of mind to know she was falling.

But in that instant, that *split-second-rush,* she remembered swinging from a threadbare rope over a watering hole in Africa. Soaring, flying, falling. Splashing. And a laugh bubbled out of her chest.

Then she hit the ground.

JENNA BLINKED HER EYES open and watched, dazed, while the most beautiful snowflakes filled the air. They were so big and white and fluffy.

Rachel dropped down beside her and snow scattered over half of Jenna's face as a result. "Jenna? Jenna, are you okay?"

"Jenna!"

She thought she heard Chance calling her name but, no. She had to be imagining things.

It took her a long moment before she could take a deep breath but the cold of the snow hitting her in the face helped clear the haze. Once she managed to breathe, once the dazed feeling wore off and she realized she'd performed a summersault mid air before landing in the snowdrift lining Rachel's house, she grinned.

"Jenna?"

She blinked the face hovering over hers into focus. *Santa Claus?*

Another blink brought clarity. And laughter.

"Go call a squad."

The order to get help brought out full-blown cackles. Maybe she'd finally lost it but she couldn't stop laughing. All these years of suppressing her inner wild child and a tumble from the roof had brought her out in force.

"Jenna."

"I'm okay," she said, barely able to get the words out.

"You're sure?"

"Yes." Years. Years and *years* of playing it safe because Jeff had always been the one messing around and tempting fate and here she'd fallen off a ladder—the equivalent of falling off a cliff. "I'm fine. Especially since you're here," she whispered, rolling into a sitting position. Oh, yeah, she'd feel it tomorrow but right now? "I'm okay."

"You might have broken something. What the hell were you doing up there?"

She made a quick assessment of potential injuries. Sore, sore, ow, sore, but nothing broken. "I'm not hurt. And I was putting up lights for Rachel."

"Lights? Tonight?" Chance's head swung back and forth as he eyed the two of them.

"It was my Christmas present," Rachel stated simply.

Jenna started giggling again, then Rachel joined in and they both laughed harder when Chance sat back on his heels and looked at them as though he thought them certifiable.

Maybe they were. But it was a fun ride getting there.

"Jenna, stop. You're scaring the poor guy. Are you sure you're okay?" Rachel asked, struggling to keep a straight face.

Jenna nodded. "I'm fine. Seriously. In fact, I think I'm better than I've been in a long time."

"We'll let a doctor be the judge of that," Chance said.

"No, I'm not hurt." She wriggled her feet, her fingers, to prove it. "See? The snow totally cushioned my fall. Well, mostly. I'm a little sore but I'm not complaining. And the only place I'm going is home." She glanced at Chance, suddenly unsure. "Are you okay?"

"Jenna, you scared twenty years off my life. You're asking me if I'm okay?"

Rachel took the throw off her shoulders and draped it over Jenna but she didn't take her eyes off Chance. "I'm glad you came back." She lifted her hand, fingering the poofy white fur on his coat. "Merry Christmas."

"MERRY CHRISTMAS," CHANCE repeated automatically, unable to believe his timing. He'd turned onto Jenna's street and was about to pull into her driveway when he saw something fall from the roof across from Jenna's house and heard an ear-splitting scream. The scream had apparently been Rachel's and, while he'd meant what he said about Jenna taking years off his life, she was laughing and looking at him like he was a sugar-plum. Damn, but the woman tied him up in knots. "Let's get you out of the cold."

He swung Jenna into his arms despite her protests that she could walk. Promising Rachel he'd take care of her friend and make sure she went to the hospital if Jenna showed any signs of injury, Chance carried her across the street and inside her house. "Stay put and don't move," he ordered once he'd lowered her to the couch. "I have to get my truck out of the middle of the street."

As he moved the vehicle, he went through the speech he'd practiced on his drive from Deer Lodge.

When you had nothing to lose, you don't fear the fear. It was how he'd grown up, and climbing and traveling had kept him from having the close-knit relationship Zane had always wanted them all to have, and Tori's accident *had* scared him away. But now that had changed to the desire to have more. Chance had never delved into the psychology mumbo-jumbo about *why* he climbed, only that he liked it and wanted to do it, but things made sense now, Jenna was right about that.

Inside, he caught her at the top of the stairs. "Where do you think you're going?"

"Shh. I need to get out of these wet clothes. I'm freezing."

"Are you sure you're okay?"

"Wanna come find out for yourself?"

All the air left his lungs. *"Jenna."*

"Go make me something warm to drink, please. I'll be right down."

She returned dressed in warm-looking sweats that showcased every curve of her luscious body.

"Stop looking at me like that," she said. "We have to talk first."

That sounded promising. "First?"

A beautiful smile teased her lips. "You probably think I'm insane."

"Sweetheart, you climbed a ladder at midnight to put Christmas lights up. I think *insane* is a given." He set the mug of tea on the table and pulled her into his arms for a kiss. "But I will say it's sexy as all get out."

That laugh. In all the time they'd been together, the only time he'd ever heard her laugh that way was at Treehouse Rock. "Talk to me, sweetheart. Unless you'd rather me go first?"

"I did fall off a roof. Maybe you should."

He pulled out a kitchen chair and urged her to sit then knelt on the floor in front of her and held her hands in his. "I'm not sure how to say this, so I'm just going to spit it out, okay? I'm not going on any more climbs with the Rock Gods. I'm done."

"Done? You're *quitting?*"

"Yes. The Rock Gods, not climbing." He explained about his idea for a new group, one more family focused and safe.

"You'd actually do that?"

"Jenna, I'm doing it for myself, too. I've never had anyone to consider before. No one who meant enough to me that I *wanted* to compromise until now. You and the kids deserve to come first. You were right. I've spent the past seventeen years trying to forget how screwed up the first thirteen years of my life were. That's why I...went to see my father. At the prison."

"Oh, Chance..."

"Yeah." A rough sound emerged from his chest. "I sat outside the gates for hours before I went in. Turns out he's just a man." She looked confused and he stroked his knuckles down her cheek. "My one main memory of him was when the cops arrested him. I saw the blood on his hands, the look on his face, the sheer rage that possessed him. And ever since then I've been afraid of turning into him."

"You couldn't." Even though she spoke instantly, the assurance sounded no less heartfelt. "That's why you've pushed everyone away?"

He nodded, loving the way Jenna held his hand. "I built him up in my mind, turned him into this monster and saw myself as being like him. That's why when things got to be too much, I'd climb. It helped."

"Then you'll keep climbing," she said firmly. "Make sure you do it safely so you'll come home to us."

He lifted one of her hands to his mouth to kiss. "All I know is that I'd rather never go climbing again if the alternative means not having you and the kids in my life. I mean that."

"It won't come to that, not since I fell off the roof."

"What do you mean?"

"Stop worrying. I'm okay. It's— I felt this *thrill*. And it made me realize I hadn't felt so alive in a long time."

"Yeah, well, you nearly scared me to death and it gave me a pretty good idea of what it's like to be the one waiting for a climber to come home."

"Good. Don't ever forget that," she said, her tone firm. "But what I meant was that the fall reminded me of who I was before I became so overwhelmed with bills and worry. The craziness of feeling like a single parent even when Jeff was alive." She held his hands, her grip tight. "It reminded me of who I used to be—the me I've been trying to find for a long time. The one who's not afraid of not always being in control."

He kissed her. "You're one of the bravest and craziest women I know."

She laughed, her lashes hanging low over her beautiful eyes.

"Jenna, my life is sweeter with you and the twins in it. The thrill I've been searching for, the one that makes me forget where I came from, the one that challenges me... I get that with you. And I want more. I want a future. Marriage and kids and college tuition bills, I want it all. But only if it's with you. I know we've got a long way to go before we can make it official but one day soon will you marry me?"

She swallowed audibly, a dazed expression on her beautiful face before she laughed, the sound low and husky and such a turn-on he struggled to remember the kids were upstairs and no doubt wouldn't be asleep long given the anticipation of Christmas morning.

"Say yes," he ordered softly, his hands buried in her hair. "Give me my Christmas wish, Jenna."

"Well, when you put it like that," she breathed. *"Yes."*

Chance sealed the deal with a kiss. It may not have happened when he'd wanted it to, but his Christmas wish had finally come true.

* * * * *

HEART & HOME

Heartwarming romances where love can
happen right when you least expect it.

COMING NEXT MONTH
AVAILABLE DECEMBER 6, 2011

#1746 THE COST OF SILENCE
Hometown U.S.A.
Kathleen O'Brien

#1747 THE TEXAN'S CHRISTMAS
The Hardin Boys
Linda Warren

#1748 BECAUSE OF THE LIST
Make Me a Match
Amy Knupp

#1749 THE BABY TRUCE
Too Many Cooks?
Jeannie Watt

#1750 A SOUTHERN REUNION
Going Back
Lenora Worth

#1751 A DELIBERATE FATHER
Suddenly a Parent
Kate Kelly

You can find more information on upcoming Harlequin® titles,
free excerpts and more at www.HarlequinInsideRomance.com.

HSRCNM1111

REQUEST YOUR FREE BOOKS!
2 FREE NOVELS PLUS 2 FREE GIFTS!

❖ Harlequin®

Super Romance®

Exciting, emotional, unexpected!

*Lucy Flemming and Ross Mitchell shared a magical,
sexy Christmas weekend together six years ago.
This Christmas, history may repeat itself when they find
themselves stranded in a major snowstorm...
and alone at last.*

Read on for a sneak peek from
IT HAPPENED ONE CHRISTMAS
by Leslie Kelly.

Available December 2011, only from Harlequin® Blaze™.

EYEING THE GRAY, THICK SKY through the expansive wall of windows, Lucy began to pack up her photography gear. The Christmas party was winding down, only a dozen or so people remaining on this floor, which had been transformed from cubicles and meeting rooms to a holiday funland. She smiled at those nearest to her, then, seeing the glances at her silly elf hat, she reached up to tug it off her head.

Before she could do it, however, she heard a voice. A deep, male voice—smooth and sexy, and so not Santa's.

"I appreciate you filling in on such short notice. I've heard you do a terrific job."

Lucy didn't turn around, letting her brain process what she was hearing. Her whole body had stiffened, the hairs on the back of her neck standing up, her skin tightening into tiny goose bumps. Because that voice sounded so familiar. *Impossibly* familiar.

It can't be.

"It sounds like the kids had a great time."

Unable to stop herself, Lucy began to turn around, wondering if her ears—and all her other senses—were deceiving her. After all, six years was a long time, the mind could play tricks. What were the odds that she'd bump into *him,* here? And today of all days. December 23.

Six years exactly. Was that really possible?

One look—and the accompanying frantic thudding of her heart—and she knew her ears and brain were working just fine. Because it was *him.*

"Oh, my God," he whispered, shocked, frozen, staring as thoroughly as she was. "Lucy?"

She nodded slowly, not taking her eyes off him, wondering why the years had made him even more attractive than ever. It didn't seem fair. Not when she'd spent the past six years thinking he must have started losing that thick, golden-brown hair, or added a spare tire to that trim, muscular form.

No.

The man was gorgeous. Truly, without-a-doubt, mouth-wateringly handsome, every bit as hot as he'd been the first time she'd laid eyes on him. She'd been twenty-two, he one year older.

They'd shared an amazing holiday season.

And had never seen one another again.

Until now.

Find out what happens in
IT HAPPENED ONE CHRISTMAS
by Leslie Kelly.
Available December 2011, only from Harlequin® Blaze™

LAURA MARIE ALTOM
brings you
another touching tale from

When family tragedy forces Wyatt Buckhorn to pair up
with his longtime secret crush, Natalie Poole, and care
for the Buckhorn clan's seven children, Wyatt worries
he's in over his head. Fearing his shameful secret will
be exposed, Wyatt tries to fight his growing attraction
to Natalie. As Natalie begins to open up to Wyatt,
he starts yearning for a family of his own—a family
with Natalie. But can Wyatt trust his heart enough
to reveal his secret?

A Baby in His Stocking

**Available December
wherever books are sold!**

SUSAN MEIER

**Experience the thrill of falling in love
this holiday season with**

Kisses on Her Christmas List

When Shannon Raleigh saw Rory Wallace staring at her
across her family's department store, she knew he would
be trouble…for her heart. Guarded, but unable to fight
her attraction, Shannon is drawn to Rory and his inquisitive
daughter. Now with only seven days to convince this
straitlaced businessman that what they feel for each other
is real, Shannon hopes for a Christmas miracle.

***Will the magic of Christmas be enough
to melt his heart?***

Available December 6, 2011.

Snowflake Bride

JILLIAN HART

Grateful when she is hired as a maid, Ruby Ballard vows to use her wages to save her family's farm. But the boss's son, Lorenzo, is entranced by this quiet beauty. He knows Ruby is the only woman he could marry, yet she refuses his courtship. As the holidays approach, he is determined to win her affections and make her his snowflake bride.

Available November 2011
wherever books are sold.

Harlequin®

ROMANTIC
SUSPENSE

USA TODAY BESTSELLING AUTHOR

MARIE FERRARELLA

Brings you another exciting installment from

CAVANAUGH
JUSTICE

A Cavanaugh Christmas

When Detective Kaitlyn Two Feathers follows a kidnapping
case outside her jurisdiction, she enlists the aid of Detective
Thomas Cavelli. Still reeling from the discovery that his
father was a Cavanaugh, Thomas takes the case, thinking
it will be a nice distraction…until Kaitlyn becomes his
ultimate distraction. As the case heats up and time
is running out, Thomas must prove to Kaitlyn that he is
trustworthy and risk it all for the one thing they both
never thought they'd find—love.

Available November 22 wherever books are sold!